The
Evil Shepherd

E. PHILIPS OPPENHEIM

1st WORLD
LIBRARY
Literary Society

The Evil Shepherd

E. Phillips Oppenheim

© 1st World Library – Literary Society, 2004
PO Box 2211
Fairfield, IA 52556
www.1stworldlibrary.org
First Edition

LCCN: 2004195290

Softcover ISBN: 1-4218-0117-5
Hardcover ISBN: 1-4218-0017-9
eBook ISBN: 1-4218-0217-1

Purchase *"The Evil Shepherd"*
as a traditional bound book at:
www.1stWorldLibrary.org/purchase.asp?ISBN=1-4218-0117-5

CHAPTER I

Francis Ledsam, alert, well-satisfied with himself and the world, the echo of a little buzz of congratulations still in his ears, paused on the steps of the modern Temple of Justice to light a cigarette before calling for a taxi to take him to his club. Visions of a whisky and soda - his throat was a little parched - and a rubber of easy-going bridge at his favourite table, were already before his eyes. A woman who had followed him from the Court touched him on the shoulder.

"Can I speak to you for a moment, Mr. Ledsam?"

The barrister frowned slightly as he swung around to confront his questioner. It was such a familiar form of address.

"What do you want?" he asked, a little curtly.

"A few minutes' conversation with you," was the calm reply. "The matter is important."

The woman's tone and manner, notwithstanding her plain, inconspicuous clothes, commanded attention. Francis Ledsam was a little puzzled. Small things meant much to him in life, and he had been looking forward almost with the zest of a schoolboy to that hour of relaxation at his club. He was impatient of even a brief delay, a sentiment which he tried to express in his response.

"What do you want to speak to me about?" he repeated bluntly. "I shall be in my rooms in the Temple to-morrow morning, any time after eleven."

"It is necessary for me to speak to you now," she insisted. "There is a tea-shop across the way. Please accompany me there."

Ledsam, a little surprised at the coolness of her request, subjected his accoster to a closer scrutiny. As he did so, his irritation diminished. He shrugged his shoulders slightly.

"If you really have business with me," he said, "I will give you a few minutes."

They crossed the street together, the woman self-possessed, negative, wholly without the embarrassment of one performing an unusual action. Her companion felt the awakening of curiosity. Zealously though she had, to all appearance, endeavoured to conceal the fact, she was without a doubt personable. Her voice and manner lacked nothing of refinement. Yet her attraction to Francis Ledsam, who, although a perfectly normal human being, was no seeker after promiscuous adventures, did not lie in these externals. As a barrister whose success at the criminal bar had been phenomenal, he had attained to a certain knowledge of human nature. He was able, at any rate, to realise that this woman was no imposter. He knew that she had vital things to say.

They passed into the tea-shop and found an empty

corner. Ledsam hung up his hat and gave an order. The woman slowly began to remove her gloves. When she pushed back her veil, her vis-à-vis received almost a shock. She was quite as good-looking as he had imagined, but she was far younger - she was indeed little more than a girl. Her eyes were of a deep shade of hazel brown, her eyebrows were delicately marked, her features and poise admirable. Yet her skin was entirely colourless. She was as pale as one whose eyes have been closed in death. Her lips, although in no way highly coloured, were like streaks of scarlet blossom upon a marble image. The contrast between her appearance and that of her companion was curiously marked. Francis Ledsam conformed in no way to the accepted physical type of his profession. He was over six feet in height, broad-shouldered and powerfully made. His features were cast in a large mould, he was of fair, almost sandy complexion, even his mouth was more humourous than incisive. His eyes alone, grey and exceedingly magnetic, suggested the gifts which without a doubt lay behind his massive forehead.

"I am anxious to avoid any possible mistake," she began. "Your name is Francis Ledsam?"

"It is," he admitted.

"You are the very successful criminal barrister," she continued, "who has just been paid an extravagant fee to defend Oliver Hilditch."

"I might take exception to the term 'extravagant'," Ledsam observed drily. "Otherwise, your information appears to be singularly correct. I do not know whether you have heard the verdict. If not, you may be interested to know that I succeeded in obtaining the man's acquittal."

"I know that you did," the woman replied. "I was in the Court when the verdict was brought in. It has since occurred to me that I should like you to understand exactly what you have done, the responsibility you have incurred."

Ledsam raised his eyebrows.

"Responsibility?" he repeated. "What I have done is simple enough. I have earned a very large fee and won my case."

"You have secured the acquittal of Oliver Hilditch," she persisted. "He is by this time a free man. Now I am going to speak to you of that responsibility. I am going to tell you a little about the man who owes his freedom to your eloquence."

It was exactly twenty minutes after their entrance into the teashop when the woman finished her monologue. She began to draw on her gloves again. Before them were two untasted cups of tea and an untouched plate of bread and butter. From a corner of the room the waitress was watching them curiously.

"Good God!" Francis Ledsam exclaimed at last, suddenly realising his whereabouts. "Do you mean to affirm solemnly that what you have been telling me is the truth?"

The woman continued to button her gloves. "It is the truth," she said.

Ledsam sat up and looked around him. He was a little

dazed. He had almost the feeling of a man recovering from the influence of some anaesthetic. Before his eyes were still passing visions of terrible deeds, of naked, ugly passion, of man's unscrupulous savagery. During those few minutes he had been transported to New York and Paris, London and Rome. Crimes had been spoken of which made the murder for which Oliver Hilditch had just been tried seem like a trifling indiscretion. Hard though his mentality, sternly matter-of-fact as was his outlook, he was still unable to fully believe in himself, his surroundings, or in this woman who had just dropped a veil over her ashen cheeks. Reason persisted in asserting itself.

"But if you knew all this," he demanded, "why on earth didn't you come forward and give evidence?"

"Because," she answered calmly, as she rose to her feet, "my evidence would not have been admissible. I am Oliver Hilditch's wife."

CHAPTER II

Francis Ledsam arrived at his club, the Sheridan, an hour later than he had anticipated. He nodded to the veteran hall-porter, hung up his hat and stick, and climbed the great staircase to the card-room without any distinct recollection of performing any of these simple and reasonable actions. In the cardroom he exchanged a few greetings with friends, accepted without comment or without the slightest tinge of gratification a little chorus of chafing congratulations upon his latest triumph, and left the room without any inclination to play, although there was a vacant place at his favourite table. From sheer purposelessness he wandered back again into the hall, and here came his first gleam of returning sensation. He came face to face with his most intimate friend, Andrew Wilmore. The latter, who had just hung up his coat and hat, greeted him with a growl of welcome.

"So you've brought it off again, Francis!"

"Touch and go," the barrister remarked. "I managed to squeak home."

Wilmore laid his hand upon his friend's shoulder and led the way towards two easy-chairs in the lounge.

"I tell you what it is, old chap," he confided, "you'll be

　　　　E. Phillips Oppenheim

making yourself unpopular before long. Another criminal at large, thanks to that glib tongue and subtle brain of yours. The crooks of London will present you with a testimonial when you're made a judge."

"So you think that Oliver Hilditch was guilty, then?" Francis asked curiously.

"My dear fellow, how do I know or care?" was the indifferent reply. "I shouldn't have thought that there had been any doubt about it. You probably know, anyway."

"That's just what I didn't when I got up to make my speech," Francis assured his friend emphatically. "The fellow was given an opportunity of making a clean breast of it, of course - Wensley, his lawyer, advised him to, in fact - but the story he told me was precisely the story he told at the inquest."

They were established now in their easy-chairs, and Wilmore summoned a waiter.

"Two large whiskies and sodas," he ordered. "Francis," he went on, studying his companion intently, "what's the matter with you? You don't look as though your few days in the country last week had done you any good."

Francis glanced around as though to be sure that they were alone.

"I was all right when I came up, Andrew," he muttered. "This case has upset me."

"Upset you? But why the dickens should it?" the other

demanded, in a puzzled tone. "It was quite an ordinary case, in its way, and you won it."

"I won it," Francis admitted.

"Your defence was the most ingenious thing I ever heard."

"Mostly suggested, now I come to think of it," the barrister remarked grimly, "by the prisoner himself."

"But why are you upset about it, anyway?" Wilmore persisted.

Francis rose to his feet, shook himself, and with his elbow resting upon the mantelpiece leaned down towards his friend. He could not rid himself altogether of this sense of unreality. He had the feeling that he had passed through one of the great crises of his life.

"I'll tell you, Andrew. You're about the only man in the world I could tell. I've gone crazy."

"I thought you looked as though you'd been seeing spooks," Wilmore murmured sympathetically.

"I have seen a spook," Francis rejoined, with almost passionate seriousness, "a spook who lifted an invisible curtain with invisible fingers, and pointed to such a drama of horrors as De Quincey, Poe and Sue combined could never have imagined. Oliver Hilditch was guilty, Andrew. He murdered the man Jordan - murdered him in cold blood."

"I'm not surprised to hear that," was the somewhat puzzled reply.

E. Phillips Oppenheim

"He was guilty, Andrew, not only of the murder of this man, his partner, but of innumerable other crimes and brutalities," Francis went on. "He is a fiend in human form, if ever there was one, and I have set him loose once more to prey upon Society. I am morally responsible for his next robbery, his next murder, the continued purgatory of those forced to associate with him."

"You're dotty, Francis," his friend declared shortly.

"I told you I was crazy," was the desperate reply. "So would you be if you'd sat opposite that woman for half-an-hour, and heard her story."

"What woman?" Wilmore demanded, leaning forward in his chair and gazing at his friend with increasing uneasiness.

"A woman who met me outside the Court and told me the story of Oliver Hilditch's life."

"A stranger?"

"A complete stranger to me. It transpired that she was his wife."

Wilmore lit a cigarette.

"Believe her?"

"There are times when one doesn't believe or disbelieve," Francis answered. "One knows."

Wilmore nodded.

"All the same, you're crazy," he declared. "Even if you did save the fellow from the gallows, you were only doing your job, doing your duty to the best of poor ability. You had no reason to believe him guilty."

"That's just as it happened," Francis pointed out. "I really didn't care at the time whether he was or not. I had to proceed on the assumption that he was not, of course, but on the other hand I should have fought just as hard for him if I had known him to be guilty."

"And you wouldn't now - to-morrow, say?"

"Never again."

"Because of that woman's story?"

"Because of the woman."

There was a short silence. Then Wilmore asked a very obvious question.

"What sort of a person was she?"

Francis Ledsam was several moments before he replied. The question was one which he had been expecting, one which he had already asked himself many times, yet he was unprepared with any definite reply.

"I wish I could answer you, Andrew," his friend confessed. "As a matter of fact, I can't. I can only speak of the impression she left upon me, and you are about the only person breathing to whom I could speak of that."

E. Phillips Oppenheim

Wilmore nodded sympathetically. He knew that, man of the world though Francis Ledsam appeared, he was nevertheless a highly imaginative person, something of an idealist as regards women, unwilling as a rule to discuss them, keeping them, in a general way, outside his daily life.

"Go ahead, old fellow," he invited. "You know I understand."

"She left the impression upon me," Francis continued quietly, "of a woman who had ceased to live. She was young, she was beautiful, she had all the gifts - culture, poise and breeding - but she had ceased to live. We sat with a marble table between us, and a few feet of oil-covered floor. Those few feet, Andrew, were like an impassable gulf. She spoke from the shores of another world. I listened and answered, spoke and listened again. And when she told her story, she went. I can't shake off the effect she had upon me, Andrew. I feel as though I had taken a step to the right or to the left over the edge of the world."

Andrew Wilmore studied his friend thoughtfully.

He was full of sympathy and understanding. His one desire at that moment was not to make a mistake. He decided to leave unasked the obvious question.

"I know," he said simply. "Are you dining anywhere?"

"I thought of staying on here," was the indifferent reply.

"We won't do anything of the sort," Wilmore insisted. "There's scarcely a soul in to-night, and the place is too humpy for a man who's been seeing spooks. Get back to your rooms and change. I'll wait here."

"What about you?"

"I have some clothes in my locker. Don't be long. And, by-the-bye, which shall it be - Bohemia or Mayfair? I'll telephone for a table. London's so infernally full, these days."

Francis hesitated.

"I really don't care," he confessed. "Now I think of it, I shall be glad to get away from here, though. I don't want any more congratulations on saving Oliver Hilditch's life. Let's go where we are least likely to meet any one we know."

"Respectability and a starched shirt-front, then," Wilmore decided. "We'll go to Claridge's."

CHAPTER III

The two men occupied a table set against the wall, not far from the entrance to the restaurant, and throughout the progress of the earlier part of their meal were able to watch the constant incoming stream of their fellow-guests. They were, in their way, an interesting contrast physically, neither of them good-looking according to ordinary standards, but both with many pleasant characteristics. Andrew Wilmore, slight and dark, with sallow cheeks and brown eyes, looked very much what he was - a moderately successful journalist and writer of stories, a keen golfer, a bachelor who preferred a pipe to cigars, and lived at Richmond because he could not find a flat in London which he could afford, large enough for his somewhat expansive habits. Francis Ledsam was of a sturdier type, with features perhaps better known to the world owing to the constant activities of the cartoonist. His reputation during the last few years had carried him, notwithstanding his comparative youth - he was only thirty-five years of age - into the very front ranks of his profession, and his income was one of which men spoke with bated breath. He came of a family of landed proprietors, whose younger sons for generations had drifted always either to the Bar or the Law, and his name was well known in the purlieus of Lincoln's Inn before he himself had made it famous. He was a persistent refuser of invitations, and his acquaintances in the fashionable world were comparatively few. Yet every now and then he felt a mild interest in the people whom his companion assiduously pointed out to him.

"A fashionable restaurant, Francis, is rather like your Law Courts - it levels people up," the latter remarked. "Louis, the head-waiter, is the judge, and the position allotted in the room is the sentence. I wonder who is going to have the little table next but one to us. Some favoured person, evidently."

Francis glanced in the direction indicated without curiosity. The table in question was laid for two and was distinguished by a wonderful cluster of red roses.

"Why is it," the novelist continued speculatively, "that, whenever we take another man's wife out, we think it necessary to order red roses?"

"And why is it," Francis queried, a little grimly, "that a dear fellow like you, Andrew, believes it his duty to talk of trifles for his pal's sake, when all the time he is thinking of something else? I know you're dying to talk about the Hilditch case, aren't you? Well, go ahead."

"I'm only interested in this last development," Wilmore confessed. "Of course, I read the newspaper reports. To tell you the truth, for a murder trial it seemed to me to rather lack colour."

"It was a very simple and straightforward case," Francis said slowly. "Oliver Hilditch is the principal partner in an American financial company which has recently opened offices in the West End. He seems to have arrived in England about two years ago, to have taken a house in Hill Street, and to have spent a great deal of money. A month or so ago, his partner from New York arrived in London, a man named Jordan of whom nothing was known. It has since transpired, however, that his journey to Europe was undertaken because he was unable to obtain certain figures relating to the business, from Hilditch. Oliver Hilditch met him at Southampton, travelled with him to London and found him a room at the Savoy. The next day, the whole of the time seems to have been spent in the office, and it is certain, from the evidence of the clerk, that some disagreement took place between the two men. They dined together, however, apparently on good terms, at the Cafe Royal, and parted in Regent Street soon after ten. At twelve o'clock, Jordan's body was picked up on the pavement in Hill Street, within a few paces of Heidrich's door. He had been stabbed through the heart with some needle-like weapon, and was quite dead."

"Was there any vital cause of quarrel between them?" Wilmore enquired.

"Impossible to say," Francis replied. "The financial position of the company depends entirely upon the value of a large quantity of speculative bonds, but as there was only one clerk employed, it was impossible to get at any figures. Hilditch declared that Jordan had only a small share in the business, from which he had drawn a considerable income for years, and that he had not the slightest cause for complaint."

"What were Hilditch's movements that evening?" Wilmore asked.

"Not a soul seems to have seen him after he left Regent Street," was the somewhat puzzled answer. "His own story was quite straightforward and has never been contradicted. He let himself into his house with a latch-key after his return from the Café Royal, drank a whisky and soda in the library, and went to bed before half-past eleven. The whole affair - "

Francis broke off abruptly in the middle of his sentence. He sat with his eyes fixed upon the door, silent and speechless.

"What in Heaven's name is the matter, old fellow?" Wilmore demanded, gazing at his companion in blank amazement.

The latter pulled himself together with an effort. The sight of the two new arrivals talking to Louis on the threshold of the restaurant, seemed for the moment to have drawn every scrap of colour from his cheeks. Nevertheless, his recovery was almost instantaneous.

"If you want to know any more," he said calmly, "you had better go and ask him to tell you the whole story himself. There he is."

"And the woman with him?" Wilmore exclaimed under his breath.

"His wife!"

CHAPTER IV

To reach their table, the one concerning which Francis and his friend had been speculating, the new arrivals, piloted by Louis, had to pass within a few feet of the two men. The woman, serene, coldly beautiful, dressed like a Frenchwoman in unrelieved black, with extraordinary attention to details, passed them by with a careless glance and subsided into the chair which Louis was holding. Her companion, however, as he recognised Francis hesitated. His expression of somewhat austere gloom was lightened. A pleasant but tentative smile parted his lips. He ventured upon a salutation, half a nod, half a more formal bow, a salutation which Francis instinctively returned. Andrew Wilmore looked on with curiosity.

"So that is Oliver Hilditch," he murmured.

"That is the man," Francis observed, "of whom last evening half the people in this restaurant were probably asking themselves whether or not he was guilty of murder. To-night they will be wondering what he is going to order for dinner. It is a strange world."

"Strange indeed," Wilmore assented. "This afternoon he was in the dock, with his fate in the balance - the condemned cell or a favoured table at Claridge's. And your meeting! One can imagine him gripping your hands, with tears in his eyes, his voice broken with emotion, sobbing out his thanks. And instead you exchange polite bows. I would not have missed this situation for anything."

"Tradesman!" Francis scoffed. "One can guess already at the plot of your next novel."

"He has courage," Wilmore declared. "He has also a very beautiful companion. Were you serious, Francis, when you told me that that was his wife?"

"She herself was my informant," was the quiet reply.

Wilmore was puzzled.

"But she passed you just now without even a glance of recognition, and I thought you told me at the club this afternoon that all your knowledge of his evil ways came from her. Besides, she looks at least twenty years younger than he does."

Francis, who had been watching his glass filled with champagne, raised it to his lips and drank its contents steadily to the last drop.

"I can only tell you what I know, Andrew," he said, as he set down the empty glass. "The woman who is with him now is the woman who spoke to me outside the Old Bailey this afternoon. We went to a tea-shop together. She told me the story of his career. I have never listened to so horrible a recital in my life."

"And yet they are here together, dining tete-a-tete, on a night when it must have needed more than ordinary courage for either of them to have been seen in public at all," Wilmore pointed out.

"It is as astounding to me as it is to you," Francis confessed. "From the way she spoke, I should never have dreamed that they were living together."

"And from his appearance," Wilmore remarked, as he called the waiter to bring some cigarettes, "I should never have imagined that he was anything else save a high-principled, well-born, straightforward sort of chap. I never saw a less criminal type of face."

They each in turn glanced at the subject of their discussion. Oliver Hilditch's good-looks had been the subject of many press comments during the last few days. They were certainly undeniable. His face was a little lined but his hair was thick and brown. His features were regular, his forehead high and thoughtful, his mouth a trifle thin but straight and shapely. Francis gazed at him like a man entranced. The hours seemed to have slipped away. He was back in the tea-shop, listening to the woman who spoke of terrible things. He felt again his shivering abhorrence of her cold, clearly narrated story. Again he shrank from the horrors from which with merciless fingers she had stripped the coverings. He seemed to see once more the agony in her white face, to hear the eternal pain aching and throbbing in her monotonous tone. He rose suddenly to his feet.

"Andrew," he begged, "tell the fellow to bring the bill outside. We'll have our coffee and liqueurs there."

Wilmore acquiesced willingly enough, but even as they turned towards the door Francis realised what was in store for him. Oliver Hilditch had risen to his feet. With a courteous little gesture he intercepted the passer-by. Francis found himself standing side by side with the man for whose life he had pleaded that afternoon, within a few feet of the woman whose terrible story seemed to have poisoned the very atmosphere he breathed, to have shown him a new horror in life, to have temporarily, at any rate, undermined every joy and ambition he possessed.

"Mr. Ledsam," Hilditch said, speaking with quiet dignity, "I hope that you will forgive the liberty I take in speaking to you here. I looked for you the moment I was free this afternoon, but found that you had left the Court. I owe you my good name, probably my life. Thanks are poor things but they must be spoken."

"You owe me nothing at all," Francis replied, in a tone which even he found harsh. "I had a brief before me and a cause to plead. It was a chapter out of my daily work."

"That work can be well done or ill," the other reminded him gently. "In your case, my presence here proves how well it was done. I wish to present you to my wife, who shares my gratitude."

Francis bowed to the woman, who now, at her husband's words, raised her eyes. For the first time he saw her smile. It seemed to him that the effort made her less beautiful.

"Your pleading was very wonderful, Mr. Ledsam," she said, a very subtle note of mockery faintly apparent in her tone. "We poor mortals find it difficult to understand that with you all that show of passionate

E. Phillips Oppenheim

earnestness is merely - what did you call it? - a chapter in your day's work? It is a great gift to be able to argue from the brain and plead as though from the heart."

"We will not detain Mr. Ledsam," Oliver Hilditch interposed, a little hastily. "He perhaps does not care to be addressed in public by a client who still carries with him the atmosphere of the prison. My wife and I wondered, Mr. Ledsam, whether you would be good enough to dine with us one night. I think I could interest you by telling you more about my case than you know at present, and it would give us a further opportunity, and a more seemly one, for expressing our gratitude."

Francis had recovered himself by this time. He was after all a man of parts, and though he still had the feeling that he had been through one of the most momentous days of his life, his savoir faire was making its inevitable reappearance. He knew very well that the idea of that dinner would be horrible to him. He also knew that he would willingly cancel every engagement he had rather than miss it.

"You are very kind," he murmured.

"Are we fortunate enough to find you disengaged," Hilditch suggested, "to-morrow evening?"

"I am quite free," was the ready response.

"That suits you, Margaret?" Hilditch asked, turning courteously to his wife.

For a single moment her eyes were fixed upon those of her prospective guest. He read their message which pleaded for his refusal, and he denied it.

"To-morrow evening will suit me as well as any other," she acquiesced, after a brief pause.

"At eight o'clock, then - number 10 b, Hill Street," Hilditch concluded.

Francis bowed and turned away with a murmured word of polite assent. Outside, he found Wilmore deep in the discussion of the merits of various old brandies with an interested maitre d'hotel.

"Any choice, Francis?" his host enquired.

"None whatever," was the prompt reply, "only, for God's sake, give me a double one quickly!"

The two men were on the point of departure when Oliver Hilditch and his wife left the restaurant. As though conscious that they had become the subject of discussion, as indeed was the case, thanks to the busy whispering of the various waiters, they passed without lingering through the lounge into the entrance hall, where Francis and Andrew Wilmore were already waiting for a taxicab. Almost as they appeared, a new arrival was ushered through the main entrance, followed by porters carrying luggage. He brushed past Francis so closely that the latter looked into his face, half attracted and half repelled by the waxen-like complexion, the piercing eyes, and the dignified carriage of the man whose arrival seemed to be creating some stir in the hotel. A reception clerk and a deputy manager had already hastened forward. The newcomer waved them back for a moment. Bare-headed, he had taken Margaret Hilditch's hands in his and raised them to his lips.

"I came as quickly as I could," he said. "There was the usual delay, of course, at Marseilles, and the trains on were terrible. So all has ended well."

Oliver Hilditch, standing by, remained speechless. It seemed for a moment as though his self-control were subjected to a severe strain.

"I had the good fortune," he interposed, in a low ,tone, "to be wonderfully defended. Mr. Ledsam here -"

He glanced around. Francis, with some idea of what was coming, obeyed an imaginary summons from the head-porter, touched Andrew Wilmore upon the shoulder, and hastened without a backward glance through the swing-doors. Wilmore turned up his coat-collar and looked doubtfully up at the rain.

"I say, old chap," he protested, "you don't really mean to walk?"

Francis thrust his hand through his friend's arm and wheeled him round into Davies Street.

"I don't care what the mischief we do, Andrew," he confided, "but couldn't you see what was going to happen? Oliver Hilditch was going to introduce me as his preserver to the man who had just arrived!"

"Are you afflicted with modesty, all of a sudden?" Wilmore grumbled.

"No, remorse," was the terse reply.

CHAPTER V

Indecision had never been one of Francis Ledsam's faults, but four times during the following day he wrote out a carefully worded telegraphic message to Mrs. Oliver Hilditch, 10 b, Hill Street, regretting his inability to dine that night, and each time he destroyed it. He carried the first message around Richmond golf course with him, intending to dispatch his caddy with it immediately on the conclusion of the round. The fresh air, however, and the concentration required by the game, seemed to dispel the nervous apprehensions with which he had anticipated his visit, and over an aperitif in the club bar he tore the telegram into small pieces and found himself even able to derive a certain half-fearful pleasure from the thought of meeting again the woman who, together with her terrible story, had never for one moment been out of his thoughts. Andrew Wilmore, who had observed his action, spoke of it as they settled down to lunch.

"So you are going to keep your engagement tonight, Francis?" he observed.

The latter nodded.

"After all, why not?" he asked, a little defiantly. "It ought to be interesting."

E. Phillips Oppenheim

"Well, there's nothing of the sordid criminal, at any rate, about Oliver Hilditch," Wilmore declared. "Neither, if one comes to think of it, does his wife appear to be the prototype of suffering virtue. I wonder if you are wise to go, Francis?"

"Why not?" the man who had asked himself that question a dozen times already, demanded.

"Because," Wilmore replied coolly, "underneath that steely hardness of manner for which your profession is responsible, you have a vein of sentiment, of chivalrous sentiment, I should say, which some day or other is bound to get you into trouble. The woman is beautiful enough to turn any one's head. As a matter of fact, I believe that you are more than half in love with her already."

Francis Ledsam sat where the sunlight fell upon his strong, forceful face, shone, too, upon the table with its simple but pleasant appointments, upon the tankard of beer by his side, upon the plate of roast beef to which he was already doing ample justice. He laughed with the easy confidence of a man awakened from some haunting nightmare, relieved to find his feet once more firm upon the ground.

"I have been a fool to take the whole matter so seriously, Andrew," he declared. "I expect to walk back to Clarges Street to-night, disillusioned. The man will probably present me with a gold pencil-case, and the woman -"

"Well, what about the woman?" Wilmore asked, after a brief pause.

"Oh, I don't know!" Francis declared, a little impatiently. "The woman is the mystery, of course. Probably my brain was a little over-excited when I came out of Court, and what I imagined to be an epic was nothing more than a tissue of exaggerations from a disappointed wife. I'm sure I'm doing the right thing to go there .... What about a four-ball this afternoon, Andrew?"

The four-ball match was played and won in normal fashion. The two men returned to town together afterwards, Wilmore to the club and Francis to his rooms in Clarges Street to prepare for dinner. At a few minutes to eight he rang the bell of number 10 b, Hill Street, and found his host and hostess awaiting him in the small drawing-room into which he was ushered. It seemed to him that the woman, still colourless, again marvellously gowned, greeted him coldly. His host, however, was almost too effusive. There was no other guest, but the prompt announcement of dinner dispelled what might have been a few moments of embarrassment after Oliver Hilditch's almost too cordial greeting. The woman laid her fingers upon her guest's coat-sleeve. The trio crossed the little hall almost in silence.

Dinner was served in a small white Georgian dining-room, with every appurtenance of almost Sybaritic luxury. The only light in the room was thrown upon the table by two purple-shaded electric lamps, and the servants who waited seemed to pass backwards and forwards like shadows in some mysterious twilight - even the faces of the three diners themselves were out of the little pool of light until they leaned forward. The dinner was chosen with taste and restraint, the wines were not only costly but rare. A watchful butler, attended now and then by a trim parlour-maid, superintended the service. Only once, when she ordered a bowl of flowers removed from the table, did their mistress address either of them. Conversation after the first few amenities speedily became almost a monologue. One man talked whilst the others listened, and the man who talked was Oliver Hilditch. He possessed the rare gift of imparting colour and actuality in a few phrases to the strange places of which he spoke, of bringing the very thrill of strange happenings into the shadowy room. It seemed that there was scarcely a country of the world which he had not visited, a country, that is to say, where men congregate, for he admitted from the first that he was a city worshipper, that the empty places possessed no charm for him.

"I am not even a sportsman," he confessed once, half apologetically, in reply to a question from his guest. "I have passed down the great rivers of the world without a thought of salmon, and I have driven through the forest lands and across the mountains behind a giant locomotive, without a thought of the beasts which might be lurking there, waiting to be killed. My only desire has been to reach the next place where men and women were."

"Irrespective of nationality?" Francis queried.

"Absolutely. I have never minded much of what race - I have. the trick of tongues rather strangely developed - but I like the feeling of human beings around me. I like the smell and sound and atmosphere of a great city. Then all my senses are awake, but life becomes almost turgid in my veins during the dreary hours of passing from one place to another."

"Do you rule out scenery as well as sport from amongst the joys of travel?" Francis enquired.

"I am ashamed to make such a confession," his host answered, "but I have never lingered for a single unnecessary moment to look at the most wonderful landscape in the world. On the other hand, I have lounged for hours in the narrowest streets of Pekin, in the markets of Shanghai, along Broadway in New York, on the boulevards in Paris, outside the Auditorium in Chicago. These are the obvious places where humanity presses the thickest, but I know of others. Some day we will talk of them."

Francis, too, although that evening, through sheer lack of sympathy, he refused to admit it, shared to some extent Hilditch's passionate interest in his fellow-creatures, and notwithstanding the strange confusion of thought into which he had been thrown during the last twenty-four hours, he felt something of the pungency of life, the thrill of new and appealing surroundings, as he sat in his high-backed chair, sipping his wonderful wine, eating almost mechanically what was set before him, fascinated through all his being by his strange company.

For three days he had cast occasional glances at this man, seated in the criminal dock with a gaoler on either side of him, his fine, nervous features gaining an added distinction from the sordidness of his surroundings. Now, in the garb of civilisation, seated amidst luxury to which he was obviously accustomed, with a becoming light upon his face and this strange, fascinating flow of words proceeding always from his lips, the man, from every external point of view, seemed amongst the chosen ones of the world. The

E. Phillips Oppenheim

contrast was in itself amazing. And then the woman! Francis looked at her but seldom, and when he did it was with a curious sense of mental disturbance; poignant but unanalysable.

It was amazing to see her here, opposite the man of whom she had told him that ghastly story, mistress of his house, to all appearance his consort, apparently engrossed in his polished conversation, yet with that subtle withholding of her real self which Francis rather imagined than felt, and which somehow seemed to imply her fierce resentment of her husband's re-entry into the arena of life. It was a situation so strange that Francis, becoming more and more subject to its influence, was inclined to wonder whether he had not met with some accident on his way from the Court, and whether this was not one of the heated nightmares following unconsciousness.

"Tell me," he asked his host, during one of the brief pauses in the conversation, "have you ever tried to analyse this interest of yours in human beings and crowded cities, this hatred of solitude and empty spaces?"

Oliver Hilditch smiled thoughtfully, and gazed at a salted almond which he was just balancing between the tips of his fingers.

"I think," he said simply, "it is because I have no soul."

CHAPTER VI

The three diners lingered for only a short time over their dessert. Afterwards, they passed together into a very delightful library on the other side of the round, stone-paved hall. Hilditch excused himself for a moment.

"I have some cigars which I keep in my dressing-room," he explained, "and which I am anxious for you to try. There is an electric stove there and I can regulate the temperature."

He departed, closing the door behind him. Francis came a little further into the room. His hostess, who had subsided into an easy-chair and was holding a screen between her face and the fire, motioned him to, seat himself opposite. He did so without words. He felt curiously and ridiculously tongue-tied. He fell to studying the woman instead of attempting the banality of pointless speech. From the smooth gloss of her burnished hair, to the daintiness of her low, black brocaded shoes, she represented, so far as her physical and outward self were concerned, absolute perfection. No ornament was amiss, no line or curve of her figure other than perfectly graceful. Yet even the fire's glow which she had seemed to dread brought no flush of colour to her cheeks. Her appearance of complete lifelessness remained. It was as though some sort of

E. Phillips Oppenheim

crust had formed about her being, a condition which her very physical perfection seemed to render the more incomprehensible.

"You are surprised to see me here living with my husband, after what I told you yesterday afternoon?" she said calmly, breaking at last the silence which had reigned between them.

"I am," he admitted.

"It seems unnatural to you, I suppose?"

"Entirely."

"You still believe all that I told you?"

"I must."

She looked at the door and raised her head a little, as though either listening or adjudging the time before her husband would return. Then she glanced across at him once more.

"Hatred," she said, "does not always drive away. Sometimes it attracts. Sometimes the person who hates can scarcely bear the other out of his sight. That is where hate and love are somewhat alike."

The room was warm but Francis was conscious of shivering. She raised her finger warningly. It seemed typical of the woman, somehow, that the message could not be conveyed by any glance or gesture.

"He is coming," she whispered.

Oliver Hilditch reappeared, carrying cigars wrapped in gold foil which he had brought with him from Cuba, the tobacco of which was a revelation to his guest. The two men smoked and sipped their coffee and brandy. The woman sat with half-closed eyes. It was obvious that Hilditch was still in the mood for speech.

"I will tell you, Mr. Ledsam," he said, "why I am so happy to have you here this evening. In the first place, I desire to tender you once more my thanks for your very brilliant efforts on my behalf. The very fact that I am able to offer you hospitality at all is without a doubt due to these."

"I only did what I was paid to do," Francis insisted, a little harshly. "You must remember that these things come in the day's work with us."

His host nodded.

"Naturally," he murmured. "There was another reason, too, why I was anxious to meet you, Mr. Ledsam," he continued. "You have gathered already that I am something of a crank. I have a profound detestation of all sentimentality and affected morals. It is a relief to me to come into contact with a man who is free from that bourgeois incubus to modern enterprise - a conscience."

"Is that your estimate of me?" Francis asked.

"Why not? You practise your profession in the criminal courts, do you not?"

"That is well-known," was the brief reply.

E. Phillips Oppenheim

"What measure of conscience can a man have," Oliver Hilditch argued blandly, "who pleads for the innocent and guilty alike with the same simulated fervour? Confess, now, Mr. Ledsam – there is no object in being hypocritical in this matter - have you not often pleaded for the guilty as though you believed them innocent?"

"That has sometimes been my duty," Francis acknowledged.

Hilditch laughed scornfully.

It is all part of the great hypocrisy of society," he proclaimed. "You have an extra glass of champagne for dinner at night and are congratulated by your friends because you have helped some poor devil to cheat the law, while all the time you know perfectly well, and so do your high-minded friends, that your whole attitude during those two hours of eloquence has been a lie. That is what first attracted me to you, Mr. Ledsam."

"I am sorry to hear it," Francis commented coldly. "The ethics of my profession -"

His host stopped him with a little wave of the hand.

"Spare me that," he begged. "While we are on the subject, though, I have a question to ask you. My lawyer told me, directly after he had briefed you, that, although it would make no real difference to your pleading, it would be just as well for me to keep up my bluff of being innocent, even in private conversation with you. Why was that?"

"For the very obvious reason," Francis told him, "that

we are not all such rogues and vagabonds as you seem to think. There is more satisfaction to me, at any rate, in saving an innocent man's life than a guilty one's."

Hilditch laughed as though amused.

"Come," he threatened, "I am going to be ill-natured. You have shown signs of smugness, a quality which I detest. I am going to rob you of some part of your self-satisfaction. Of course I killed Jordan. I killed him in the very chair in which you are now sitting."

There was a moment's intense silence. The woman was still fanning herself lazily. Francis leaned forward in his place.

"I do not wish to hear this!" he exclaimed harshly.

"Don't be foolish," his host replied, rising to his feet and strolling across the room. "You know the whole trouble of the prosecution. They couldn't discover the weapon, or anything like it, with which the deed was done. Now I'll show you something ingenious."

Francis followed the other's movements with fascinated eyes. The woman scarcely turned her head. Hilditch paused at the further end of the room, where there were a couple of gun cases, some fishing rods and a bag, of golf clubs. From the latter he extracted a very ordinary-looking putter, and with it in his hands strolled back to them.

"Do you play golf, Ledsam?" he asked. "What do you think of that?"

Francis took the putter into his hand. It was a very

ordinary club, which had apparently seen a good deal of service, so much, indeed, that the leather wrapping at the top was commencing to unroll. The maker's name was on the back of the blade, also the name of the professional from whom it had been purchased. Francis swung the implement mechanically with his wrists.

"There seems to be nothing extraordinary about the club," he pronounced. "It is very much like a cleek I putt with myself."

"Yet it contains a secret which would most certainly have hanged me," Oliver Hilditch declared pleasantly. "See!"

He held the shaft firmly in one hand and bent the blade away from it. In a moment or two it yielded and he commenced to unscrew it. A little exclamation escaped from Francis' lips. The woman looked on with tired eyes.

"The join in the steel," Hilditch pointed out, "is so fine as to be undistinguishable by the naked eye. Yet when the blade comes off, like this, you see that although the weight is absolutely adjusted, the inside is hollow. The dagger itself is encased in this cotton wool to avoid any rattling. I put it away in rather a hurry the last time I used it, and as you see I forgot to clean it."

Francis staggered back and gripped at the mantelpiece. His eyes were filled with horror. Very slowly, and with the air of one engaged upon some interesting task, Oliver Hilditch had removed the blood-stained sheath of cotton wool from around the thin blade of a marvellous-looking stiletto, on which was also a long stain of encrusted blood.

"There is a handle," he went on, "which is perhaps the most ingenious thing of all. You touch a spring here, and behold!"

He pressed down two tiny supports which opened upon hinges about four inches from the top of the handle. There was now a complete hilt.

"With this little weapon," he explained, "the point is so sharpened and the steel so wonderful that it is not necessary to stab. It has the perfection of a surgical instrument. You have only to lean it against a certain point in a man's anatomy, lunge ever so little and the whole thing is done. Come here, Mr. Ledsam, and I will show you the exact spot."

Francis made no movement. His eyes were fixed upon the weapon.

"If I had only known!" he muttered.

"My dear fellow, if you had," the other protested soothingly, "you know perfectly well that it would not have made the slightest difference. Perhaps that little break in your voice would not have come quite so naturally, the little sweep of your arm towards me, the man whom a moment's thoughtlessness might sweep into Eternity, would have been a little stiffer, but what matter? You would still have done your best and you would probably still have succeeded. You don't care about trifling with Eternity, eh? Very well, I will find the place for you."

Hilditch's fingers strayed along his shirt-front until he

E. Phillips Oppenheim

found a certain spot. Then he leaned the dagger against it, his forefinger and second finger pressed against the hilt. His eyes were fixed upon his guest's. He seemed genuinely interested. Francis, glancing away for a moment, was suddenly conscious of a new horror. The woman had leaned a little forward in her easy-chair until she had attained almost a crouching position. Her eyes seemed to be measuring the distance from where she sat to that quivering thread of steel.

"You see, Ledsam," his host went on, "that point driven now at that angle would go clean through the vital part of my heart. And it needs no force, either - just the slow pressure of these two fingers. What did you say, Margaret?" he enquired, breaking off abruptly.

The woman was seated upon the very edge of her chair, her eyes rivetted upon the dagger. There was no change in her face, not a tremor in her tone.

"I said nothing," she replied. "I did not speak at all. I was just watching."

Hilditch turned back to his guest.

"These two fingers," he repeated, "and a flick of the wrist - very little more than would be necessary for a thirty yard putt right across the green."

Francis had recovered himself, had found his bearings to a certain extent.

"I am sorry that you have told me this, Mr. Hilditch," he said, a little stiffly.

"Why?" was the puzzled reply. "I thought you would be interested."

"I am interested to this extent," Francis declared, "I shall accept no more cases such as yours unless I am convinced of my client's innocence. I look upon your confession to me as being in the worst possible taste, and I regret very much my efforts on your behalf."

The woman was listening intently. Hilditch's expression was one of cynical wonder. Francis rose to his feet and moved across to his hostess.

"Mrs. Hilditch," he said, "will you allow me to make my apologies? Your husband and I have arrived at an understanding - or perhaps I should say a misunderstanding - which renders the acceptance of any further hospitality on my part impossible."

She held out the tips of her fingers.

"I had no idea," she observed, with gentle sarcasm, "that you barristers were such purists morally. I thought you were rather proud of being the last hope of the criminal classes."

"Madam," Francis replied, "I am not proud of having saved the life of a self-confessed murderer, even though that man may be your husband."

Hilditch was laughing softly to himself as he escorted his departing guest to the door.

"You have a quaint sense of humour," Francis remarked.

"Forgive me," Oliver Hilditch begged, "but your last few words rather appealed to me. You must be a person of very scanty perceptions if you could spend the evening here and not understand that my death is the one thing in the world which would make my wife happy."

Francis walked home with these last words ringing in his ears. They seemed with him even in that brief period of troubled sleep which came to him when he had regained his rooms and turned in. They were there in the middle of the night when he was awakened, shivering, by the shrill summons of his telephone bell. He stood quaking before the instrument in his pajamas. It was the voice which, by reason of some ghastly premonition, he had dreaded to hear - level, composed, emotionless.

"Mr. Ledsam?" she enquired.

"I am Francis Ledsam," he assented. "Who wants me?"

"It is Margaret Hilditch speaking," she announced. "I felt that I must ring up and tell you of a very strange thing which happened after you left this evening."

"Go on," he begged hoarsely.

"After you left," she went on, "my husband persisted in playing with that curious dagger. He laid it against his heart, and seated himself in the chair which Mr. Jordan had occupied, in the same attitude. It was what he called a reconstruction. While he was holding it there, I think that he must have had a fit, or it may have been remorse, we shall never know. He called out and I hurried across the room to him. I tried to snatch the dagger away - I did so, in fact - but I must have been too late. He had already applied that slight movement of the fingers which was necessary. The doctor has just left. He says that death must have been instantaneous."

"But this is horrible!" Francis cried out into the well of darkness.

"A person is on the way from Scotland Yard," the voice continued, without change or tremor. "When he has satisfied himself, I am going to bed. He is here now. Good-night!"

Francis tried to speak again but his words beat against a wall of silence. He sat upon the edge of the bed, shivering. In that moment of agony he seemed to hear again the echo of Oliver Hilditch's mocking words:

"My death is the one thing in the world which would make my wife happy!"

CHAPTER VII

There was a good deal of speculation at the Sheridan Club, of which he was a popular and much envied member, as to the cause for the complete disappearance from their midst of Francis Ledsam since the culmination of the Hilditch tragedy.

"Sent back four topping briefs, to my knowledge, last week," one of the legal luminaries of the place announced to a little group of friends and fellow-members over a before-dinner cocktail.

"Griggs offered him the defence of William Bull, the Chippenham murderer, and he refused it," another remarked. "Griggs wrote him personally, and the reply came from the Brancaster Golf Club! It isn't like Ledsam to be taking golfing holidays in the middle of the session."

"There's nothing wrong with Ledsam," declared a gruff voice from the corner. "And don't gossip, you fellows, at the top of your voices like a lot of old women. He'll be calling here for me in a moment or two."

They all looked around. Andrew Wilmore rose slowly to his feet and emerged from behind the sheets of an evening paper. He laid his hand upon the shoulder of a friend, and glanced towards the door.

"Ledsam's had a touch of, nerves," he confided. "There's been nothing else the matter with him. We've been down at the Dormy House at Brancasterand he's as right as a trivet now. That Hilditch affair did him in completely."

"I don't see why," one of the bystanders observed. "He got Hilditch off all right. One of the finest addresses to a jury I ever heard."

That's just the point," Wilmore explained "You see, Ledsam had no idea that Hilditch was really guilty, and for two hours that afternoon he literally fought for his life, and in the end wrested a verdict from the jury, against the judge's summing up, by sheer magnetism or eloquence or whatever you fellows like to call it. The very night after, Hilditch confesses his guilt and commits suicide."

"I still don't see where Ledsam's worry comes in," the legal luminary remarked. "The fact that the man was guilty is rather a feather in the cap of his counsel. Shows how jolly good his pleading must have been."

"Just so," Wilmore agreed, "but Ledsam, as you know, is a very conscientious sort of fellow, and very sensitive, too. The whole thing was a shock to him."

"It must have been a queer experience," a novelist remarked from the outskirts of the group, "to dine with a man whose life you have juggled away from the law, and then have him explain his crime to you, and the exact manner of its accomplishment. Seems to bring one amongst the goats, somehow."

"Bit of a shock, no doubt," the lawyer assented, "but I

still don't understand Ledsam's sending back all his briefs. He's not going to chuck the profession, is he?"

"Not by any means," Wilmore declared. "I think he has an idea, though, that he doesn't want to accept any briefs unless he is convinced that the person whom he has to represent is innocent, and lawyers don't like that sort of thing, you know. You can't pick and choose, even when you have Leadsam's gifts."

"The fact of it is," the novelist commented, "Francis Ledsam isn't callous enough to be associated with you money-grubbing dispensers of the law. He'd be all right as Public Prosecutor, a sort of Sir Galahad waving the banner of virtue, but he hates to stuff his pockets at the expense of the criminal classes."

"Who the mischief are the criminal classes?" a police court magistrate demanded. "Personally, I call war profiteering criminal, I call a good many Stock Exchange deals criminal, and," he added, turning to a member of the committee who was hovering in the background, "I call it criminal to expect. us to drink French vermouth like this."

"There is another point of view," the latter retorted. "I call it a crime to expect a body of intelligent men to administer without emolument to the greed of such a crowd of rotters. You'll get the right stuff next week."

The hall-porter approached and addressed Wilmore.

"Mr. Ledsam is outside in a taxi, sir," he announced.

"Outside in a taxi?" the lawyer repeated. "Why on earth can't he come in?"

"I never heard such rot," another declared. "Let's go and rope him in."

"Mr. Ledsam desired me to say, sir," the hall porter continued, "to any of his friends who might be here, that he will be in to lunch to-morrow."

"Leave him to me till then," Wilmore begged. "He'll be all right directly. He's simply altering his bearings and taking his time about it. If he's promised to lunch here to-morrow, he will. He's as near as possible through the wood. Coming up in the train, he suggested a little conversation to-night and afterwards the normal life. He means it, too. There's nothing neurotic about Ledsam."

The magistrate nodded.

"Run along, then, my merry Andrew," he said, "but see that Ledsam keeps his word about to-morrow."

Andrew Wilmore plunged boldly into the forbidden subject later on that evening, as the two men sat side by side at one of the wall tables in Soto's famous club restaurant. They had consumed an excellent dinner. An empty champagne bottle had just been removed, double liqueur brandies had taken its place. Francis, with an air of complete and even exuberant humanity, had lit a huge cigar. The moment seemed propitious.

"Francis," his friend began, "they say at the club that you refused to be briefed in the Chippenham affair."

"Quite true," was the calm reply. "I told Griggs that I wouldn't have anything to do with it."

Wilmore knew then that all was well. Francis' old air of strength and decision had returned. His voice was firm, his eyes were clear and bright. His manner seemed even to invite questioning.

"I think I know why," Wilmore said, "but I should like you to tell me in your own words."

Francis glanced around as though to be sure that they were not overheard.

"Because," he replied, dropping his voice a little but still speaking with great distinctness, "William Bull is a cunning and dangerous criminal whom I should prefer to see hanged."

"You know that?"

"I know that."

"It would be a great achievement to get him off," Wilmore persisted. "The evidence is very weak in places."

"I believe that I could get him off," was the confident reply. "That is why I will not touch the brief. I think," Francis continued, "that I have already conveyed it to you indirectly, but here you are in plain words, Andrew. I have made up my mind that I will defend no man in future unless I am convinced of his innocence."

"That means -"

"It means practically the end of my career at the bar," Francis admitted. "I realise that absolutely: Fortunately, as you know, I am not dependent upon my earnings, and I have had a wonderful ten years."

"This is all because of the Hilditch affair, I suppose?"

"Entirely."

Wilmore was still a little puzzled.

"You seem to imagine that you have something on your conscience as regards that business," he said boldly.

"I have," was the calm reply.

"Come," Wilmore protested, "I don't quite follow your line of thought. Granted that Hilditch was a desperate criminal whom by the exercise of your special gifts you saved from the law, surely his tragic death balanced the account between you and Society?"

"It might have done," Francis admitted, "if he had really committed suicide."

Wilmore was genuinely startled. He looked at his companion curiously.

"What the devil do you mean, old chap?" he demanded. "Your own evidence at the inquest was practically conclusive as to that."

Francis glanced around him with apparent indifference but in reality with keen and stealthy care. On their right was a glass division, through which the sound of their voices could not possibly penetrate. On their left was an empty space, and a table beyond was occupied by a well-known cinema magnate engaged in testing the attractions in daily life of a would-be film star. Nevertheless, Francis' voice was scarcely raised above a whisper.

"My evidence at the coroner's inquest," he confided, "was a subtly concocted tissue of lies. I committed perjury freely. That is the real reason why I've been a little on the nervy side lately, and why I took these few months out of harness."

"Good God!" Wilmore exclaimed, setting down untasted the glass of brandy which be had just raised to his lips.

"I want to finish this matter up," Francis continued calmly, "by making a clean breast of it to you, because from to-night I am starting afresh, with new interests in my life, what will practically amount to a new career. That is why I preferred not to dine at the club to-night, although I am looking forward to seeing them all again. I wanted instead to have this conversation with you. I lied at the inquest when I said that the relations between Oliver Hilditch and his wife that night seemed perfectly normal. I lied when I said that I knew of no cause for ill-will between them. I lied when I said that I left them on friendly terms. I lied when I said that Oliver Hilditch seemed depressed and nervous. I lied when I said that he expressed the deepest remorse for what he had done. There was every indication that night, of the hate which I happen to know existed between the woman and the man. I have not the faintest doubt in my mind but that she murdered him. In my judgment, she was perfectly justified in doing so."

There followed a brief but enforced silence as some

late arrivals passed their table. The room was well-ventilated but Andrew Wilmore felt suddenly hot and choking. A woman, one of the little group of new-comers, glanced towards Francis curiously.

"Francis Ledsam, the criminal barrister," her companion whispered, - " the man who got Oliver Hilditch off. The man with him is Andrew Wilmore, the novelist. Discussing a case, I expect."

CHAPTER VIII

The little party of late diners passed on their way to the further end of the room, leaving a wave of artificiality behind, or was it, Andrew Wilmore wondered, in a moment of half-dazed speculation, that it was they and the rest of the gay company who represented the real things, and he and his companion who were playing a sombre part in some unreal and gloomier world. Francis' voice, however, when he recommenced his diatribe, was calm and matter-of-fact enough.

"You see," he continued, argumentatively, "I was morally and actually responsible for the man's being brought back into Society. And far worse than that, I was responsible for his being thrust back again upon his wife. Ergo, I was also responsible for what she did that night. The matter seems as plain as a pikestaff to me. I did what I could to atone, rightly or wrongly it doesn't matter, because it is over and done with. There you are, old fellow, now you know what's been making me nervy. I've committed wholesale perjury, but I acted according to my conscience and I think according to justice. The thing has worried me, I admit, but it has passed, and I'm glad it's off my chest. One more liqueur, Andrew, and if you want to we'll talk about my plans for the future."

The brandy was brought. Wilmore studied his friend

curiously, not without some relief. Francis had lost the harassed and nervous appearance upon which his club friends had commented, which had been noticeable, even, to a diminishing extent, upon the golf course at Brancaster. He was alert and eager. He had the air of a man upon the threshold of some enterprise dear to his heart.

"I have been through a queer experience," Francis continued presently, as he sipped his second liqueur. "Not only had I rather less than twelve hours to make up my mind whether I should commit a serious offence against the law, but a sensation which I always hoped that I might experience, has come to me in what I suppose I must call most unfortunate fashion."

"The woman?" Wilmore ventured.

Francis assented gloomily. There was a moment's silence. Wilmore, the metaphysician, saw then a strange thing. He saw a light steal across his friend's stern face. He saw his eyes for a moment soften, the hard mouth relax, something incredible, transforming, shine, as it were, out of the man's soul in that moment of self-revelation. It was gone like the momentary passing of a strange gleam of sunshine across a leaden sea, but those few seconds were sufficient. Wilmore knew well enough what had happened.

"Oliver Hilditch's wife," Francis went on, after a few minutes' pause, "presents an enigma which at present I cannot hope to solve. The fact that she received her husband back again, knowing what he was and what he was capable of, is inexplicable to me. The woman herself is a mystery. I do not know what lies behind her extraordinary immobility. Feeling she must have,

E. Phillips Oppenheim

and courage, or she would never have dared to have ridded herself of the scourge of her life. But beyond that my judgment tells me nothing. I only know that sooner or later I shall seek her out. I shall discover all that I want to know, one way or the other. It may be for happiness - it may be the end of the things that count."

"I guessed this," Wilmore admitted, with a little shiver which he was wholly unable to repress.

Francis nodded.

"Then keep it to yourself, my dear fellow," he begged, "like everything else I am telling you tonight. I have come out of my experience changed in many ways," he continued, "but, leaving out that one secret chapter, this is the dominant factor which looms up before me. I bring into life a new aversion, almost a passion, Andrew, born in a tea-shop in the city, and ministered to by all that has happened since. I have lost that sort of indifference which my profession engenders towards crime. I am at war with the criminal, some-times, I hope, in the Courts of Justice, but forever out of them. I am no longer indifferent as to whether men do good or evil so long as they do not cross my path. I am a hunter of sin. I am out to destroy. There's a touch of melodrama in this for you, Andrew," he concluded, with a little laugh, "but, my God, I'm in earnest!"

"What does this mean so far as regards the routine of your daily life?" Wilmore asked curiously.

"Well, it brings us to the point we discussed down at Brancaster," Francis replied. "It will affect my work to this extent. I shall not accept any brief unless, after reading the evidence, I feel convinced that the accused is innocent."

"That's all very well," Wilmore observed, "but you know what it will mean, don't you? Lawyers aren't likely to single you out for a brief without ever feeling sure whether you will accept it or not."

"That doesn't worry me," Francis declared. "I don't need the fees, fortunately, and I can always pick up enough work to keep me going by attending Sessions. One thing I can promise you - I certainly shall not sit in my rooms and wait for things to happen. Mine is a militant spirit and it needs the outlet of action."

"Action, yes, but how?" Wilmore queried. "You can't be always hanging about the courts, waiting for the chance of defending some poor devil who's been wrongfully accused - there aren't enough of them, for one thing. On the other hand, you can't walk down Regent Street, brandishing a two-edged sword and hunting for pickpockets."

Francis smiled.

"Nothing so flamboyant, I can assure you, Andrew," he replied; "nor shall I play the amateur detective with his mouth open for mysteries. But listen," he went on earnestly. "I've had some experience, as you know, and, notwithstanding the Oliver Hilditch's of the world, I can generally tell a criminal when I meet him face to face. There are plenty of them about, too, Andrew - as many in this place as any other. I am not going to be content with a negative position as regards evildoers. I am going to set my heel on as many of the human vermin of this city as I can find."

"A laudable, a most exhilarating and delightful pursuit! `human vermin,' too, is excellent. It opens up a new and fascinating vista for the modern sportsman. My congratulations!"

It was an interruption of peculiar and wonderful significance, but Francis did not for the moment appreciate the fact. Turning his head, he simply saw a complete stranger seated unaccountably at the next table, who had butted into a private conversation and whose tone of gentle sarcasm, therefore, was the more offensive.

"Who the devil are you, sir," he demanded, "and where did you come from?"

The newcomer showed no resentment at Francis' little outburst. He simply smiled with deprecating amiability - a tall, spare man, with lean, hard face, complexion almost unnaturally white; black hair, plentifully besprinkled with grey; a thin, cynical mouth, notwith-standing its distinctly humourous curve, and keen, almost brilliant dark eyes. He was dressed in ordinary dinner garb; his linen and jewellery was indeed in the best possible taste. Francis, at his second glance, was troubled with a vague sense of familiarity.

"Let me answer your last question first, sir," the intruder begged. "I was seated alone, several tables away, when the couple next to you went out, and having had pointed out to me the other evening at Claridge's Hotel, and knowing well by repute, the great barrister, Mr. Francis Ledsam, and his friend the world-famed novelist, Mr. Andrew Wilmore, I - er - unobtrusively made my way, half a yard at a time, in your direction - and here I am. I came stealthily, you may object? Without a doubt. If I had come in any other fashion, I should have disturbed a conversation in which I was much interested."

"Could you find it convenient," Francis asked, with icy politeness, "to return to your own table, stealthily or not, as you choose?"

The newcomer showed no signs of moving.

"In after years," he declared, "you would be the first to regret the fact if I did so. This is a momentous meeting. It gives me an opportunity of expressing my deep gratitude to you, Mr. Ledsam, for the wonderful evidence you tendered at the inquest upon the body of my son-in-law, Oliver Hilditch."

Francis turned in his place and looked steadily at this unsought-for companion, learning nothing, however, from the half-mocking smile and imperturbable expression.

"Your son-in-law?" he repeated. "Do you mean to say that you are the father of - of Oliver Hilditch's wife?"

"Widow," the other corrected gently. "I have that honour. You will understand, therefore, that I feel myself on this, the first opportunity, compelled to tender my sincere thanks for evidence so chivalrously offered, so flawlessly truthful."

Francis was a man accustomed to self-control, but he clenched his hands so that his finger nails dug into his flesh. He was filled with an insane and unreasoning resentment against this man whose words were biting into his conscience. Nevertheless, he kept his tone level.

"I do not desire your gratitude," he said, "nor, if you will permit me to say so, your further acquaintance."

The stranger shook his head regretfully.

"You are wrong," he protested. "We were bound, in any case, to know one another. Shall I tell you why? You have just declared yourself anxious to set your heel upon the criminals of the world. I have the distinction of being perhaps the most famous patron of that maligned class now living - and my neck is at your service."

"You appear to me," Francis said suavely, "to be a buffoon."

It might have been fancy, but Francis could have sworn that he saw the glitter of a sovereign malevolence in the other's dark eyes. If so, it was but a passing weakness, for a moment later the half good-natured, half cynical smile was back again upon the man's lips.

"If so, I am at least a buffoon of parts," was the prompt rejoinder. "I will, if you choose, prove myself."

There was a moment's silence. Wilmore was leaning forward in his place, studying the newcomer earnestly. An impatient invective was somehow stifled upon Francis' lips.

"Within a few yards of this place, sometime before the closing hour to-night," the intruder continued, earnestly yet with a curious absence of any human quality in his hard tone, "there will be a disturbance, and probably what you would call a crime will be committed. Will you use your vaunted gifts to hunt down the desperate criminal, and, in your own picturesque phraseology, set your heel upon his neck? Success may bring you fame, and the trail may lead - well, who knows where?"

Afterwards, both Francis and Andrew Wilmore marvelled at themselves, unable at any time to find any reasonable explanation of their conduct, for they answered this man neither with ridicule, rudeness nor civility. They simply stared at him, impressed with the convincing arrogance of his challenge and unable to find words of reply. They received his mocking farewell without any form of reciprocation or sign of resentment. They watched him leave the room, a dignified, distinguished figure, sped on his way with marks of the deepest respect by waiters, maitres d'hotels and even the manager himself. They behaved, indeed, as they both admitted afterwards, like a couple of moonstruck idiots. When he had finally disappeared, however, they looked at one another and the spell was broken.

"Well, I'm damned!" Francis exclaimed. "Soto, come here at once."

The manager hastened smilingly to their table.

"Soto," Francis invoked, "tell us quickly - tell us the name of the gentleman who has just gone out, and who he is?"

Soto was amazed.

"You don't know Sir Timothy Brast, sir?" he exclaimed. "Why, he is supposed to be one of the richest men in the world! He spends money like water. They say that when he is in England, his place down the river alone costs a thousand pounds a week. When he gives a party here, we can find nothing good enough. He is our most generous client."

"Sir Timothy Brast," Wilmore repeated. "Yes, I have heard of him."

"Why, everybody knows Sir Timothy," Soto went on eloquently. "He is the greatest living patron of boxing. He found the money for the last international fight."

"Does he often come in alone like this?" Francis asked curiously.

"Either alone," Soto replied, "or with a very large party. He entertains magnificently."

"I've seen his name in the paper in connection with something or other, during the last few weeks," Wilmore remarked reflectively.

"Probably about two months ago, sir," Soto suggested. "He gave a donation of ten thousand pounds to the Society for the Prevention of Cruelty to Animals, and they made him a Vice President.... In one moment, sir."

The manager hurried away to receive a newly-arrived guest. Francis and his friend exchanged a wondering glance.

"Father of Oliver Hilditch's wife," Wilmore observed,

"the most munificent patron of boxing in the world, Vice President of the Society for the Prevention of Cruelty to Animals, and self-confessed arch-criminal! He pulled our legs pretty well!"

"I suppose so," Francis assented absently.

Wilmore glanced at his watch.

"What about moving on somewhere?" he suggested. "We might go into the Alhambra for half-an-hour, if you like. The last act of the show is the best."

Francis shook his head.

"We've got to see this thing out," he replied. "Have you forgotten that our friend promised us a sensation before we left?"

Wilmore began to laugh a little derisively. Then, suddenly aware of some lack of sympathy between himself and his friend, he broke off and glanced curiously at the latter.

"You're not taking him seriously, are you?" he enquired.

Francis nodded.

"Certainly I am," he confessed.

"You don't believe that he was getting at us?"

"Not for a moment."

"You believe that something is going to happen here in

E. Phillips Oppenheim

this place, or quite close?"

"I am convinced of it," was the calm reply.

Wilmore was silent. For a moment he was troubled with his old fears as to his friend's condition. A glance, however, at Francis' set face and equable, watchful air, reassured him.

"We must see the thing through, of course, then," he assented. "Let us see if we can spot the actors in the coming drama."

CHAPTER IX

It happened that the two men, waiting in the vestibule of the restaurant for Francis' car to crawl up to the entrance through the fog which had unexpectedly rolled up, heard the slight altercation which was afterwards referred to as preceding the tragedy. The two young people concerned were standing only a few feet away, the girl pretty, a little peevish, an ordinary type; her companion, whose boyish features were marred with dissipation, a very passable example of the young man about town going a little beyond his tether.

"It's no good standing here, Victor!" the girl exclaimed, frowning. "The commissionaire's been gone ages already, and there are two others before us for taxis."

"We can't walk," her escort replied gloomily. "It's a foul night. Nothing to do but wait, what? Let's go back and have another drink."

The girl stamped her satin-shod foot impatiently.

"Don't be silly," she expostulated. "You know I promised Clara we'd be there early."

"All very well," the young man grumbled, "but what

can we do? We shall have to wait our turn."

"Why can't you slip out and look for a taxi yourself?" she suggested. "Do, Victor," she added, squeezing his arm. "You're so clever at picking them up:"

He made a little grimace, but lit a cigarette and turned up his coat collar.

"I'll do my best" he promised. "Don't go on without me."

"Try up towards Charing Cross Road, not the other way," she advised earnestly.

"Right-oh!" he replied, which illuminative form of assent, a word spoken as he plunged unwillingly into the thick obscurity on the other side of the revolving doors, was probably the last he ever uttered on earth.

Left alone, the girl began to shiver, as though suddenly cold. She turned around and glanced hurriedly back into the restaurant. At that moment she met the steady, questioning scrutiny of Francis' eyes. She stood as though transfixed. Then came the sound which every one talked of for months afterwards, the sound which no one who heard it ever forgot - the death cry of Victor Bidlake, followed a second afterwards by a muffled report. A strain of frenzied surprise seemed mingled with the horror. Afterwards, silence.

There was the sound of some commotion outside, the sound of hurried footsteps and agitated voices. Then a terrible little procession appeared. Something - it seemed to be a shapeless heap of clothes - was carried in and laid upon the floor, in the little space between the revolving doors and the inner entrance. Two blue-liveried attendants kept back the horrified but curious crowd. Francis, vaguely recognised as being somehow or other connected with the law, was one of the few people allowed to remain whilst a doctor, fetched out from the dancing-room, kneeled over the prostrate form. He felt that he knew beforehand the horrible verdict which the latter whispered in his ear after his brief examination.

"Quite dead! A ghastly business!"

Francis gazed at the hole in the shirt-front, disfigured also by a scorching stain.

"A bullet?" he asked.

The doctor nodded.

"Fired within a foot of the poor fellow's heart," he whispered. "The murderer wasn't taking any chances, whoever he was."

"Have the police been sent for?"

The head-porter stepped forward.

"There was a policeman within a few yards of the spot, sir," he replied. "He's gone down to keep every one away from the place where we found the body. We've telephoned to Scotland Yard for an inspector."

The doctor rose to his feet.

"Nothing more can be done," he pronounced. "Keep the people out of here whilst I go and fetch my hat and coat. Afterwards, I'll take the body to the mortuary when the ambulance arrives."

An attendant pushed his way through the crowd of people on the inner side of the door.

"Miss Daisy Hyslop, young lady who was with Mr. Bidlake, has just fainted in the ladies' room, sir," he announced. "Could you come?"

"I'll be there immediately," the doctor promised.

The rest of the proceedings followed a normal course. The police arrived, took various notes, the ambulance followed a little later, the body was removed, and the little crowd of guests, still infected with a sort of awed excitement, were allowed to take their leave. Francis and Wilmore drove almost in silence to the former's rooms in Clarges Street.

"Come up and have a drink, Andrew," Francis invited.

"I need it," was the half-choked response.

Francis led the way in silence up the two flights of stairs into his sitting-room, mixed whiskies and sodas from the decanter and syphon which stood upon the sideboard, and motioned his friend to an easy-chair. Then he gave form to the thought which had been haunting them both.

"What about our friend Sir Timothy Brast?" he enquired. "Do you believe now that he was pulling our legs?"

Wilmore dabbed his forehead with his handkerchief. It

was a chilly evening, but there were drops of perspiration still standing there.

"Francis," he confessed, "it's horrible! I don't think realism like this attracts me. It's horrible! What are we going to do?"

"Nothing for the present," was the brief reply. "If we were to tell our story, we should only be laughed at. What there is to be done falls to my lot."

"Had the police anything to say about it?" Wilmore asked.

"Only a few words," Francis replied. "Shopland has it in hand. A good man but unimaginative. I've come across him in one or two cases lately. You'll find a little bit like this in the papers to-morrow: 'The murder is believed to have been committed by one of the gang of desperadoes who have infested the west-end during the last few months.' You remember the assault in the Albany Court Yard, and the sandbagging in Shepherd Market only last week?"

"That seems to let Sir Timothy out," Wilmore remarked.

"There are many motives for crime besides robbery," Francis declared. "Don't be afraid, Andrew, that I am going to turn amateur detective and make the unravelment of this case all the more difficult for Scotland Yard. If I interfere, it will be on a certainty. Andrew, don't think I'm mad but I've taken up the challenge our great philanthropist flung at me to-night. I've very little interest in who killed this boy Victor Bidlake, or why, but I'm convinced of one thing - Brast knew about it, and if he is posing as a patron of crime on a great scale, sooner or later I shall get him. He may think himself safe, and he may have the courage of Beelzebub - he seems rather that type - but if my presentiment about him - comes true, his number's up. I can almost divine the meaning of his breaking in upon our conversation to-night. He needs an enemy - he is thirsting for danger. He has found it!"

Wilmore filled his pipe thoughtfully. At the first whiff of tobacco he began to feel more normal.

"After all, Francis," he said, "aren't we a little over-strung to-night? Sir Timothy Brast is no adventurer. He is a prince in the city, a persona grata wherever he chooses to go. He isn't a hanger-on in Society. He isn't even dependent upon Bohemia for his entertainment. You can't seriously imagine that a man with his possessions is likely to risk his life and liberty in becoming the inspiration of a band of cutthroats?"

Francis smiled. He, too, had lit his pipe and had thrown himself into his favourite chair. He smiled confidently across at his friend.

"A millionaire with brains," he argued, "is just the one person in the world likely to weary of all ordinary forms of diversion. I begin to remember things about him already. Haven't you heard about his wonderful parties down at The Walled House?"

Wilmore struck the table by his side with his clenched fist.

"By George, that's it!" he exclaimed. "Who hasn't!"

"I remember Baker talking about one last year," Francis continued, "never any details, but all kinds of mysterious hints - a sort of mixture between a Roman orgy and a chapter from the 'Arabian Nights' - singers from Petrograd, dancers from Africa and fighting men from Chicago."

"The fellow's magnificent, at any rate," Wilmore remarked.

His host smoked furiously for a moment.

"That's the worst of these multi-millionaires," he declared. "They think they can rule the world, traffic in human souls, buy morals, mock at the law. We shall see!"

"Do you know the thing that I found most interesting about him?" Wilmore asked.

"His black opals," the other suggested. "You're by the way of being a collector, aren't you?"

Wilmore shook his head.

"The fact that he is the father of Oliver Hilditch's widow."

Francis sat quite still for a moment. There was a complete change in his expression. He looked like a man who has received a shock.

"I forgot that," he muttered.

CHAPTER X

Francis met Shopland one morning about a week later, on his way from Clarges Street to his chambers in the Temple. The detective raised his hat and would have passed on, but Francis accosted him.

"Any progress, Mr. Shopland?" he enquired.

The detective fingered his small, sandy moustache. He was an insignificant-looking little man, undersized, with thin frame and watery eyes. His mouth, however, was hard, and there were some tell-tale little lines at its corners.

"None whatever, I am sorry to say, Mr. Ledsam," he admitted. "At present we are quite in the dark."

"You found the weapon, I hear?"

Shopland nodded.

"It was just an ordinary service revolver, dating from the time of the war, exactly like a hundred thousand others. The enquiries we were able to make from it came to nothing."

"Where was it picked up?"

"In the middle of the waste plot of ground next to Soto's. The murderer evidently threw it there the moment he had discharged it. He must have been wearing rubber-soled shoes, for not a soul heard him go."

Francis nodded thoughtfully.

"I wonder," he said, after a slight pause, "whether it ever occurred to you to interview Miss Daisy Hyslop, the young lady who was with Bidlake on the night of his murder?"

"I called upon her the day afterwards," the detective answered.

"She had nothing to say?"

"Nothing whatever."

"Indirectly, of course," Francis continued, "the poor girl was the cause of his death. If she had not insisted upon his going out for a taxicab, the man who was loitering about would probably have never got hold of him."

The detective glanced up furtively at the speaker. He seemed to reflect for a moment.

"I gathered," he said, "in conversation with the commissionaire, that Miss Hyslop was a little impatient that night. It seems, however, that she was anxious to get to a ball which was being given down in Kensington."

"There was a ball, was there?" Francis asked.

E. Phillips Oppenheim

"Without a doubt," the detective replied. "It was given by a Miss Clara Bultiwell. She happens to remember urging Miss Hyslop to come on as early as possible."

"So that's that," Francis observed.

"Just so, Mr. Ledsam," the detective murmured.

They were walking along the Mall now, eastwards. The detective, who seemed to have been just a saunterer, had accommodated himself to Francis' destination.

"Let me see, there was nothing stolen from the young man's person, was there?" Francis asked presently.

"Apparently nothing at all, sir."

"And I gather that you have made every possible enquiry as to the young man's relations with his friends?"

"So far as one can learn, sir, they seem to have been perfectly amicable."

"Of course," Francis remarked presently, "this may have been quite a purposeless affair. The deed may have been committed by a man who was practically a lunatic, without any motive or reason whatever."

"Precisely so, sir," the detective agreed.

"But, all the same, I don't think it was."

"Neither do I, sir."

Francis smiled slightly.

"Shopland," he said, "if there is no further external evidence to be collected, I suggest that there is only one person likely to prove of assistance to you."

"And that one person, sir?"

"Miss Daisy Hyslop."

"The young lady whom I have already seen?"

Francis nodded.

"The young lady whom you have already seen," he assented. "At the same time, Mr. Shopland, we must remember this. If Miss Hyslop has any knowledge of the facts which are behind Mr. Bidlake's murder, it is more likely to be to her interest to keep them to herself, than to give them away to the police free gratis and for nothing. Do you follow me?"

"Precisely, sir."

"That being so," Francis continued, "I am going to make a proposition to you for what it is worth. Where were you going when I met you this morning, Shopland?"

"To call upon you in Clarges Street, sir."

"What for?"

"I was going to ask you if you would be so kind as to call upon Miss Daisy Hyslop, sir."

Francis smiled.

"Great minds," he murmured. "I will see the young lady this afternoon, Shopland."

The detective raised his hat. They had reached the spot where his companion turned off by the Horse Guards Parade.

"I may hope to hear from you, then, sir?"

"Within the course of a day or two, perhaps earlier," Francis promised.

Francis continued his walk along the Embankment to his chambers in the Temple. He glanced in the outer office as he passed to his consulting room.

"Anything fresh, Angrave?" he asked his head-clerk.

"Nothing whatever, sir," was the quiet reply.

He passed on to his own den - a bare room with long windows looking out over the gardens. He glanced at the two or three letters which lay on his desk, none of them of the least interest, and leaning back in his chair commenced to fill his pipe. There was a knock at the door. Fawsitt, a young beginner at the bar, in whom he had taken some interest and who deviled for him, presented himself.

"Can I have a word with you, Mr. Ledsam?" he asked.

"By all means," was the prompt response. "Sit down."

Fawsitt seated himself on the other side of the table.

He had a long, thin face, dark, narrow eyes, unwholesome complexion, a slightly hooked nose, and teeth discoloured through constant smoking. His fingers, too, bore the tell-tale yellow stains.

"Mr. Ledsam," he said, "I think, with your permission, I should like to leave at the end of my next three months."

Francis glanced across at him.

"Sorry to hear that, Fawsitt. Are you going to work for any one else?"

"I haven't made arrangements yet, sir," the young man replied. "I thought of offering myself to Mr. Barnes."

"Why do you want to leave me?" Francis asked.

"There isn't enough for me to do, sir."

Francis lit his pipe.

"It's probably just a lull, Fawsitt," he remarked.

"I don't think so, sir."

"The devil! You've been gossiping with some of these solicitors' clerks, Fawsitt."

"I shouldn't call it gossiping, sir. I am always interested to hear anything that may concern our - my future. I have reason to believe, sir, that w e are being passed over for briefs."

"The reason being?"

"One can't pick and choose, sir. One shouldn't, anyway."

Francis smiled.

"You evidently don't approve of any measure of personal choice as to the work which one takes up."

"Certainly I do not, sir, in our profession. The only brief I would refuse would be a losing or an ill-paid one. I don't conceive it to be our business to prejudge a case."

"I see," Francis murmured. "Go on, Fawsitt."

"There's a rumour about," the young man continued, "that you are only going to plead where the chances are that your client is innocent."

"There's some truth in that," Francis admitted.

"If I could leave a little before the three months, sir, I should be glad," Fawsitt said. "I look at the matter from an entirely different point of view."

"You shall leave when you like, of course, Fawsitt, but tell me what that point of view is?"

"Just this, sir. The simplest-minded idiot who ever stammered through his address, can get an innocent prisoner off if he knows enough of the facts and the law. To my mind, the real triumph in our profession is to be able to unwind the meshes of damning facts and force a verdict for an indubitably guilty client."

"How does the moral side of that appeal to you?" his

senior enquired.

"I didn't become a barrister to study morals, or even to consider them," was the somewhat caustic reply. "When once a brief is in my mind, it is a matter of brain, cunning and resource. The guiltier a man, the greater the success if you can get him off."

"And turn him loose again upon Society?"

"It isn't our job to consider that, sir. The moral question is only confusing in the matter. Our job is to make use of the law for the benefit of our client. That's what we're paid for. That's the measure of our success or failure."

Francis nodded.

"Very reasonably put, Fawsitt," he conceded. "I'll give you a letter to Barnes whenever you like."

"I should be glad if you would do so, sir," the young man said. "I'm only wasting my time here ...."

Francis wrote a letter of recommendation to Barnes, the great K.C., considered a stray brief which had found its way in, and strolled up towards the Milan as the hour approached luncheon-time. In the American bar of that palatial hotel he found the young man he was looking for - a flaxen-haired youth who was seated upon one of the small tables, with his feet upon a chair, laying down the law to a little group of acquaintances. He greeted Francis cordially but without that due measure of respect which nineteen should accord to thirty-five.

"Cheerio, my elderly relative!" he exclaimed. "Have a cocktail."

Francis nodded assent.

"Come into this corner with me for a moment, Charles," he invited. "I have a word for your ear."

The young man rose and sat by his uncle's side on a settee.

"In my declining years," the latter began, "I find myself reverting to the follies of youth. I require a letter of introduction from you to a young lady of your acquaintance."

"The devil! Not one of my own special little pets, I hope?"

"Her name is Miss Daisy Hyslop," Francis announced.

Lord Charles Southover pursed his lips and whistled. He glanced at Francis sideways.

"Is this the beginning of a campaign amongst the butterflies," he enquired, "because, if so, I feel it my duty, uncle, to address to you a few words of solemn warning. Miss Daisy Hyslop is hot stuff."

"Look here, young fellow," Francis said equably, "I don't know what the state of your exchequer is -"

"I owe you forty," Lord Charles interrupted. "Spring another tenner, make it fifty, that is, and the letter of introduction I will write for you will bring tears of gratitude to your eyes."

"I'll spring the tenner," Francis promised, "but you'll write just what I tell you - no more and no less."

"Anything extra for keeping mum at home?" the young man ventured tentatively.

"You're a nice sort of nephew to have!" Francis declared. "Abandon these futile attempts at blackmail and just come this way to the writing-table."

"You've got the tenner with you?" the young man asked anxiously.

Francis produced a well-filled pocketbook. His nephew led the way to a writing-table, lit a cigarette which he stuck into the corner of his mouth, and in painstaking fashion wrote the few lines which Francis dictated. The ten pounds changed hands.

"Have one with me for luck?" the young man invited brightly. "No? Perhaps you're right," he added, in valedictory fashion. "You'd better keep your head clear for Daisy!"

CHAPTER XI

Miss Daisy Hyslop received Francis that afternoon, in the sitting-room of her little suite at the Milan. Her welcoming smile was plaintive and a little subdued, her manner undeniably gracious. She was dressed in black, a wonderful background for her really gorgeous hair, and her deportment indicated a recent loss.

"How nice of you to come and see me," she murmured, with a lingering touch of the fingers. "Do take that easy-chair, please, and sit down and talk to me. Your roses were beautiful, but whatever made you send them to me?"

"Impulse," he answered.

She laughed softly.

"Then please yield to such impulses as often as you feel them," she begged. "I adore flowers. Just now, too," she added, with a little sigh, "anything is welcome which helps to keep my mind off my own affairs."

"It was very good of you to let me come," he declared. "I can quite understand that you don't feel like seeing many people just now."

Francis' manner, although deferential and courteous, had nevertheless some quality of aloofness in it to which she was unused and which she was quick to recognise. The smile, faded from her face. She seemed suddenly not quite so young.

"Haven't I seen you before somewhere quite lately?" she asked, a little sharply.

"You saw me at Soto's, the night that Victor Bidlake was murdered," he reminded her. "I stood quite close to you both while you were waiting for your taxi."

The animation evoked by this call from a presumably new admirer, suddenly left her. She became nervous and constrained. She glanced again at his card.

"Don't tell me," she begged, "that you have come to ask me anyquestions about that night! I simply could not bear it. The police have been here twice, and I had nothing to tell them, absolutely nothing."

"Quite right," he assented soothingly. "Police have such a clumsy way of expecting valuable information for nothing. I'm always glad to hear of their being disappointed."

She studied her visitor for a moment carefully. Then she turned to the table by her side, picked up a note and read it through.

"Lord Southover tells me here," she said, "that you are just a pal of his who wants to make my acquaintance. He doesn't say why."

"Is that necessary?" Francis asked good-naturedly.

She moved in her chair a little nervously, crossing and uncrossing her legs more than once. Her white silk stockings underneath her black skirt were exceedingly effective, a fact of which she never lost consciousness, although at that moment she was scarcely inspired to play the coquette.

"I'd like to think it wasn't," she admitted frankly.

"I've seen you repeatedly upon the stage," he told her, "and, though musical comedy is rather out of my line, I have always admired you immensely."

She studied him once more almost wistfully.

"You look very nice," she acknowledged, "but you don't look at all the kind of man who admires girls who do the sort of rubbish I do on the stage."

"What do I look like?" he asked, smiling.

"A man with a purpose," she answered.

"I begin to think," he ventured, "that we shall get on. You are really a very astute young lady."

"You are quite sure you're not one of these amateur detectives one reads about?" she demanded.

"Certainly not," he assured her. "I will confess that I am interested in Victor Bidlake's death, and I should like to discover the truth about it, but I have a reason for that which I may tell you some day. It has nothing whatever to do with the young man himself. To the best of my belief, I never saw or heard of him before in my life. My interest lies with another person. You have lost a great friend, I know. If you felt disposed to tell me the whole story, it might make such a difference."

She sighed. Her confidence was returning - also her self-pity. The latter at once betrayed itself.

"You see," she confided, "Victor and I were engaged to be married, so naturally I let him help me a little. I shan't be able to stay on here now. They are bothering me about their bill already," she added, with a side-glance at an envelope which stood on a table by her side.

He drew a little nearer to her.

"Miss Hyslop - " he began.

"Daisy," she interrupted.

"Miss Daisy Hyslop, then," he continued, smiling, "I suggested just now that I did not want to come and bother you for information without any return. If I can be of any assistance to you in that matter," he added, glancing towards the envelope, "I shall be very pleased."

She sighed gratefully.

"Just till Victor's people return to town," she said. "I know that they mean to do something for me."

"How much?" he asked.

"Two hundred pounds would keep me going," she told him.

He wrote out a cheque. Miss Hyslop drew a sigh of relief as she laid it on one side with the envelope. Then she swung round in her chair to face him where he sat at the writing-table.

"I am afraid you will think that what I have to tell is very insignificant," she confessed. "Victor was one of those boys who always fancied themselves bored. He was bored with polo, bored with motoring, bored with the country and bored with town. Then quite suddenly during the last few weeks he seemed changed. All that he would tell me was that he had found a new interest in life. I don't know what it was but I don't think it was a nice one. He seemed to drop all his old friends, too, and go about with a new set altogether - not a nice set at all. He used to stay out all night, and he quite gave up going to dances and places where he could take me. Once or twice he came here in the afternoon, dead beat, without having been to bed at all, and before he could say half-a-dozen words he was asleep in my easy-chair. He used to mutter such horrible things that I had to wake him up."

"Was he ever short of money?" Francis asked.

She shook her head.

"Not seriously," she answered. "He was quite well-off, besides what his people allowed him. I was going to have a wonderful settlement as soon as our engagement was announced. However, to go on with what I was telling you, the very night before - it happened - he came in to see me, looking like nothing on earth. He cried like a baby, behaved like a lunatic, and called himself all manner of names. He had had a great deal too much to drink, and I gathered that he had seen something horrible. It was then he asked me to dine with him the next night, and told me that he was going to break altogether with his new friends. Something in connection with them seemed to have given him a terrible fright."

Francis nodded. He had the tact to abandon his curiosity at this precise point.

"The old story," he declared, "bad company and rotten habits. I suppose some one got to know that the young man usually carried a great deal of money about with him."

"It was so foolish of him," she assented eagerly: "I warned him about it so often. The police won't listen to it but I am absolutely certain that he was robbed. I noticed when he paid the bill that he had a great wad of bank-notes which were never discovered afterwards."

Francis rose to his feet.

"What are you doing to-night?" he enquired.

"Nothing," she acknowledged eagerly.

"Then let's dine somewhere and see the show at the Frivolity," he suggested.

"You dear man!" she assented with enthusiasm. "The one thing I wanted to do, and the one person I wanted to do it with."

CHAPTER XII

It was after leaving Miss Daisy Hyslop's flat that the event to which Francis Ledsam had been looking forward more than anything else in the world, happened. It came about entirely by chance. There were no taxis in the Strand. Francis himself had finished work for the day, and feeling disinclined for his usual rubber of bridge, he strolled homewards along the Mall. At the corner of Green Park, he came face to face with the woman who for the last few months had scarcely been out of his thoughts. Even in that first moment he realised to his pain that she would have avoided him if she could. They met, however, where the path narrowed, and he left her no chance to avoid him. That curious impulse of conventionality which opens a conversation always with cut and dried banalities, saved them perhaps from a certain amount of embarrassment. Without any conscious suggestion, they found themselves walking side by side.

"I have been wanting to see you very much indeed," he said. "I even went so far as to wonder whether I dared call."

"Why should you?" she asked. "Our acquaintance began and ended in tragedy. There is scarcely any purpose in carrying it further."

He looked at her for a moment before replying. She was wearing black, but scarcely the black of a woman who sorrows. She was still frigidly beautiful, redolent, in all the details of her toilette, of that almost negative perfection which he had learnt to expect from her. She suggested to him still that same sense of aloofness from the actualities of life.

"I prefer not to believe that it is ended," he protested. "Have you so many friends that you have no room for one who has never consciously done you any harm?"

She looked at him with some faint curiosity in her immobile features.

"Harm? No! On the contrary, I suppose I ought to thank you for your evidence at the inquest."

"Some part of it was the truth," he replied.

"I suppose so," she admitted drily. "You told it very cleverly."

He looked her in the eyes.

"My profession helped me to be a good witness," he said. "As for the gist of my evidence, that was between my conscience and myself."

"Your conscience?" she repeated. "Are there really men who possess such things?"

"I hope you will discover that for yourself some day," he answered. "Tell me your plans? Where are you living?"

"For the present with my father in Curzon Street."

"With Sir Timothy Brast?"

She assented.

"You know him?" she asked indifferently.

"Very slightly," Francis replied. "We talked together, some nights ago, at Soto's Restaurant. I am afraid that I did not make a very favourable impression upon him. I gathered, too, that he has somewhat eccentric tastes."

"I do not see a great deal of my father," she said. "We met, a few months ago, for the first time since my marriage, and things have been a little difficult between us - just at first. He really scarcely ever puts in an appearance at Curzon Street. I dare say you have heard that he makes a hobby of an amazing country house which he has down the. river."

"The Walled House?" he ventured.

She nodded.

"I see you have heard of it. All London, they tell me, gossips about the entertainments there."

"Are they really so wonderful?" he asked.

"I have never been to one," she replied. "As a matter of fact, I have spent scarcely any time in England since my marriage. My husband, as I remember he told you, was fond of travelling."

Notwithstanding the warm spring air he was conscious

of a certain chilliness. Her level, indifferent tone seemed to him almost abnormally callous. A horrible realisation flashed for a moment in his brain. She was speaking of the man whom she had killed!

"Your father overheard a remark of mine," Francis told her. "I was at Soto's with a friend - Andrew Wilmore, the novelist – and to tell you the truth we were speaking of the shock I experienced when I realised that I had been devoting every effort of which I was capable, to saving the life of - shall we say a criminal? Your father heard me say, in rather a flamboyant manner, perhaps, that in future I declared war against all crime and all criminals."

She smiled very faintly, a smile which had in it no single element of joy or humour.

"I can quite understand my father intervening," she said. "He poses as being rather a patron of artistically-perpetrated crime. Sue is his favourite author, and I believe that he has exceedingly grim ideas as to duelling and fighting generally. He was in prison once for six months at New Orleans for killing a man who insulted my mother. Nothing in the world would ever have convinced him that he had not done a perfectly legitimate thing."

"I am expecting to find him quite an interesting study, when I know him better," Francis pronounced. "My only fear is that he will count me an unfriendly person and refuse to have anything to do with me."

"I am not at all sure," she said indifferently, "that it would not be very much better for you if he did."

"I cannot admit that," he answered, smiling. "I think that our paths in life are too far apart for either of us to influence the other. You don't share his tastes, do you?"

"Which ones?" she asked, after a moment's silence.

"Well, boxing for one," he replied. "They tell me that he is the greatest living patron of the ring, both here and in America."

"I have never been to a fight in my life," she confessed. "I hope that I never may."

"I can't go so far as that," he declared, "but boxing isn't altogether one of my hobbies. Can't we leave your father and his tastes alone for the present? I would rather talk about - ourselves. Tell me what you care about most in life?"

"Nothing," she answered listlessly.

"But that is only a phase," he persisted. "You have had terrible trials, I know, and they must have affected your outlook on life, but you are still young, and while one is young life is always worth having."

"I thought so once," she assented. "I don't now."

"But there must be - there will be compensations," he assured her. "I know that just now you are suffering from the reaction - after all you have gone through. The memory of that will pass."

"The memory of what I have gone through will never pass," she answered.

There was a moment's intense silence, a silence pregnant with reminiscent drama. The little room rose up before his memory - the woman's hopeless, hating eyes, the quivering thread of steel, the dead man's mocking words. He seemed at that moment to see into the recesses of her mind. Was it remorse that troubled her, he wondered? Did she lack strength to realise that in that half-hour at the inquest he had placed on record for ever his judgment of her deed? Even to think of it now was morbid. Although he would never have confessed it even to himself, there was growing daily in his mind some idea of reward. She had never thanked him - he hoped that she never would - but he had surely a right to claim some measure of her thoughts, some alight place in her life.

"Please look at me," he begged, a little abruptly.

She turned her head in some surprise. Francis was almost handsome in the clear Spring sunlight, his face alight with animation, his deep-set grey eyes full of amused yet anxious solicitude. Even as she appreciated these things and became dimly conscious of his eager interest, her perturbation seemed to grow.

"Well?" she ventured.

"Do I look like a person who knew what he was talking about?" he asked.

"On the whole, I should say that you did," she admitted.

"Very well, then," he went on cheerfully, "believe me when I say that the shadow which depresses you all the time now will pass. I say this confidently," he added, his voice softening, "because I hope to be allowed to help. Haven't you guessed that I am very glad indeed to see you again?"

She came to a sudden standstill. They had just passed through Lansdowne Passage and were in the quiet end of Curzon Street.

"But you must not talk to me like that!" she expostulated.

"Why not?" he demanded. "We have met under strange and untoward circumstances, but are you so very different from other women?"

For a single moment she seemed infinitely more human, startled, a little nervous, exquisitely sympathetic to an amazing and unexpected impression. She seemed to look with glad but terrified eyes towards the vision of possible things - and then to realise that it was but a trick of the fancy and to come shivering back to the world of actualities.

"I am very different," she said quietly. "I have lived my life. What I lack in years has been made up to me in horror. I have no desire now but to get rid of this aftermath of years as smoothly and quickly as possible. I do not wish any man, Mr. Ledsam, to talk to me as you are doing."

"You will not accept my friendship?"

"It is impossible," she replied.

"May I be allowed to call upon you?" he went on, doggedly.

"I do not receive visitors," she answered.

They were walking slowly up Curzon Street now. She had given him every opportunity to leave her, opportunities to which he was persistently blind. Her obstinacy had been a shock to him.

"I am sorry," he said, "but I cannot accept my dismissal like this. I shall appeal to your father. However much he may dislike me, he has at least common-sense."

She looked at him with a touch of the old horror in her coldly-questioning eyes.

"In your way you have been kind to me," she admitted. "Let me in return give you a word of advice. Let me beg you to have nothing whatever to do with my father, in friendship or in enmity. Either might be equally disastrous. Either, in the long run, is likely to cost you dear."

"If that is your opinion of your father, why do you live with him?" he asked.

She had become entirely callous again. Her smile, with its mocking quality, reminded him for a moment of the man whom they were discussing.

"Because I am a luxury and comfort-loving parasite," she answered deliberately, "because my father gladly pays my accounts at Lucille and Worth and Reville, because I have never learnt to do without things. And please remember this. My father, so far as I am concerned, has no faults. He is a generous and courteous companion. Nevertheless, number 70 b,

Curzon Street is no place for people who desire to lead normal lives."

And with that she was gone. Her gesture of dismissal was so complete and final that he had no courage for further argument. He had lost her almost as soon as he had found her.

CHAPTER XIII

Four men were discussing the verdict at the adjourned inquest upon Victor Bidlake, at Soto's American Bar about a fortnight later. They were Robert Fairfax, a young actor in musical comedy, peter Jacks, a cinema producer, Gerald Morse, a dress designer, and Sidney Voss, a musical composer and librettist, all habitues of the place and members of the little circle towards which the dead man had seemed, during the last few weeks of his life, to have become attracted. At a table a short distance away, Francis Ledsam was seated with a cocktail and a dish of almonds before him. He seemed to be studying an evening paper and to be taking but the scantiest notice of the conversation at the bar.

"It just shows," Peter Jacks declared, "that crime is the easiest game in the world. Given a reasonable amount of intelligence, and a murderer's business is about as simple as a sandwich-man's."

"The police," Gerald Morse, a pale-faced, anaemic-looking youth, declared, "rely upon two things, circumstantial evidence and motive. In the present case there is no circumstantial evidence, and as to motive, poor old Victor was too big a fool to have an enemy in the world."

Sidney Voss, who was up for the Sheridan Club and

E. Phillips Oppenheim

had once been there, glanced respectfully across at Francis.

"You ought to know something about crime and criminals, Mr. Ledsam," he said. "Have you any theory about the affair?"

Francis set down the glass from which he had been drinking, and, folding up the evening paper, laid it by the side of him.

"As a matter of fact," he answered calmly, "I have."

The few words, simply spoken, yet in their way charged with menace, thrilled through the little room. Fairfax swung round upon his stool, a tall, aggressive-looking youth whose good-looks were half eaten up with dissipation. His eyes were unnaturally bright, the cloudy remains in his glass indicated absinthe.

"Listen, you fellows!" he exclaimed. "Mr. Francis Ledsam, the great criminal barrister, is going to solve the mystery of poor old Victor's death for us!"

The three other young men all turned around from the bar. Their eyes and whole attention seemed rivetted upon Francis. No one seemed to notice the newcomer who passed quietly to a chair in the background, although he was a person of some note and interest to all of them. Imperturbable and immaculate as ever, Sir Timothy Brast smiled amiably upon the little gathering, summoned a waiter and ordered a Dry Martini.

"I can scarcely promise to do that," Francis said slowly, his eyes resting for a second or two upon each of the four faces. "Exact solutions are a little out of my line. I think I can promise to give you a shock, though, if you're strong enough to stand it."

There was another of those curiously charged si ences. The bartender paused with the cocktail shaker still in his hand. Voss began to beat nervously upon the counter with his knuckles.

"We can stand anything but suspense," he declared. "Get on with your shock-giving."

"I believe that the person responsible for the death of Victor Bidlake is in this room at the present moment," Francis declared.

Again the silence, curious, tense and dramatic. Little Jimmy, the bartender, who had leaned forward to listen, stood with his mouth slightly open and the cocktail-shaker which was in his hand leaked drops upon the counter. The first conscious impulse of everybody seemed to be to glance suspiciously around the room. The four young men at the bar, Jimmy and one waiter, Francis and Sir Timothy Brast, were its only occupants.

"I say, you know, that's a bit thick, isn't it?" Sidney Voss stammered at last. "I wasn't in the place at all, I was in Manchester, but it's a bit rough on these other chaps, Victor's pals."

"I was dining at the Cafe Royal," Jacks declared, loudly.

Morse drew a little breath.

"Every one knows that I was at Brighton," he muttered.

"I went home directly the bar here closed," Jimmy said, in a still dazed tone. "I heard nothing about it till the next morning."

"Alibis by the bushel," Fairfax laughed harshly. "As for me, I was doing my show - every one knows that. I was never in the place at all."

"The murder was not committed in the place," Francis commented calmly.

Fairfax slid off his stool. A spot of colour blazed in his pale cheeks, the glass which he was holding snapped in his fingers. He seemed suddenly possessed.

"I say, what the hell are you getting at?" he cried. "Are you accusing me - or any of us Victor's pals?"

"I accuse no one," Francis replied, unperturbed. "You invited a statement from me and I made it."

Sir Timothy Brast rose from his place and made his way to the end of the counter, next to Fairfax and nearest Francis. He addressed the former. There was an inscrutable smile upon his lips, his manner was reassuring.

"Young gentleman," he begged, "pray do not disturb yourself. I will answer for it that neither you nor any of your friends are the objects of Mr. Leadsam's suspicion. Without a doubt, it is I to whom his somewhat bold statement refers."

They all stared at him, immersed in another crisis,

bereft of speech. He tapped a cigarette upon the counter and lit it. Fairfax, whose glass had just been refilled by the bartender, was still ghastly pale, shaking with nervousness and breathing hoarsely. Francis, tense and alert in his chair, watched the speaker but said nothing.

"You see," Sir Timothy continued, addressing himself to the four young men at the bar, "I happen to have two special aversions in life. One is sweet champagne and the other amateur detectives - their stories, their methods and everything about them. I chanced to sit upstairs in the restaurant, within hearing of Mr. Ledsam and his friend Mr. Wilmore, the novelist, the other night, and I heard Mr. Ledsam, very much to my chagrin, announce his intention of abandoning a career in which he has, if he will allow me to say so," - with a courteous bow to Francis - "attained considerable distinction, to indulge in the moth-eaten, flamboyant and melodramatic antics of the lesser Sherlock Holmes. I fear that I could not resist the opportunity of - I think you young men call it - pulling his leg."

Every one was listening intently, including Shopland, who had just drifted into the room and subsided into a chair near Francis.

"I moved my place, therefore," Sir Timothy continued, "and I whispered in Mr. Ledsam's ear some rodomontade to the effect that if he were planning to be the giant crime-detector of the world, I was by ambition the arch-criminal - or words to that effect. And to give emphasis to my words, I wound up by prophesying a crime in the immediate vicinity of the place within a few hours."

"A somewhat significant prophecy, under the circumstances," Francis remarked, reaching out for a dish of salted almonds and drawing them towards him.

Sir Timothy shrugged his shoulders deprecatingly.

"I will confess," he admitted, "that I had not in my mind an affair of such dimensions. My harmless remark, however, has produced cataclysmic effects. The conversation to which I refer took place on the night of young Bidlake's murder, and Mr. Ledsam, with my somewhat, I confess, bombastic words in his memory, has pitched upon me as the bloodthirsty murderer."

"Hold on for a moment, sir," Peter Jacks begged, wiping the perspiration from his forehead. "We've got to have another drink quick. Poor old Bobby here looks knocked all of a heap, and I'm kind of jumpy myself. You'll join us, sir?"

"I thank you," was the courteous reply. "I do not as a rule indulge to the extent of more than one cocktail, but I will recognise the present as an exceptional occasion. To continue, then," he went on, after the glasses had been filled, "I have during the last few weeks experienced the ceaseless and lynx-eyed watch of Mr. Ledsam and presumably his myrmidons. I do not know whether you are all acquainted with my name, but in case you are not, let me introduce myself. I am Sir Timothy Brast, Chairman, as I dare say you know, of the United Transvaal Gold Mines, Chairman, also, of two of the principal hospitals in London, Vice President of the Society for the Prevention of Cruelty to Animals, a patron of sport in many forms, a traveller in many countries, and a recipient of the honour of knighthood from His Majesty, in recognition of my services for various philanthropic works. These facts, however, have availed me nothing now that the bungling amateur investigator into crime has pointed the finger of suspicion towards me. My servants and neighbours have alike been plagued to death with cunning questions as to my life and habits. I have been watched in the streets and watched in my harmless amusements. My simple life has been peered into from every perspective and direction. In short, I am suspect. Mr. Ledsam's terrifying statement a few minutes ago was directed towards me and me only."

There were murmurs of sympathy from the four young men, who each in his own fashion appeared to derive consolation from Sir Timothy's frank and somewhat caustic statement. Francis, who had listened unmoved to this flow of words, glanced towards the door behind which dark figures seemed to be looming.

"That is all you have to say, Sir Timothy?" he asked politely.

"For the present, yes," was the guarded reply. "I trust that I have succeeded in setting these young gentlemen's minds at ease."

"There is one of them," Francis said gravely, "whose mind not even your soothing words could lighten."

Shopland had risen unobtrusively to his feet. He laid his hand suddenly on Fairfax's shoulder and whispered in his ear. Fairfax, after his first start, seemed cool enough. He stretched out his hand towards the glass which as yet he had not touched; covered it with his fingers for a moment and drained its contents. The gently sarcastic smile left Sir Timothy's lips. His eyebrows met in a quick frown, his eyes glittered.

"What is the meaning of this?" he demanded sharply.

A policeman in plain clothes had advanced from the door. The manager hovered in the background. Shopland saw that all was well.

"It means," he announced, "that I have just arrested Mr. Robert Fairfax here on a charge of wilful murder. There is a way out through the kitchens, I believe. Take his other arm, Holmes. Now, gentlemen, if you please."

There were a few bewildered exclamations - then a dramatic hush. Fairfax had fallen forward on his stool. He seemed to have relapsed into a comatose state. Every scrap of colour was drained from his sallow cheeks, his eyes were covered with a film and he was breathing heavily. The detective snatched up the glass from which the young man had been drinking, and smelt it.

"I saw him drop a tablet in just now," Jimmy faltered. "I thought it was one of the digestion pills he uses sometimes."

Shopland and the policeman placed their hands underneath the armpits of the unconscious man.

"He's done, sir," the former whispered to Francis. "We'll try and get him to the station if we can."

CHAPTER XIV

The greatest tragedies in the world, provided they happen to other people, have singularly little effect upon the externals of our own lives. There was certainly not a soul in Soto's that night who did not know that Bobby Fairfax had been arrested in the bar below for the murder of Victor Bidlake, had taken poison and died on the way to the police station. Yet the same number of dinners were ordered and eaten, the same quantity of wine drunk. The management considered that they had shown marvellous delicacy of feeling by restraining the orchestra from their usual musical gymnastics until after the service of dinner. Conversation, in consequence, buzzed louder than ever. One speculation in particular absorbed the attention of every single person in the room - why had Bobby Fairfax, at the zenith of a very successful career, risked the gallows and actually accepted death for the sake of killing Victor Bidlake, a young man with whom, so far as anybody knew, he had no cause of quarrel whatever? There were many theories, many people who knew the real facts and whispered them into a neighbour's ear, only to have them contradicted a few moments later. Yet, Curiously enough, the two men who knew most about it were the two most silent men in the room, for each was dining alone. Francis, who had remained only in the hope that something of the sort might happen, was conscious of a queer sense

E. Phillips Oppenheim

of excitement when, with the service of coffee, Sir Timothy, glass in hand, moved up from a table lower down and with a word of apology took the vacant place by his side. It was what he had desired, and yet he felt a thrill almost of fear at Sir Timothy's murmured words. He felt that he was in the company of one who, if not an enemy, at any rate had no friendly feeling towards him.

"My congratulations, Mr. Ledsam," Sir Timothy said quietly. "You appear to have started your career with a success."

"Only a partial one," Francis acknowledged, "and as a matter of fact I deny that I have started in any new career. It was easy enough to make use of a fluke and direct the intelligence of others towards the right person, but when the real significance of the thing still eludes you, one can scarcely claim a triumph."

Sir Timothy gently knocked the ash from the very fine cigar which he was smoking.

"Still, your groundwork was good," he observed.

Francis shrugged his shoulders.

"That," he admitted, "was due to chance."

"Shall we exchange notes?" Sir Timothy suggested gently. "It might be interesting."

"As you will," Francis assented. "There is no particular secret in the way I stumbled upon the truth. I was dining here that night, as you know, with Andrew Wilmore, and while he was ordering the dinner and talking to some friends, I went down to the American Bar to have a cocktail. Miss Daisy Hyslop and Fairfax were seated there alone and talking confidentially. Fairfax was insisting that Miss Hyslop should do something which puzzled her. She consented reluctantly, and Fairfax then hurried off to the theatre. Later on, Miss Hyslop and the unfortunate young man occupied a table close to ours, and I happened to notice that she made a point of leaving the restaurant at a particular time. While they were waiting in the vestibule she grew very impatient. I was standing behind them and I saw her glance at the clock just before she insisted upon her companion's going out himself to look for a taxicab. Ergo, one enquires at Fairfax's theatre. For that exact three-quarters of an hour he is off the stage. At that point my interest in the matter ceases. Scotland Yard was quite capable of the rest."

"Disappointing," Sir Timothy murmured. "I thought at first that you were over-modest. I find chat I was mistaken. It was chance alone which set you on the right track."

"Well, there is my story, at any rate," Francis declared. "With how much of your knowledge of the affair are you going to indulge me?"

Sir Timothy slowly revolved his brandy glass.

"Well," he said, "I will tell you this. The two young men concerned, Bidlake and Fairfax, were both guests of mine recently at my country house. They had discovered for one another a very fierce and reasonable antipathy. With that recurrence to primitivism with which I have always been a hearty sympathiser, they

E. Phillips Oppenheim

agreed, instead of going round their little world making sneering remarks about each other, to fight it out."

"At your suggestion, I presume?" Francis interposed.

"Precisely," Sir Timothy assented. "I recommended that course, and I offered them facilities for bringing the matter to a crisis. The fight, indeed, was to have come off the day after the unfortunate episode which anticipated it."

"Do you mean to tell me that you knew - " Francis began.

Sir Timothy checked him quietly but effectively.

"I knew nothing," he said, "except this. They were neither of them young men of much stomach, and I knew that the one who was the greater coward would probably try to anticipate the matter by attacking the other first if he could. I knew that Fairfax was the greater coward - not that there was much to choose between them - and I also knew that he was the injured person. That is really all there is about it. My somewhat theatrical statement to you was based upon probability, and not upon any certain foreknowledge. As you see, it came off."

"And the cause of their quarrel?" Francis asked.

"There might have been a hundred reasons," Sir Timothy observed. "As a matter of fact, it was the eternal one. There is no need to mention a woman's name, so we will let it go at that."

There was a moment's silence - a strange, unforgettable

moment for Francis Ledsam, who seemed by some curious trick of the imagination to have been carried away into an impossible and grotesque world. The hum of eager conversation, the popping of corks, the little trills of feminine laughter, all blended into one sensual and not unmusical chorus, seemed to fade from his ears. He fancied himself in some subterranean place of vast dimensions, through the grim galleries of which men and women with evil faces crept like animals. And towering above them, unreal in size, his scornful face an epitome of sin, the knout which he wielded symbolical and ghastly, driving his motley flock with the leer of the evil shepherd, was the man from whom he had already learnt to recoil with horror. The picture came and went in a flash. Francis found himself accepting a courteously offered cigar from his companion.

"You see, the story is very much like many others," Sir Timothy murmured, as he lit a fresh Cigar himself and leaned back with the obvious enjoyment of the cultivated smoker. "In every country of the world, the animal world as well as the human world, the male resents his female being taken from him. Directly he ceases to resent it, he becomes degenerate. Surely you must agree with me, Mr. Leddam?

"It comes to this, then," Francis pronounced delibe- rately, "that you stage-managed the whole affair."

Sir Timothy smiled.

"It is my belief, Mr. Ledsam," he said, "that you grow more and more intelligent every hour."

Sir Timothy glanced presently at his thin gold watch

and put it back in his pocket regretfully.

"Alas!" he sighed, "I fear that I must tear myself away. I particularly want to hear the last act of 'Louise.' The new Frenchwoman sings, and my daughter is alone. You will excuse me."

Francis nodded silently. His companion's careless words had brought a sudden dazzling vision into his mind. Sir Timothy scrawled his name at the foot of his bill.

"It is one of my axioms in life, Mr. Ledsam," he continued, "that there is more pleasure to be derived from the society of one's enemies than one's friends. If I thought you sufficiently educated in the outside ways of the world to appreciate this, I would ask if you cared to accompany me?"

Francis did not hesitate for a moment.

"Sir Timothy," he said, "I have the greatest detestation for you, and I am firmly convinced that you represent all the things in life abhorrent to me. On the other hand, I should very much like to hear the last act of 'Louise,' and it would give me the greatest pleasure to meet your daughter. So long as there is no misunderstanding."

Sir Timothy laughed.

"Come," he said, "we will get our hats. I am becoming more and more grateful to you, Mr. Ledsam. You are supplying something in my life which I have lacked. You appeal alike to my sense of humour and my imagination. We will visit the opera together."

CHAPTER XV

The two men left Soto's together, very much in the fashion of two ordinary acquaintances sallying out to spend the evening together. Sir Timothy's Rolls-Royce limousine was in attendance, and in a few minutes they were threading the purlieus of Covent Garden. It was here that an incident occurred which afforded Francis considerable food for thought during the next few days.

It was a Friday night, and one or two waggons laden with egetable produce were already threading their way through the difficult thoroughfares. Suddenly Sir Timothy, who was looking out of the window, pressed the button of the car, which was at once brought to a standstill. Before the footman could reach the door Sir Timothy was out in the street. For the first time Francis saw him angry. His eyes were blazing. His voice - Francis had followed him at once into the street - shook with passion. His hand had fallen heavily upon the shoulder of a huge carter, who, with whip in hand, was belabouring a thin scarecrow of a horse.

"What the devil are you doing?" Sir Timothy demanded.

The man stared at his questioner, and the instinctive antagonism of race vibrated in his truculent reply. The

E. Phillips Oppenheim

carter was a beery-faced, untidy-looking brute, but powerfully built and with huge shoulders. Sir Timothy, straight as a dart, without overcoat or any covering to his thin evening clothes, looked like a stripling in front of him.

"I'm whippin' 'er, if yer want to know," was the carter's reply. "I've got to get up the 'ill, 'aven't I? Garn and mind yer own business!"

"This is my business," Sir Timothy declared, laying his hand upon the neck of the horse. "I am an official of the Society for the Prevention of Cruelty to Animals. You are laying yourself open to a fine for your treatment of this poor brute."

"I'll lay myself open for a fine for the treatment of something else, if you don't quid 'old of my 'oss," the carter retorted, throwing his whip back into the waggon and coming a step nearer. "D'yer 'ear? I don't want any swells interferin' with my business. You 'op it. Is that strite enough? 'Op it, quick!"

Sir Timothy's anger seemed to have abated. There was even the beginning of a smile upon his lips. All the time his hand caressed the neck of the horse. Francis noticed with amazement that the poor brute had raised his head and seemed to be making some faint effort at reciprocation.

"MY good man," Sir Timothy said, "you seem to be one of those brutal persons unfit to be trusted with an animal. However -"

The car carter had heard quite enough. Sir Timothy's tone seemed to madden him. He clenched his fist and rushed in.

"You take that for interferin', you big toff!" he shouted.

The result of the man's effort at pugilism was almost ridiculous. His arms appeared to go round like windmills beating the air. It really seemed as though he had rushed upon the point of Sir Timothy's knuckles, which had suddenly shot out like the piston of an engine. The carter lay on his back for a moment. Then he staggered viciously to his feet.

"Don't," Sir Timothy begged, as he saw signs of another attack. "I don't want to hurt you. I have been amateur champion of two countries. Not quite fair, is it?"

"Wot d'yer want to come interferin' with a chap's business for?" the man growled, dabbing his cheek with a filthy handkerchief but keeping at a respectful distance.

"It happens to be my business also," Sir Timothy replied, "to interfere whenever I see animals ill-treated. Now I don't want to be unreasonable. That animal has done all the work it ought to do in this world. How much is she worth to you?"

Through the man's beer-clogged brain a gleam of cunning began to find its way. He looked at the Rolls-Royce, with the two motionless servants on the box, at Francis standing by, at Sir Timothy, even to his thick understanding the very prototype of a "toff."

"That 'oss," he said, "ain't what she was, it's true, but there's a lot of work in 'er yet. She may not be much to look at but she's worth forty quid to me - ay, and one to spit on!"

Sir Timothy counted out some notes from the pocketbook which he had produced, and handed them to the man.

"Here are fifty pounds," he said. "The mare is mine. Johnson!"

The second man sprang from his seat and came round.

"Unharness that mare," his master ordered, "help the man push his trolley back out of the way, then lead the animal to the mews in Curzon Street. See that she is well bedded down and has a good feed of corn. To-morrow I shall send her down to the country, but I will come and have a look at her first."

The man touched his hat and hastened to commence his task. The carter, who had been busy counting the notes, thrust them into his pocket with a grin.

"Good luck to yer, guvnor!" he shouted out, in valedictory fashion. "'Ope I meets yer again when I've an old crock on the go."

Sir Timothy turned his head.

"If ever I happen to meet you, my good man," he threatened, "using your whip upon a poor beast who's doing his best, I promise you you won't get up in two minutes, or twenty .... We might walk the last few yards, Mr. Ledsam."

The latter acquiesced at once, and in a moment or two

they were underneath the portico of the Opera House. Sir Timothy had begun to talk about the opera but Francis was a little distrait. His companion glanced at him curiously.

"You are puzzled, Mr. Ledsam?" he remarked.

"Very," was the prompt response.

Sir Timothy smiled.

"You are one of these primitive Anglo-Saxons," he said, "who can see the simple things with big eyes, but who are terribly worried at an unfamiliar constituent. You have summed me up in your mind as a hardened brute, a criminal by predilection, a patron of murderers. Ergo, you ask yourself why should I trouble to save a poor beast of a horse from being chastised, and go out of my way to provide her with a safe asylum for the rest of her life? Shall I help you, Mr. Ledsam?"

"I wish you would," Francis confessed.

They had passed now through the entrance to the Opera House and were in the corridor leading to the grand tier boxes. On every side Sir Timothy had been received with marks of deep respect. Two bowing attendants were preceding them. Sir Timothy leaned towards his companion.

"Because," he whispered, "I like animals better than human beings."

Margaret Hilditch, her chair pushed back into the recesses of the box, scarcely turned her head at her father's entrance.

"I have brought an acquaintance of yours, Margaret," the latter announced, as he hung up his hat. "You remember Mr. Ledsam?"

Francis drew a little breath of relief as he bowed over her hand. For the second time her inordinate composure had been assailed. She was her usual calm and indifferent self almost immediately, but the gleam of surprise, and he fancied not unpleasant surprise, had been unmistakable.

"Are you a devotee, Mr. Ledsam?" she asked.

"I am fond of music," Francis answered, "especially this opera."

She motioned to the chair in the front of the box, facing the stage.

"You must sit there," she insisted. "I prefer always to remain here, and my father always likes to face the audience. I really believe," she went on, "that he likes to catch the eye of the journalist who writes little gossipy items, and to see his name in print."

"But you yourself?" Francis ventured.

"I fancy that my reasons for preferring seclusion should be obvious enough," she replied, a little bitterly.

"My daughter is inclined, I fear, to be a little morbid," Sir Timothy said, settling down in his place.

Francis made no reply. A triangular conversation of this sort was almost impossible. The members of the orchestra were already climbing up to their places, in preparation for the overture to the last act. Sir Timothy rose to his feet.

"You will excuse me for a moment," he begged. "I see a lady to whom I must pay my respects."

Francis drew a sigh of relief at his departure. He turned at once to his companion.

"Did you mind my coming?" he asked.

"Mind it?" she repeated, with almost insolent nonchalance. "Why should it affect me in any way? My father's friends come and go. I have no interest in any of them."

"But," he protested, "I want you to be interested in me."

She moved a little uneasily in her place. Her tone, nevertheless, remained icy.

"Could you possibly manage to avoid personalities in your conversation, Mr. Ledsam?" she begged.

"I have tried already to tell you how I feel about such things."

She was certainly difficult. Francis realised that with a little sigh.

"Were you surprised to see me with your father?" he asked, a little inanely.

"I cannot conceive what you two have found in common," she admitted.

"Perhaps our interest in you," he replied. "By-the-bye, I have just seen him perform a quixotic but a very fine action," Francis said. "He stopped a carter from thrashing his horse; knocked him down, bought the horse from him and sent it home."

She was mildly interested.

"An amiable side of my father's character which no one would suspect," she remarked. "The entire park of his country house at Hatch End is given over to broken-down animals."

"I am one of those," he confessed, "who find this trait amazing."

"And I am another," she remarked coolly. "If any one settled down seriously to try and understand my father, he would need the spectacles of a De Quincey, the outlook of a Voltaire, and the callousness of a Borgia. You see, he doesn't lend himself to any of the recognised standards."

"Neither do you," he said boldly.

She looked away from him across the House, to where Sir Timothy was talking to a man and woman in one of the ground-floor boxes. Francis recognised them with some surprise - an agricultural Duke and his daughter, Lady Cynthia Milton, one of the most, beautiful and famous young women in London.

"Your father goes far afield for his friends," Francis remarked.

"My father has no friends," she replied. "He has many

acquaintances. I doubt whether he has a single confidant. I expect Cynthia is trying to persuade him to invite her to his next party at The Walled House."

"I should think she would fail, won't she?" he asked.

"Why should you think that?"

Francis shrugged his shoulders slightly.

"Your father's entertainments have the reputation of being somewhat unique," he remarked. "You do not, by-the-bye, attend them yourself."

"You must remember that I have had very few opportunities so far," she observed. "Besides, Cynthia has tastes which I do not share."

"As, for instance?"

"She goes to the National Sporting Club. She once travelled, I know, over a hundred miles to go to a bull fight."

"On the whole," Francis said, "I am glad that you do not share her tastes."

"You know her?" Margaret enquired.

"Indifferently well," Francis replied. "I knew her when she was a child, and we seem to come together every now and then at long intervals. As a debutante she was charming. Lately it seems to me that she has got into the wrong set."

"What do you call the wrong set?"

He hesitated for a moment.

"Please don't think that I am laying down the law," he said. "I have been out so little, the last few years, that I ought not, perhaps, to criticise. Lady Cynthia, however, seems to me to belong to the extreme section of the younger generation, the section who have a sort of craze for the unusual, whose taste in art and living is distorted and bizarre. You know what I mean, don't you - black drawing-rooms, futurist wall-papers, opium dens and a cocaine box! It's to some extent affectation, of course, but it's a folly that claims its victims."

She studied him for a moment attentively. His leanness was the leanness of muscular strength and condition, his face was full of vigour and determination.

"You at least have escaped the abnormal," she remarked. "I am not quite sure how the entertainments at The Walled House would appeal to you, but if my father should invite you there, I should advise you not to go."

"Why not?" he asked.

She hesitated for a moment.

"I really don't know why I should trouble to give you advice," she said. "As a matter of fact, I don't care whether you go or not. In any case, you are scarcely likely to be asked."

"I am not sure that I agree with you," he protested. "Your father seems to have taken quite a fancy to me."

"And you?" she murmured.

"Well, I like the way he bought that horse," Francis admitted. "And I am beginning to realise that there may be something in the theory which he advanced when he invited me to accompany him here this evening - that there is a certain piquancy in one's intercourse with an enemy, which friendship lacks. There may be complexities in his character which as yet I have not appreciated."

The curtain had gone up and the last act of the opera had commenced. She leaned back in her chair. Without a word or even a gesture, he understood that a curtain had been let down between them. He obeyed her unspoken wish and relapsed into silence. Her very absorption, after all, was a hopeful sign. She would have him believe that she felt nothing, that she was living outside all the passion and sentiment of life. Yet she was absorbed in the music .... Sir Timothy came back and seated himself silently. It was not until the tumult of applause which broke out after the great song of the French ouvrier, that a word passed between them.

"Cavalisti is better," Sir Timothy commented. "This man has not the breadth of passion. At times he is merely peevish."

She shook her head.

"Cavalisti would be too egotistical for the part," she said quietly. "It is difficult."

Not another word was spoken until the curtain fell. Francis lingered for a moment over the arrangement of her cloak. Sir Timothy was already outside, talking to some acquaintances.

"It has been a great pleasure to see you like this unexpectedly," he said, a little wistfully.

"I cannot imagine why," she answered, with an undernote of trouble in her tone. "Remember the advice I gave you before. No good can come of any friendship between my father and you."

"There is this much of good in it, at any rate," he answered, as he held open. the door for her. "It might give me the chance of seeing you sometimes."

"That is not a matter worth considering," she replied.

"I find it very much worth considering," he whispered, losing his head for a moment as they stood close together in the dim light of the box, and a sudden sense of the sweetness of her thrilled his pulses. "There isn't anything in the world I want so much as to see you oftener - to have my chance."

There was a momentary glow in her eyes. Her lips quivered. The few words which he saw framed there - he fancied of reproof - remained unspoken. Sir Timothy was waiting for them at the entrance.

"I have been asking Mrs. Hilditch's permission to call in Curzon Street," Francis said boldly.

"I am sure my daughter will be delighted," was the cold but courteous reply.

Margaret herself made no comment. The car drew up

and she stepped into it - a tall, slim figure, wonderfully graceful in her unrelieved black, her hair gleaming as though with some sort of burnish, as she passed underneath the electric light. She looked back at him with a smile of farewell as he stood bareheaded upon the steps, a smile which reminded him somehow of her father, a little sardonic, a little tender, having in it some faintly challenging quality. The car rolled away. People around were g gossiping - rather freely.

"The wife of that man Oliver Hilditch," he heard a woman say, "the man who was tried for murder, and committed suicide the night after his acquittal. Why, that can't be much more than three months ago."

"If you are the daughter of a millionaire," her escort observed, "you can defy convention."

"Yes, that was Sir Timothy Brast," another man was saying. "He's supposed to be worth a cool five millions."

"If the truth about him were known," his companion confided, dropping his voice, "it would cost him all that to keep out of the Old Bailey. They say that his orgies at Hatch End - Our taxi. Come on, Sharpe."

Francis strolled thoughtfully homewards.

E. Phillips Oppenheim

CHAPTER XVI

Francis Ledsam was himself again, the lightest-hearted and most popular member of his club, still a brilliant figure in the courts, although his appearances there were less frequent, still devoting the greater portion of his time, to his profession, although his work in connection with it had become less spectacular. One morning, at the corner of Clarges Street and Curzon Street, about three weeks after his visit to the Opera, he came face to face with Sir Timothy Brast.

"Well, my altruistic peerer into other people's affairs, how goes it?" the latter enquired pleasantly.

"How does it seem, my arch-criminal, to be still breathing God's fresh air?" Francis retorted in the same vein. "Make the most of it. It may not last for ever."

Sir Timothy smiled. He was looking exceedingly well that morning, the very prototype of a man contented with life and his part in it. He was wearing a morning coat and silk hat, his patent boots were faultlessly polished, his trousers pressed to perfection, his grey silk tie neat and fashionable. Notwithstanding his waxenlike pallor, his slim figure and lithe, athletic walk seemed to speak of good health.

"You may catch the minnow," he murmured. "The big

fish swim on. By-the-bye," he added, "I do not notice that your sledge-hammer blows at crime are having much effect. Two undetected murders last week, and one the week before. What Are you about, my astute friend?"

"Those are matters for Scotland Yard," Francis replied, with an indifferent little wave of the hand which held his cigarette. "Details are for the professional. I seek that corner in Hell where the thunders are welded and the poison gases mixed. In other words, I seek for the brains of crime."

"Believe me, we do not see enough of one another, my young friend," Sir Timothy said earnestly. "You interest me more and more every time we meet. I like your allegories, I like your confidence, which in any one except a genius would seem blatant. When can we dine together and talk about crime?"

"The sooner the better," Francis replied promptly. "Invite me, and I will cancel any other engagement I might happen to have."

Sir Timothy considered for a moment. The June sunshine was streaming down upon them and the atmosphere was a little oppressive.

"Will you dine with me at Hatch End to-night?" he asked. "My daughter and I will be alone."

"I should be delighted," Francis replied promptly. "I ought to tell you, perhaps, that I have called three times upon your daughter but have not been fortunate enough to find her at home."

Sir Timothy was politely apologetic.

"I fear that my daughter is a little inclined to be morbid," he confessed. "Society is good for her. I will undertake that you are a welcome guest."

"At what time do I come and how shall I find your house?" Francis enquired.

"You motor down, I suppose?" Sir Timothy observed. "Good! In Hatch End any one will direct you. We dine at eight. You had better come down as soon as you have finished your day's work. Bring a suitcase and spend the night."

"I shall be delighted," Francis replied.

"Do not," Sir Timothy continued, "court disappointment by over-anticipation. You have without doubt heard of my little gatherings at Hatch End. They are viewed, I am told, with grave suspicion, alike by the moralists of the City and, I fear, the police. I am not inviting you to one of those gatherings. They are for people with other tastes. My daughter and I have been spending a few days alone in the little bungalow by the side of my larger house. That is where you will find us - The Sanctuary, we call it."

"Some day," Francis ventured, "I shall hope to be asked to one of your more notorious gatherings. For the present occasion I much prefer the entertainment you offer."

"Then we are both content," Sir Timothy said, smiling. "Au revoir!"

Francis walked across Green Park, along the Mall, down Horse Guards Parade, along the Embankment to his rooms on the fringe of the Temple. Here he found his clerk awaiting his arrival in some disturbance of spirit.

"There is a young gentleman here to see you, sir," he announced. "Mr. Reginald Wilmore his name is, I think."

"Wilmore?" Francis repeated. "What have you done with him?"

"He is in your room, sir. He seems very impatient. He has been out two or three times to know how long I thought you would be."

Francis passed down the stone passage and entered his room, a large, shady apartment at the back of the building. To his surprise it was empty. He was on the point of calling to his clerk when he saw that the writing-paper on his desk had been disturbed. He went over and read a few lines written in a boy's hasty writing:

DEAR Mr. LEDSAM:

I am in a very strange predicament and I have come to ask your advice. You know my brother Andrew well, and you may remember playing tennis with me last year. I am compelled -

At that point the letter terminated abruptly. There was a blot and a smudge. The pen lay where it seemed to have rolled -on the floor. The ink was not yet dry. Francis called to his clerk.

E. Phillips Oppenheim

"Angrave," he said, "Mr. Wilmore is not here."

The clerk looked around in obvious surprise.

"It isn't five minutes since he came out to my office, sir!" he exclaimed. "I heard him go back again afterwards."

Francis shrugged his shoulders.

"Perhaps he decided not to wait and you didn't hear him go by."

Angrave shook his head.

"I do not see how he could have left the place without my hearing him, sir," he declared. "The door of my office has been open all the time, and I sit opposite to it. Besides, on these stone floors one can hear any one so distinctly."

"Then what," Francis asked, "has become of him?"

The clerk shook his head.

"I haven't any idea, sir," he confessed.

Francis plunged into his work and forgot all about the matter. He was reminded of it, however, at luncheon-time, when, on entering the dining-room of the club, he saw Andrew Wilmore seated alone at one of the small tables near the wall. He went over to him at once.

"Hullo, Andrew," he greeted him, "what are you doing here by yourself ?"

"Bit hipped, old fellow," was the depressed reply. "Sit down, will you?"

Francis sat down and ordered his lunch.

"By-the-bye," he said, "I had rather a mysterious visit this morning from your brother Reggie."

Wilmore stared at him for a moment, half in relief, half in amazement.

"Good God, Francis, you don't say so!" he exclaimed. "How was he? What did he want? Tell me about it at once? We've been worried to death about the boy."

"Well, as a matter of fact, I didn't see him," Francis explained. "He arrived before I reached my rooms - as you know, I don't live there - waited some time, began to write me this note," - drawing the sheet of paper from his pocket - "and when I got there had disappeared without leaving a message or anything."

Wilmore adjusted his pince nez with trembling fingers. Then he read the few lines through.

"Francis," he said, when he had finished them, "do you know that this is the first word we've heard of him for three days?"

"Great heavens!" Francis exclaimed. "He was living with his mother, wasn't he?"

"Down at Kensington, but he hasn't been there since Monday," Andrew replied. "His mother is in a terrible state. And now this, I don't understand it at all."

"Was the boy hard up?"

"Not more than most young fellows are," was the puzzled reply. "His allowance was due in a few days, too. He had money in the bank, I feel sure. He was saving up for a motorcar."

"Haven't I seen him once or twice at restaurants lately?" Francis enquired. "Soto's, for instance?"

"Very likely," his brother assented. "Why not? He's fond of dancing, and we none of us ever encouraged him to be a stay-at-home."

"Any particular girl was he interested in?"

"Not that we know of. Like most young fellows of his age, he was rather keen on young women with some connection with the stage, but I don't believe there was any one in particular. Reggie was too fond of games to waste much time that way. He's at the gymnasium three evenings a week."

"I wish I'd been at the office a few minutes earlier this morning," Francis observed. "I tell you what, Andrew. I have some pals down at Scotland Yard, and I'll go down and see them this afternoon. They'll want a photograph, and to ask a few questions, I dare say, but I shouldn't talk about the matter too much."

"You're very kind, Francis," his friend replied, "but it isn't so easy to sit tight. I was going to the police myself this afternoon."

"Take my advice and leave it to me," Francis begged. "I have a particular pal down at Scotland Yard who I know will be interested, and I want him to take up the case."

"You haven't any theory, I suppose?" Wilmore asked, a little wistfully.

Francis shook his head.

"Not the ghost of one," he admitted. "The reason I am advising you to keep as quiet as possible, though, is just this. If you create a lot of interest in a disappearance, you have to satisfy the public curiosity when the mystery is solved."

"I see," Wilmore murmured. "All the same, I can't imagine Reggie getting mixed up in anything discreditable."

"Neither can I, from what I remember of the boy," Francis agreed. "Let me see, what was he doing in the City?"

"He was with Jameson & Scott, the stockbrokers," Wilmore replied. "He was only learning the business and he had no responsibilities. Curiously enough, though, when I went to see Mr. Jameson he pointed out one or two little matters that Reggie had attended to, which looked as though he were clearing up, somehow or other."

"He left no message there, I suppose?"

"Not a line or a word. He gave the porter five shillings, though, on the afternoon before he disappeared - a man who has done some odd jobs for him."

"Well, a voluntary disappearance is better than an involuntary one," Francis remarked. "What was his usual programme when he left the office?"

"He either went to Queen's and played racquets, or he went straight to his gymnasium in the Holborn. I telephoned to Queen's. He didn't call there on the Wednesday night, anyhow."

"Where's the gymnasium?"

"At 147 a Holborn. A lot of city young men go there late in the evening, but Reggie got off earlier than most of them and used to have the place pretty well to himself. I think that's why he stuck to it."

Francis made a note of the address.

"I'll get Shopland to step down there some time," he said. "Or better still, finish your lunch and we'll take a taxi there ourselves. I'm going to the country later on, but I've half-an-hour to spare. We can go without our coffee and be there in ten minutes."

"A great idea," Wilmore acquiesced. "It's probably the last place Reggie visited, anyway."

CHAPTER XVII

The gymnasium itself was a source of immense surprise to both Francis and Wilmore. It stretched along the entire top storey of a long block of buildings, and was elaborately fitted with bathrooms, a restaurant and a reading-room. The trapezes, bars, and all the usual appointments were of the best possible quality. The manager, a powerful-looking man dressed with the precision of the prosperous city magnate, came out of his office to greet them.

"What can I do for you, gentlemen?" he enquired.

"First of all," Francis replied, "accept our heartiest congratulations upon your wonderful gymnasium."

The man bowed.

"It is the best appointed in the country, sir," he said proudly. "Absolutely no expense has been spared in fitting it up. Every one of our appliances is of the latest possible description, and our bathrooms are an exact copy of those in a famous Philadelphia club."

"What is the subscription?" Wilmore asked.

"Five shillings a year."

"And how many members?"

"Two thousand."

The manager smiled as he saw his two visitors exchange puzzled glances.

"Needless to say, sir," he added, "we are not self-supporting. We have very generous patrons."

"I lave heard my brother speak of this place as being quite wonderful," Wilmore remarked, "but I had no idea that it was upon this scale."

"Is your brother a member?" the man asked.

"He is. To tell you the truth, we came here to ask you a question about him."

"What is his name?"

"Reginald Wilmore. He was here, I think, last Wednesday night."

While Wilmore talked, Francis watched. He was conscious of a curious change in the man's deportment at the mention of Reginald Wilmore's name. From being full of bumptious, almost condescending good-nature, his expression had changed into one of stony incivility. There was something almost sinister in the tightly-closed lips and the suspicious gleam in his eyes.

"What questions did you wish to ask?" he demanded.

"Mr. Reginald Wilmore has disappeared," Francis explained simply. "He came here on leaving the office last Monday. He has not been seen or heard of since."

"Well?" the manager asked.

"We came to ask whether you happen to remember his being here on that evening, and whether he gave any one here any indication of his future movements. We thought, perhaps, that the instructor who was with him might have some information."

"Not a chance," was the uncompromising reply. "I remember Mr. Wilmore being here perfectly. He was doing double turns on the high bar. I saw more of him myself than any one. I was with him when he went down to have his swim."

"Did he seem in his usual spirits?" Wilmore ventured.

"I don't notice what spirits my pupils are in," the man answered, a little insolently. "There was nothing the matter with him so far as I know."

"He didn't say anything about going away?"

"Not a word. You'll excuse me, gentlemen - "

"One moment," Francis interrupted. "We came here ourselves sooner than send a detective. Enquiries are bound to be made as to the young man's disappearance, and we have reason to know that this is the last place at which he was heard of. It is not unreasonable, therefore, is it, that we should come to you for information?"

"Reasonable or unreasonable, I haven't got any," the man declared gruffly. "If Mr. Wilmore's cleared out, he's cleared out for some reason of his own. It's not my business and I don't know anything about it."

"You understand," Francis persisted, "that our interest in young Mr. Wilmore is entirely a friendly one?"

"I don't care whether it's friendly or unfriendly. I tell you I don't know anything about him. And," he added, pressing his thumb upon the button for the lift, "I'll wish you two gentlemen good afternoon. I've business to attend to."

Francis looked at him curiously.

"Haven't I seen you somewhere before?" he asked, a little abruptly.

"I can't say. My name is John Maclane."

"Heavy-weight champion about seven years ago?"

"I was," the man acknowledged. "You may have seen me in the ring. Now, gentlemen, if you please."

The lift had stopped opposite to them. The manager's gesture of dismissal was final.

"I am sorry, Mr. Maclane, if we have annoyed you with our questions," Francis said. "I wish you could remember a little more of Mr. Wilmore's last visit."

"Well, I can't, and that's all there is to it," was the blunt reply. "As to being annoyed, I am only annoyed when my time's wasted. Take these gents down, Jim. Good afternoon!"

The door was slammed to and they shot downwards. Francis turned to the lift man.

"Do you know a Mr. Wilmore who comes here sometimes?" he asked.

"Not likely!" the man scoffed. "They're comin' and goin' all the time from four o'clock in the afternoon till eleven at night. If I heard a name I shouldn't remember it. This way out, gentlemen."

Wilmore's hand was in his pocket but the man turned deliberately away. They walked out into the street.

"For downright incivility," the former observed, "commend me to the attendants of a young men's gymnasium!"

Francis smiled.

"All the same, old fellow," he said, "if you worry for another five minutes about Reggie, you're an ass."

At six o'clock that evening Francis turned his two-seater into a winding drive bordered with rhododendrons, and pulled up before the porch of a charming two-storied bungalow, covered with creepers, and with French-windows opening from every room onto the lawns. A man-servant who had heard the approach of the car was already standing in the porch. Sir Timothy, in white flannels and a panama hat, strolled across the lawn to greet his approaching guest.

"Excellently timed, my young friend," he said. "You will have time for your first cocktail before you change. My daughter you know, of course. Lady

Cynthia Milton I think you also know."

Francis shook hands with the two girls who were lying under the cedar tree. Margaret Hilditch seemed to him more wonderful than ever in her white serge boating clothes. Lady Cynthia, who had apparently just arrived from some function in town, was still wearing muslin and a large hat.

"I am always afraid that Mr. Ledsam will have forgotten me," she observed, as she gave him her hand. "The last time I met you was at the Old Bailey, when you had been cheating the gallows of a very respectable wife murderer. Poynings, I think his name was."

"I remember it perfectly," Francis assented. "We danced together that night, I remember, at your aunt's, Mrs. Malcolm's, and you were intensely curious to know how Poynings had spent his evening."

"Lady Cynthia's reminder is perhaps a little unfortunate," Sir Timothy observed. "Mr. Ledsam is no longer the last hope of the enterprising criminal. He has turned over a new leaf. To secure the services of his silver tongue, you have to lay at his feet no longer the bags of gold from your ill-gotten gains but the white flower of the blameless life."

"This is all in the worst possible taste," Margaret Hilditch declared, in her cold, expressionless tone. "You might consider my feelings."

Lady Cynthia only laughed.

"My dear Margaret," she said, "if I thought that you had any, I should never believe that you were your father's daughter. Here's to them, anyway," she added, accepting the cocktail from the tray which the butler had just brought out. "Mr. Ledsam, are you going to attach yourself to me, or has Margaret annexed you?"

"I have offered myself to Mrs. Hilditch," Francis rejoined promptly, "but so far I have made no impression."

"Try her with a punt and a concertina after dinner," Lady Cynthia suggested. "After all, I came down here to better my acquaintance with my host. You flirted with me disgracefully when I was a debutante, and have never taken any notice of me since. I hate infidelity in a man. Sir Timothy, I shall devote myself to you. Can you play a concertina?"

"Where the higher forms of music are concerned," he replied, "I have no technical ability. I should prefer to sit at your feet."

"While I punt, I suppose?"

"There are backwaters," he suggested.

Lady Cynthia sipped her cocktail appreciatively.

"I wonder how it is," she observed, "that in these days, although we have become callous to everything else in life, cocktails and flirtations still attract us. You shall take me to a backwater after dinner, Sir Timothy. I shall wear my silver-grey and take an armful of those black cushions from the drawing-room. In that half light, there is no telling what success I may not achieve."

Sir Timothy sighed.

"Alas!" he said, "before dinner is over you will probably have changed your mind."

"Perhaps so," she admitted, "but you must remember that Mr. Ledsam is my only alternative, and I am not at all sure that he likes me. I am not sufficiently Victorian for his taste."

The dressing-bell rang. Sir Timothy passed his arm through Francis'.

"The sentimental side of my domain;" he said, "the others may show you. My rose garden across the stream has been very much admired. I am now going to give you a glimpse of The Walled House, an edifice the possession of which has made me more or less famous."

He led the way through a little shrubbery, across a further strip of garden and through a door in a high wall, which he opened with a key attached to his watch-chain. They were in an open park now, studded with magnificent trees, in the further corner of which stood an imposing mansion, with a great domed roof in the centre, and broad stone terraces, one of which led down to the river. The house itself was an amazingly blended mixture of old and new, with great wings supported by pillars thrown out on either side. It seemed to have been built without regard to any definite period of architecture, and yet to have attained a certain coherency - a far-reaching structure, with long lines of outbuildings. In the park itself were a score or more of horses, and in the distance beyond a long line of loose boxes with open doors. Even as they stood there, a grey sorrel mare had trotted up to their side and laid her head against Sir Timothy's shoulder. He caressed her surreptitiously, affecting not to notice the approach of other animals from all quarters.

"Let me introduce you to The Walled House," its owner observed, "so called, I imagine, because this wall, which is a great deal older than you or I, completely encloses the estate. Of course, you remember the old house, The Walled Palace, they called it? It belonged for many years to the Lynton family, and afterwards to the Crown."

"I remember reading of your purchase," Francis said, "and of course I remember the old mansion. You seem to have wiped it out pretty effectually."

"I was obliged to play the vandal," his host confessed. "In its previous state, the house was picturesque but uninhabitable. As you see it now, it is an exact reproduction of the country home of one of the lesser known of the Borgias - Sodina, I believe the lady's name was. You will find inside some beautiful arches, and a sense of space which all modern houses lack. It cost me a great deal of money, and it is inhabited, when I am in Europe, about once a fortnight. You know the river name for it? 'Timothy's Folly!'"

"But what on earth made you build it, so long as you don't care to live there?" Francis enquired.

Sir Timothy smiled reflectively.

"Well," he explained, "I like sometimes to entertain, and I like to entertain, when I do, on a grand scale. In London, if I give a party, the invitations are almost automatic. I become there a very insignificant link in the chain of what is known as Society, and Society practically helps itself to my entertainment, and sees that everything is done according to rule. Down here things are entirely different. An invitation to The Walled House is a personal matter. Society has nothing whatever to do with my functions here. The reception-rooms, too, are arranged according to my own ideas. I have, as you may have heard, the finest private gymnasium in England. The ballroom and music-room and private theatre, too, are famous."

"And do you mean to say that you keep that huge place empty?" Francis asked curiously.

"I have a suite of rooms there which I occasionally occupy," Sir Timothy replied, "and there are always thirty or forty servants and attendants of different sorts who have their quarters there. I suppose that my daughter and I would be there at the present moment but for the fact that we own this cottage. Both she and I, for residential purposes, prefer the atmosphere there."

"I scarcely wonder at it," Francis agreed.

They were surrounded now by various quadrupeds. As well as the horses, half-a-dozen of which were standing patiently by Sir Timothy's side, several dogs had made their appearance and after a little preliminary enthusiasm had settled down at his feet. He leaned over and whispered something in the ear of the mare who had come first. She trotted off, and the others followed suit in a curious little procession. Sir Timothy watched them, keeping his head turned away from Francis.

"You recognise the mare the third from the end?" he pointed out. "That is the animal I bought in Covent Garden. You see how she has filled out?"

"I should never have recognised her," the other confessed.

"Even Nero had his weaknesses," Sir Timothy remarked, waving the dogs away. "My animals' quarters are well worth a visit, if you have time. There is a small hospital, too, which is quite up to date."

"Do any of the horses work at all?" Francis asked.

Sir Timothy smiled.

"I will tell you a very human thing about my favourites," he said. "In the gardens on the other side of the house we have very extensive lawns, and my head groom thought he would make use of one of a my horses who had recovered from a serious accident and was really quite a strong beast, for one of the machines. He found the idea quite a success, and now he no sooner appears in the park with a halter than, instead of stampeding, practically every one of those horses comes cantering up with the true volunteering spirit. The one which he selects, arches his neck and goes off to work with a whole string of the others following. Dodsley - that is my groom's name - tells me that he does a great deal more mowing now than he need, simply because they worry him for the work. Gratitude, you see, Mr. Ledsam, sheer gratitude. If you were to provide a dozen alms-houses for your poor dependants, I wonder how many of them would be anxious to mow your lawn.... Come, let me show you your room now."

They passed back through the postern-gate into the gardens of The Sanctuary. Sir Timothy led the way towards the house.

"I am glad that you decided to spend the night, Mr. Ledsam," he said. "The river sounds a terribly hackneyed place to the Londoner, but it has beauties which only those who live with it can discover. Mind your head. My ceilings are low."

Francis followed his host along many passages, up and down stairs, until he reached a little suite of rooms at the extreme end of the building. The man-servant who had unpacked his bag stood waiting. Sir Timothy glanced around critically.

"Small but compact," he remarked. "There is a little sitting-room down that stair, and a bathroom beyond. If the flowers annoy you, throw them out of the window. And if you prefer to bathe in the river to-morrow morning, Brooks here will show you the diving pool. I am wearing a short coat myself to-night, but do as you please. We dine at half-past eight."

Sir Timothy disappeared with a courteous little inclination of the head. Francis dismissed the man-servant at once as being out of keeping with his quaint and fascinating surroundings. The tiny room with its flowers, its perfume of lavender, its old-fashioned chintzes, and its fragrant linen, might still have been a room in a cottage. The sitting-room, with its veranda looking down upon the river, was provided with cigars, whisky and soda and cigarettes; a bookcase, with a rare copy of Rabelais, an original Surtees, a large paper Decameron, and a few other classics. Down another couple of steps was a perfectly white bathroom, with shower and plunge. Francis wandered from room to room, and finally threw himself into a chair on the veranda to smoke a cigarette. From the river below him came now and then the sound of voices. Through the trees on his right he could catch a glimpse, here and there, of the strange pillars and green domed roof of the Borghese villa.

CHAPTER XVIII

It was one of those faultless June evenings when the
only mission of the faintly stirring breeze seems to be
to carry perfumes from garden to garden and to make
the lightest of music amongst the rustling leaves. The
dinner-table had been set out of doors, underneath the
odorous cedar-tree. Above, the sky was an arc of the
deepest blue through which the web of stars had
scarcely yet found its way. Every now and then came
the sound of the splash of oars from the river; more
rarely still, the murmur of light voices as a punt passed
up the stream. The little party at The Sanctuary sat
over their coffee and liqueurs long after the fall of the
first twilight, till the points of their cigarettes glowed
like little specks of fire through the enveloping
darkness. Conversation had been from the first
curiously desultory, edited, in a way, Francis felt, for
his benefit. There was an atmosphere about his host
and Lady Cynthia, shared in a negative way by
Margaret Hilditch, which baffled Francis. It seemed to
establish more than a lack of sympathy - to suggest,
even, a life lived upon a different plane. Yet every now
and then their references to everyday happenings were
trite enough. Sir Timothy had assailed the recent craze
for drugs, a diatribe to which Lady Cynthia had
listened in silence for reasons which Francis could
surmise.

"If one must soothe the senses," Sir Timothy declared, "for the purpose of forgetting a distasteful or painful present, I cannot see why the average mind does not turn to the contemplation of beauty in some shape or other. A night like to-night is surely sedative enough. Watch these lights, drink in these perfumes, listen to the fall and flow of the water long enough, and you would arrive at precisely the same mental inertia as though you had taken a dose of cocaine, with far less harmful an aftermath."

Lady Cynthia shrugged her shoulders.

"Cocaine is in one's dressing-room," she objected, "and beauty is hard to seek in Grosvenor Square."

"The common mistake of all men," Sir Timothy continued, "and women, too, for the matter of that, is that we will persist in formulating doctrines for other people. Every man or woman is an entity of humanity, with a separate heaven and a separate hell. No two people can breathe the same air in the same way, or see the same picture with the same eyes."

Lady Cynthia rose to her feet and shook out the folds of her diaphanous gown, daring alike in its shape-lessness and scantiness. She lit a cigarette and laid her hand upon Sir
Timothy's arm.

"Come," she said, "must I remind you of your promise? You are to show me the stables at The Walled House before it is dark."

"You would see them better in the morning," he reminded her, rising with some reluctance to his feet.

"Perhaps," she answered, "but I have a fancy to see them now."

Sir Timothy looked back at the table.

"Margaret," he said, "will you look after Mr. Ledsam for a little time? You will excuse us, Ledsam? We shall not be gone long."

They moved away together towards the shrubbery and the door in the wall behind. Francis resumed his seat.

"Are you not also curious to penetrate the mysteries behind the wall, Mr. Ledsam?" Margaret asked.

"Not so curious but that I would much prefer to remain here," he answered.

"With me?"

"With you."

She knocked the ash from her cigarette. She was looking directly at him, and he fancied that there was a gleam of curiosity in her beautiful eyes. There was certainly a little more abandon about her attitude. She was leaning back in a corner of her high-backed chair, and her gown, although it lacked the daring of Lady Cynthia's, seemed to rest about her like a cloud of blue-grey smoke.

"What a curious meal!" she murmured. "Can you solve a puzzle for me, Mr. Ledsam?"

"I would do anything for you that I could," he answered.

"Tell me, then, why my father asked you here to-night? I can understand his bringing you to the opera, that was just a whim of the moment, but an invitation down here savours of deliberation. Studiously polite though you are to one another, one is conscious all the time of the hostility beneath the surface."

"I think that so far as your father is concerned, it is part of his peculiar disposition," Francis replied. "You remember he once said that he was tired of entertaining his friends - that there was more pleasure in having an enemy at the board."

"Are you an enemy, Mr. Ledsam?" she asked curiously.

He rose a little abruptly to his feet, ignoring her question. There were servants hovering in the background.

"Will you walk with me in the gardens?" he begged. "Or may I take you upon the river?"

She rose to her feet. For a moment she seemed to hesitate.

"The river, I think," she decided. "Will you wait for three minutes while I get a wrap. You will find some punts moored to the landing-stage there in the stream. I like the very largest and most comfortable."

Francis strolled to the edge of the stream, and made his choice of punts. Soon a servant appeared with his arms full of cushions, and a moment or two later, Margaret herself, wrapped in an ermine cloak. She smiled a little deprecatingly as she picked her way across the lawn.

"Don't laugh at me for being such a chilly mortal, please," she enjoined. "And don't be afraid that I am going to propose a long expedition. I want to go to a little backwater in the next stream."

She settled herself in the stern and they glided down the narrow thoroughfare. The rose bushes from the garden almost lapped the water as they passed. Behind, the long low cottage, the deserted dinner-table, the smooth lawn with its beds of scarlet geraniums and drooping lilac shrubs in the background, seemed like a scene from fairyland, to attain a perfection of detail unreal, almost theatrical.

"To the right when you reach the river, please," she directed. "You will find there is scarcely any current. We turn up the next stream."

There was something almost mysterious, a little impressive, about the broad expanse of river into which they presently turned. Opposite were woods and then a sloping lawn. From a house hidden in the distance they heard the sound of a woman singing. They even caught the murmurs of applause as she concluded. Then there was silence, only the soft gurgling of the water cloven by the punt pole. They glided past the front of the great unlit house, past another strip of woodland, and then up a narrow stream.

"To the left here," she directed, "and then stop."

They bumped against the bank. The little backwater into which they had turned seemed to terminate in a bed of lilies whose faint fragrance almost enveloped them. The trees on either side made a little arch of darkness.

"Please ship your pole and listen," Margaret said dreamily. "Make yourself as comfortable as you can. There are plenty of cushions behind you. This is where I come for silence."

Francis obeyed her orders without remark. For a few moments, speech seemed impossible. The darkness was so intense that although he was acutely conscious of her presence there, only a few feet away, nothing but the barest outline of her form was visible. The silence which she had brought him to seek was all around them. There was just the faintest splash of water from the spot where the stream and the river met, the distant barking of a dog, the occasional croaking of a frog from somewhere in the midst of the bed of lilies. Otherwise the silence and the darkness were like a shroud. Francis leaned forward in his place. His hands, which gripped the sides of the punt, were hot. The serenity of the night mocked him.

"So this is your paradise," he said, a little hoarsely.

She made no answer. Her silence seemed to him more thrilling than words. He leaned forward. His hands fell upon the soft fur which encompassed her. They rested there. Still she did not speak. He tightened his grasp, moved further forward, the passion surging through his veins, his breath almost failing him. He was so near now that he heard her breathing, saw her face, as pale as ever. Her lips were a little parted, her eyes looked out, as it seemed to him, half in fear, half in hope. He bent lower still. She neither shrank away nor invited him.

E. Phillips Oppenheim

"Dear!" he whispered.

Her arms stole from underneath the cloak, her fingers rested upon his shoulders. He scarcely knew whether it was a caress or whether she were holding him from her. In any case it was too late. With a little sob of passion his lips were pressed to hers. Even as she closed her eyes, the scent of the lilies seemed to intoxicate him.

He was back in his place without conscious movement. His pulses were quivering, the passion singing in his blood, the joy of her faint caress living proudly in his memory. It had been the moment of his life, and yet even now he felt sick at heart with fears, with the torment of her passiveness. She had lain there in his arms, he had felt the thrill of her body, some quaint inspiration had told him that she had sought for joy in that moment and had not wholly failed. Yet his anxiety was tumultuous, overwhelming. Then she spoke, and his heart leaped again. Her voice was more natural. It was not a voice which he had ever heard before.

"Give me a cigarette, please - and I want to go back."

He leaned over her again, struck a match with trembling fingers and gave her the cigarette. She smiled at him very faintly.

"Please go back now," she begged. "Smoke yourself, take me home slowly and say nothing."

He obeyed, but his knees were shaking when he stood up. Slowly, a foot at a time, they passed from the mesh of the lilies out into the broad stream. Almost as they did so, the yellow rim of the moon came up over the low hills. As they turned into their own stream, the light was strong enough for him to see her face. She lay there like a ghost, her eyes half closed, the only touch of colour in the shining strands of her beautiful hair. She roused herself a little as they swung around. He paused, leaning upon the pole.

"You are not angry?" he asked.

"No, I am not angry," she answered. "Why should I be? But I cannot talk to you about it tonight."

They glided to the edge of the landing-stage. A servant appeared and secured the punt.

"Is Sir Timothy back yet?" Margaret enquired.

"Not yet, madam."

She turned to Francis.

"Please go and have a whisky and soda in the smoking-room," she said, pointing to the open French windows. "I am going to my favourite seat. You will find me just across the bridge there."

He hesitated, filled with a passionate disinclination to leave her side even for a moment. She seemed to understand but she pointed once more to the room.

"I should like very much," she added, "to be alone for five minutes. If you will come and find me then - please!"

Francis stepped through the French windows into the smoking-room, where all the paraphernalia for satisfying thirst were set out upon the sideboard. He helped himself to whisky and soda and drank it absently, with his eyes fixed upon the clock. In five minutes he stepped once more back into the gardens, soft and brilliant now in the moonlight. As he did so, he heard the click of the gate in the wall, and footsteps. His host, with Lady Cynthia upon his arm, came into sight and crossed the lawn towards him. Francis, filled though his mind was with other thoughts, paused for a moment and glanced towards them curiously. Lady Cynthia seemed for a moment to have lost all her weariness. Her eyes were very bright, she walked with a new spring in her movements. Even her voice, as she addressed Francis, seemed altered.

"Sir Timothy has been showing me some of the wonders of his villa - do you call it a villa or a palace?" she asked.

"It is certainly not a palace," Sir Timothy protested, "and I fear that it has scarcely the atmosphere of a villa. It is an attempt to combine certain ideas of my own with the requirements of modern entertainment. Come and have a drink with use Ledsam."

"I have just had one," Francis replied. "Mrs. Hilditch is in the rose garden and I am on my way to join her."

He passed on and the two moved towards the open French windows. He crossed the rustic bridge that led into the flower garden, turned down the pergola and came to a sudden standstill before the seat which Margaret had indicated. It was empty, but in the corner lay the long-stalked lily which she had picked in the backwater. He stood there for a moment, transfixed. There were other seats and chairs in the garden, but he knew before he started his search that it was in vain. She had gone. The flower, drooping a little now though the stalk was still wet with the moisture of the river, seemed to him like her farewell.

CHAPTER XIX

Francis was surprised, when he descended for breakfast the next morning, to find the table laid for one only. The butler who was waiting, handed him the daily papers and wheeled the electric heater to his side.

"Is no one else breakfasting?" Francis asked.

"Sir Timothy and Mrs. Hilditch are always served in their rooms, sir. Her ladyship is taking her coffee upstairs."

Francis ate his breakfast, glanced through the Times, lit a cigarette and went round to the garage for his car. The butler met him as he drove up before the porch.

"Sir Timothy begs you to excuse him this morning, sir," he announced. "His secretary has arrived from town with a very large correspondence which they are now engaged upon."

"And Mrs. Hilditch?" Francis ventured.

"I have not seen her maid this morning, sir," the man replied, "but Mrs. Hilditch never rises before midday. Sir Timothy hopes that you slept well, sir, and would like you to sign the visitors' book."

Francis signed his name mechanically, and was turning away when Lady Cynthia called to him from the stairs. She was dressed for travelling and followed by a maid, carrying her dressing-case.

"Will you take me up to town, Mr. Ledsam?" she asked.

"Delighted," he answered.

Their dressing-cases were strapped together behind and Lady Cynthia sank into the cushions by his side. They drove away from the house, Francis with a backward glance of regret. The striped sun-blinds had been lowered over all the windows, thrushes and blackbirds were twittering on the lawn, the air was sweet with the perfume of flowers, a boatman was busy with the boats. Out beyond, through the trees, the river wound its placid way.

"Quite a little paradise," Lady Cynthia murmured.

"Delightful," her companion assented. "I suppose great wealth has its obligations, but why any human being should rear such a structure as what he calls his Borghese villa, when he has a charming place like that to live in, I can't imagine."

Her silence was significant, almost purposeful. She unwound the veil from her motoring turban, took it off altogether and attached it to the cushions of the car with a hatpin.

"There," she said, leaning back, "you can now gaze upon a horrible example to the young women of to-day. You can see the ravages which late hours, innumerable cocktails, a thirst for excitement, a contempt of the simple pleasures of life, have worked upon my once comely features. I was quite good-looking, you know, in the days you first knew me."

"You were the most beautiful debutante of your season," he agreed.

"What do you think of me now?" she asked.

She met his gaze without flinching. Her face was unnaturally thin, with disfiguring hollows underneath her cheekbones; her lips lacked colour; even her eyes were lustreless. Her hair seemed to lack brilliancy. Only her silken eyebrows remained unimpaired, and a certain charm of expression which nothing seemed able to destroy.

"You look tired," he said.

"Be honest, my dear man," she rejoined drily. "I am a physical wreck, dependent upon cosmetics for the looks which I am still clever enough to palm off on the uninitiated."

"Why don't you lead a quieter life?" he asked. "A month or so in the country would put you all right."

She laughed a little hardly. Then for a moment she looked at him appraisingly.

"I was going to speak to you of nerves," she said, "but how would you ever understand? You look as though you had not a nerve in your body. I can't think how you manage it, living in London. I suppose you do exercises and take care of what you eat and drink."

"I do nothing of the sort," he assured her indignantly. "I eat and drink whatever I fancy. I have always had a direct object in life - my work - and I believe that has kept me fit and well. Nerve troubles come as a rule, I think, from the under-used brain."

"I must have been born with a butterfly disposition," she said. "I am quite sure that mine come because I find it so hard to be amused. I am sure I am most enterprising. I try whatever comes along, but nothing satisfies me."

"Why not try being in love with one of these men who've been in love with you all their lives?"

She laughed bitterly.

"The men who have cared for me and have been worth caring about," she said, "gave me up years ago. I mocked at them when they were in earnest, scoffed at sentiment, and told them frankly that when I married it would only be to find a refuge for broader life. The right sort wouldn't have anything to say to me after that, and I do not blame them. And here is the torture of it. I can't stand the wrong sort near me - physically, I mean. Mind, I believe I'm attracted towards people with criminal tastes and propensities. I believe that is what first led me towards Sir Timothy. Every taste I ever had in life seems to have become besmirched. I'm all the time full of the craving to do horrible things, but all the same I can't bear to be touched. That's the torment of it. I wonder if you can understand?"

"I think I can," he answered. "Your trouble lies in having the wrong friends and in lack of self-discipline. If you were my sister, I'd take you away for a fortnight and put you on the road to being cured."

"Then I wish I were your sister," she sighed.

"Don't think I'm unsympathetic," he went on, "because I'm not. Wait till we've got into the main road here and I'll try and explain."

They were passing along a country lane, so narrow that twigs from the hedges, wreathed here and there in wild roses, brushed almost against their cheeks. On their left was the sound of a reaping-machine and the perfume of new-mown hay. The sun was growing stronger at every moment. A transitory gleam of pleasure softened her face.

"It is ages since I smelt honeysuckle," she confessed, "except in a perfumer's shop. I was wondering what it reminded me of."

"That," he said, as they turned out into the broad main road, with its long vista of telegraph poles, "is because you have been neglecting the real for the sham, flowers themselves for their artificially distilled perfume. What I was going to try and put into words without sounding too priggish, Lady Cynthia," he went on, "is this. It is just you people who are cursed with a restless brain who are in the most dangerous position, nowadays. The things which keep us healthy and normal physically - games, farces, dinner-parties of young people, fresh air and exercise - are the very things which after a time fail to satisfy the person with imagination. You want more out of life, always the something you don't understand, the something beyond. And so you keep on trying new things, and for every new thing you try, you drop an old one. Isn't it something like that?"

"I suppose it is," she admitted wearily.

"Drugs take the place of wholesome wine," he went on, warming to his subject. "The hideous fascination of flirting with the uncouth or the impossible some way or another, stimulates a passion which simple means have ceased to gratify. You seek for the unusual in every way - in food, in the substitution of absinthe for your harmless Martini, of cocaine for your stimulating champagne. There is a horrible wave of all this sort of thing going on to-day in many places, and I am afraid," he concluded, "that a great many of our very nicest young women are caught up in it."

"Guilty," she confessed, "Now cure me."

"I could point out the promised land, but how, could I lead you to it?" he answered.

"You don't like me well enough," she sighed.

"I like you better than you believe," he assured her, slackening his speed a little. "We have met, I suppose, a dozen times in our lives. I have danced with you here and there, talked nonsense once, I remember, at a musical reception -"

"I tried to flirt with you then," she interrupted.

He nodded.

"I was in the midst of a great case," he said, and everything that happened to me outside it was swept out of my mind day by day. What I was going to say is that I have always liked you, from the moment when your mother presented me to you at your first dance."

"I wish you'd told me so," she murmured.

"It wouldn't have made any difference," he declared. "I wasn't in a position to think of a duke's daughter, in those days. I don't suppose I am now."

"Try," she begged hopefully.

He smiled back at her. The reawakening of her sense of humour was something.

"Too late," he regretted. "During the last month or so the thing has come to me which we all look forward to, only I don't think fate has treated me kindly. I have always loved normal ways and normal people, and the woman I care for is different."

"Tell me about her?" she insisted.

"You will be very surprised when I tell you her name," he said. "It is Margaret Hilditch."

She looked at him for a moment in blank astonishment.

"Heavens!" she exclaimed. "Oliver Hilditch's wife!"

"I can't help that," he declared, a little doggedly. "She's had a miserable time, I know. She was married to a scamp. I'm not quite sure that her father isn't as bad a one. Those things don't make any difference."

"They wouldn't with you," she said softly. "Tell me, did you say anything to her last night?"

"I did," he replied. "I began when we were out alone together. She gave me no encouragement to speak of, but at any rate she knows."

Lady Cynthia leaned a little forward in her place.

"Do you know where she is now?"

He was a little startled.

"Down at the cottage, I suppose. The butler told me that she never rose before midday."

"Then for once the butler was mistaken," his companion told him. "Margaret Hilditch left at six o'clock this morning. I saw her in travelling clothes get into the car and drive away."

"She left the cottage this morning before us?" Francis repeated, amazed.

"I can assure you that she did," Lady Cynthia insisted. "I never sleep, amongst my other peculiarities," she went on bitterly, "and I was lying on a couch by the side of the open window when the car came for her. She stopped it at the bend of the avenue - so that it shouldn't wake us up, I suppose. I saw her get in and drive away."

Francis was silent for several moments. Lady Cynthia watched him curiously.

"At any rate," she observed, "in whatever mood she went away this morning, you have evidently succeeded in doing what I have never seen any one else do - breaking through her indifference. I shouldn't have thought that anything short of an earthquake would have stirred Margaret, these days."

"These days?" he repeated quickly. "How long have you known her?"

"We were at school together for a short time," she told him. "It was while her father was in South America. Margaret was a very different person in those days."

"However was she induced to marry a person like Oliver Hilditch?" Francis speculated.

His companion shrugged her shoulders.

"Who knows?" she answered indifferently. "Are you going to drop me?"

"Wherever you like."

"Take me on to Grosvenor Square, if you will, then," she begged, "and deposit me at the ancestral mansion. I am really rather annoyed about Margaret," she went on, rearranging her veil. "I had begun to have hopes that you might have revived my taste for normal things."

"If I had had the slightest intimation - " he murmured.

"It would have made no difference," she interrupted dolefully. "Now I come to think of it, the Margaret whom I used to know - and there must be plenty of her left yet - is just the right type of woman for you."

They drew up outside the house in Grosvenor Square. Lady Cynthia held out her hand.

"Come and see me one afternoon, will you?" she invited.

"I'd like to very much," he replied.

She lingered on the steps and waved her hand to him - a graceful, somewhat insolent gesture.

"All the same, I think I shall do my best to make you forget Margaret," she called out. "Thanks for the lift up. A bientot!"

CHAPTER XX

Francis drove direct from Grosvenor Square to his chambers in the Temple, and found Shopland, his friend from Scotland Yard, awaiting his arrival.

"Any news?" Francis enquired.

"Nothing definite, I am sorry, to say," was the other's reluctant admission.

Francis hung up his hat, threw himself into his easy-chair and lit a cigarette.

"The lad's brother is one of my oldest friends, Shopland," he said. "He is naturally in a state of great distress."

The detective scratched his chin thoughtfully.

"I said 'nothing definite' just now, sir," he observed. "As a rule, I never mention suspicions, but with you it is a different matter. I haven't discovered the slightest trace of Mr. Reginald Wilmore, or the slightest reason for his disappearance. He seems to have been a well-conducted young gentleman, a little extravagant, perhaps, but able to pay his way and with nothing whatever against him. Nothing whatever, that is to say, except one almost insignificant thing."

"And that?"

"A slight tendency towards bad company, sir. I have heard of his being about with one or two whom we are keeping our eye upon."

"Bobby Fairfax's lot, by any chance?"

Shopland nodded.

"He was with Jacks and Miss Daisy Hyslop, a night or two before he disappeared. I am not sure that a young man named Morse wasn't of the party, too."

"What do you make of that lot?" Francis asked curiously. "Are they gamesters, dope fiends, or simply vicious?"

The detective was silent. He was gazing intently at his rather square-toed shoes.

"There are rumours, sir," he said, presently, "of things going on in the West End which want looking into very badly - very badly indeed. You will remember speaking to me of Sir Timothy Brast?"

"I remember quite well," Francis acknowledged.

"I've nothing to go on," the other continued. "I am working almost on your own lines, Mr. Ledsam, groping in the dark to find a clue, as it were, but I'm beginning to have ideas about Sir Timothy Brast, just ideas."

"As, for instance?"

"Well, he stands on rather queer terms with some of his acquaintances, sir. Now you saw, down at Soto's Bar, the night we arrested Mr. Fairfax, that not one of those young men there spoke to Sir Timothy as though they were acquainted, nor he to them. Yet I happened to find out that every one of them, including Mr. Fairfax himself, was present at a party Sir Timothy Brast gave at his house down the river a week or two before."

"I'm afraid there isn't much in that," Francis declared. "Sir Timothy has the name of being an eccentric person everywhere, especially in this respect - he never notices acquaintances. I heard, only the other day, that while he was wonderfully hospitable and charming to all his guests, he never remembered them outside his house."

Shopland nodded.

"A convenient eccentricity," he remarked, a little drily. "I have heard the same thing myself. You spent the night at his country cottage, did you not, Mr. Ledsam? Did he offer to show you over The Walled House?"

"How the dickens did you know I was down there?" Francis demanded, with some surprise. "I was just thinking as I drove up that I hadn't left my address either here or at Clarges Street."

"Next time you visit Sir Timothy," the detective observed, "I should advise you to do so. I knew you were there, Mr. Ledsam, because I was in the neighbourhood myself. I have been doing a little fishing, and keeping my eye on that wonderful estate of Sir Timothy's."

Francis was interested.

"Shopland," he said, "I believe that our intelligences, such as they are, are akin."

"What do you suspect Sir Timothy of?" the detective asked bluntly.

"I suspect him of nothing," Francis replied. "He is simply, to my mind, an incomprehensible, somewhat sinister figure, who might be capable of anything. He may have very excellent qualities which he contrives to conceal, or he may be an arch-criminal. His personality absolutely puzzles me."

There was a knock at the door and Angrave appeared. Apparently he had forgotten Shopland's presence, for he ushered in another visitor.

"Sir Timothy Brast to see you, sir," he announced.

The moment was one of trial to every one, admirably borne. Shopland remained in his chair, with only a casual glance at the newcomer. Francis rose to his feet with a half-stifled expression of anger at the clumsiness of his clerk. Sir Timothy, well-shaven and groomed, attired in a perfectly-fitting suit of grey flannel, nodded to Francis in friendly fashion and laid his Homburg hat upon the table with the air of a familiar.

"My dear Ledsam," he said, "I do hope that you will excuse this early call. I could only have been an hour behind you on the road. I dare say you can guess what I have come to see you about. Can we have a word together?"

"Certainly," was the ready reply. "You remember my friend Shopland, Sir Timothy? It was Mr. Shopland who arrested young Fairfax that night at Soto's."

"I remember him perfectly," Sir Timothy declared. "I fancied, directly I entered, that your face was familiar," he added, turning to Shopland. "I am rather ashamed of myself about that night. My little outburst must have sounded almost ridiculous to you two. To tell you the truth, I quite failed at that time to give Mr. Ledsam credit for gifts which I have since discovered him to possess."

"Mr. Shopland and I are now discussing another matter," Francis went on, pushing a box of cigarettes towards Sir Timothy, who was leaning against the table in an easy attitude. "Don't go, Shopland, for a minute. We were consulting together about the disappearance of a young man, Reggie Wilmore, the brother of a friend of mine - Andrew Wilmore, the novelist."

"Disappearance?" Sir Timothy repeated, as he lit a cigarette. "That is rather a vague term."

"The young man has been missing from home for over a week," Francis said, "and left no trace whatever of his whereabouts. He was not in financial trouble, he does not seem to have been entangled with any young woman, he had not quarrelled with his people, and he seems to have been on the best of terms with the principal at the house of business where he was employed. His disappearance, therefore, is, to say the least of it, mysterious."

Sir Timothy assented gravely.

"The lack of motive to which you allude," he pointed out, "makes the case interesting. Still, one must remember that London is certainly the city of modern mysteries. If a new 'Arabian Nights' were written, it might well be about London. I dare say Mr. Shopland will agree with me," he continued, turning courteously towards the detective, "that disappearances of this sort are not nearly so uncommon as the uninitiated would believe. For one that is reported in the papers, there are half-a-dozen which are not. Your late Chief Commissioner, by-the-bye," he added meditatively, "once a very intimate friend of mine, was my informant."

"Where do you suppose they disappear to?", Francis enquired.

"Who can tell?" was the speculative reply. "For an adventurous youth there are a thousand doors which lead to romance. Besides, the lives of none of us are quite so simple as they seem. Even youth has its secret chapters. This young man, for instance, might be on his way to Australia, happy in the knowledge that he has escaped from some murky chapter of life which will now never be known. He may write to his friends, giving them a hint. The whole thing will blow over."

"There may be cases such as you suggest, Sir Timothy," the detective said quietly. "Our investigations, so far as regards the young man in question, however, do not point that way."

Sir Timothy turned over his cigarette to look at the name of the maker.

"Excellent tobacco," he murmured. "By-the-bye, what did you say the young man's name was?"

"Reginald Wilmore," Francis told him.

"A good name," Sir Timothy murmured. "I am sure I wish you both every good fortune in your quest. Would it be too much to ask you now, Mr. Ledsam, for that single minute alone?"

"By no means," Francis answered.

"I'll wait in the office, if I may," Shopland suggested, rising to his feet. "I want to have another word with you before I go."

"My business with Mr. Ledsam is of a family nature," Sir Timothy said apologetically, as Shopland passed out. "I will not keep him for more than a moment."

Shopland closed the door behind him. Sir Timothy waited until he heard his departing footsteps. Then he turned back to Francis.

Mr. Ledsam," he said, "I have come to ask you if you know anything of my daughter's whereabouts?"

"Nothing whatever," Francis replied. "I was on the point of ringing you up to ask you the same question."

"Did she tell you that she was leaving The Sanctuary?"

"She gave me not the slightest intimation of it," Francis assured his questioner, "in fact she invited me to meet her in the rose garden last night. When I arrived there, she was gone. I have heard nothing from her since."

"You spent the evening with her?"

"To my great content."

"What happened between you?"

"Nothing happened. I took the opportunity, however, of letting your daughter understand the nature of my feelings for her."

"Dear me! May I ask what they are?"

"I will translate them into facts," Francis replied. "I wish your daughter to become my wife."

"You amaze me!" Sir Timothy exclaimed, with the old mocking smile at his lips. "How can you possibly contemplate association with the daughter of a man whom you suspect and distrust as you do me?"

"If I suspect and distrust you, it is your own fault," Francis reminded him. "You have declared yourself to be a criminal and a friend of criminals. I am inclined to believe that you have spoken the truth. I care for that fact just as little as I care for the fact that you are a millionaire, or that Margaret has been married to a murderer. I intend her to become my wife."

"Did you encourage her to leave me?"

"I did not. I had not the slightest idea that she had left The Sanctuary until Lady Cynthia told me, halfway to London this morning."

Sir Timothy was silent for several moments.

"Have you any idea in your own mind," he persisted, "as to where she has gone and for what purpose?"

"Not the slightest in the world," Francis declared. "I am just as anxious to hear from her; and to know where she is, as you seem to be."

Sir Timothy sighed.

"I am disappointed," he admitted. "I had hoped to obtain some information from you. I must try in another direction."

"Since you are here, Sir Timothy," Francis said, as his visitor prepared to depart, "may I ask whether you have an objection to my marrying your daughter?"

Sir Timothy frowned.

"The question places me in a somewhat difficult position," he replied coldly. "In a certain sense I have a liking for you. You are not quite the ingenuous nincompoop I took you for on the night of our first meeting. On the other hand, you have prejudices against me. My harmless confession of sympathy with criminals and their ways seems to have stirred up a cloud of suspicion in your mind. You even employ a detective to show the world what a fool he can look, sitting in a punt attempting to fish, with one eye on the supposed abode of crime."

"I have nothing whatever to do with the details of Shopland's investigations," Francis protested. "He is in search of Reggie Wilmore."

"Does he think I have secret dungeons in my new abode," Sir Timothy demanded, "or oubliettes in which I keep and starve brainless youths for some nameless purpose? Be reasonable, Mr. Ledsam. What the devil benefit could accrue to me from abducting or imprisoning or in any way laying my criminal hand upon this young man?"

"None whatever that we have been able to discover as yet," Francis admitted.

"A leaning towards melodrama, admirable in its way, needs the leaven of a well-balanced discretion and a sense of humour," Sir Timothy observed. "The latter quality is as a rule singularly absent amongst the myrmidons of Scotland Yard. I do not think that Mr. Shopland will catch even fish in the neighbourhood of The Walled House. As regards your matrimonial proposal, let us waive that until my daughter returns."

"As you will," Francis agreed. "I will be frank to this extent, at any rate. If I can persuade your daughter to marry me, your consent will not affect the matter."

"I can leave Margaret a matter of two million pounds," Sir Timothy said pensively.

"I have enough money to support my wife myself," Francis observed.

"Utopian but foolish," Sir Timothy declared. "All the same, Mr. Ledsam, let me tell you this. You have a curious attraction for me. When I was asked why I had invited you to The Sanctuary last night, I frankly could not answer the question. I didn't know. I don't know. Your dislike of me doesn't seem to affect the question. I was glad to have you there last night. It pleases me to hear you talk, to hear your views of things. I feel that I shall have to be very careful, Mr. Ledsam, or -"

"Or what?" Francis demanded.

"Or I shall even welcome the idea of having you for a son-in-law," Sir Timothy concluded reluctantly. "Make my excuses to Mr. Shopland. Au revoir!"

Shopland came in as the door closed behind the departing visitor. He listened to all that Francis had to say, without comment.

"If The Walled House," he said at last, "is so carefully guarded that Sir Timothy has been informed of my watching the place and has been made aware of my mild questionings, it must be because there is something to conceal. I may or may not be on the track of Mr. Reginald Wilmore, but," the detective concluded, "of one thing I am becoming convinced - The Walled House will pay for watching."

CHAPTER XXI

It was a day when chance was kind to Francis. After leaving his rooms at the Temple, he made a call at one of the great clubs in Pall Mall, to enquire as to the whereabouts of a friend. On his way back towards the Sheridan, he came face to face with Margaret Hilditch, issuing from the doors of one of the great steamship companies. For a moment he almost failed to recognise her. She reminded him more of the woman of the tea-shop. Her costume, neat and correct though it was, was studiously unobtrusive. Her motoring veil, too, was obviously worn to assist her in escaping notice.

She, too, came to a standstill at seeing him. Her first ejaculations betrayed a surprise which bordered on consternation. Then Francis, with a sudden inspiration, pointed to the long envelope which she was carrying in her hand.

"You have been to book a passage somewhere!" he exclaimed.

"Well?"

The monosyllable was in her usual level tone. Nevertheless, he could see that she was shaken:

"You were going away without seeing me again?"' he

asked reproachfully.

"Yes!" she admitted.

"Why?"

She looked up and down a little helplessly.

"I owe you no explanation for my conduct," she said. "Please let me pass."

"Could we talk for a few minutes, please?" he begged. "Tell me where you were going?"

"Oh, back to lunch, I suppose," she answered.

"Your father has been up, looking for you," he told her.

"I telephoned to The Sanctuary," she replied. "He had just left."

"I am very anxious," he continued, "not to distress you, but I cannot let you go away like this. Will you come to my rooms and let us talk for a little time?"

She made no answer. Somehow, he realised that speech just then was difficult. He called a taxi and handed her in. They drove to Clarges Street in silence. He led the way up the stairs, gave some quick orders to his servant whom he met coming down, ushered her into his sitting-room and saw her ensconced in an easy-chair.

"Please take off that terrible veil," he begged.

"It is pinned on to my hat," she told him.

"Then off with both," he insisted. "You can't eat luncheon like that. I'm not going to try and bully you. If you've booked your passage to Timbuctoo and you really want to go - why, you must. I only want the chance of letting you know that I am coming after you."

She took off her hat and veil and threw them on to the sofa, glancing sideways at a mirror let into the door of a cabinet.

"My hair is awful," she declared:

He laughed gaily, and turned around from the sideboard, where he was busy mixing cocktails.

"Thank heavens for that touch of humanity!" he exclaimed. "A woman who can bother about her hair when she takes her hat off, is never past praying for. Please drink this."

She obeyed. He took the empty glass away from her. Then he came over to the hearthrug by her side.

"Do you know that I kissed you last night?" he reminded her.

"I do," she answered. "That is why I have just paid eighty-four pounds for a passage to Buenos Ayres."

"I should have enjoyed the trip," he said. "Still, I'm glad I haven't to go."

"Do you really mean that you would have come after me?" she asked curiously.

"Of course I should," he assured her. "Believe me, there isn't such an obstinate person in the world as the man of early middle-age who suddenly discovers the woman he means to marry."

"But you can't marry me," she protested.

"Why not?" he asked.

"Because I was Oliver Hilditch's wife, for one thing."

"Look here," he said, "if you had been Beelzebub's wife, it wouldn't make the least difference to me. You haven't given me much of a chance to tell you so yet, Margaret, but I love you."

She sat a little forward in her chair. Her eyes were fixed upon his wonderingly.

"But how can you?" she exclaimed. "You know, nothing of me except my associations, and they have been horrible. What is there to love in me? I am a frozen-up woman. Everything is dead here," she went on, clasping her hand to her heart. "I have no sentiment, no passion, nothing but an animal desire to live my life luxuriously and quickly."

He smiled confidently. Then, with very little warning, he sank on one knee, drew her face to his, kissed her lips and then her eyes.

"Are you so sure of all these things, Margaret?" he whispered. "Don't you think it is, perhaps, because there has been no one to care for you as I do - as I shall - to the end of my days? The lily you left on your chair last night was like you - fair and stately and beautiful, but a little bruised. You will come back as it has done, come back to the world. My love will bring you. My care. Believe it, please!"

Then he saw the first signs of change in her face. There was the faintest shade of almost shell-like pink underneath the creamy-white of her cheeks. Her lips were trembling a little, her eyes were misty. With a sudden passionate little impulse, her arms were around his neck, her lips sought his of their own accord.

"Let me forget," she sobbed. "Kiss me let me forget!"

Francis' servant was both heavy-footed and discreet. When he entered the room with a tray, his master was standing at the sideboard.

"I've done the best I could, sir," he announced, a little apologetically. "Shall I lay the cloth?"

"Leave everything on the tray, Brooks," Francis directed. "We will help ourselves. In an hour's time bring coffee."

The man glanced around the room.

"There are glasses on the sideboard, sir, and the corkscrew is here. I think you will have everything you want."

He departed, closing the door behind him. Francis held out his hands to Margaret. She rose slowly to her feet, looked in the glass helplessly and then back at him. She was very beautiful but a little dazed.

"Are we going to have luncheon?" she asked.

"Of course," he answered. "Did you think I meant to starve you?"

He picked up the long envelope which she had dropped upon the carpet, and threw it on to the sofa. Then he drew up two chairs to the table, and opened a small bottle of champagne.

"I hope you won't mind a picnic," he said. "Really, Brooks hasn't done so badly - pate de foie gras, hot toast and Devonshire butter. Let me spread some for you. A cold chicken afterwards, and some strawberries. Please be hungry, Margaret."

She laughed at him. It occurred to him suddenly, with a little pang, that he had never heard her laugh before. It was like music.

"I'm too happy," she murmured.

"Believe me," he assured her, as he buttered a piece of toast, "happiness and hunger might well be twins. They go so well together. Misery can take away one's appetite. Happiness, when one gets over the gulpiness of it, is the best tonic in the world. And I never saw any one, dear, with whom happiness agreed so well," he added, pausing in his task to bend over and kiss her. "Do you know you are the most beautiful thing on earth? It is a lucky thing we are going to live in England, and that these are sober, matter-of-fact days, or I should find myself committed to fighting duels all the time."

She had a momentary relapse. A look of terror suddenly altered her face. She caught at his wrist.

"Don't!" she cried. "Don't talk about such things!"

He was a little bewildered. The moment passed. She laughed almost apologetically.

"Forgive me," she begged, "but I hate the thought of fighting of any sort. Some day I'll explain."

"Clumsy ass I was!" he declared, completing his task and setting the result before her. "Now how's that for a first course? Drink a little of your wine."

He leaned his glass against hers.

"My love," he whispered, "my love now, dear, and always, and you'll find it quite strong enough," he went on, "to keep you from all the ugly things. And now away with sentiment. I had a very excellent but solitary breakfast this morning, and it seems a long time ago."

"It seems amazing to think that you spent last night at The Sanctuary," she reflected.

"And that you and I were in a punt," he reminded her, "in the pool of darkness where the trees met, and the lilies leaned over to us."

"And you nearly upset the punt."

"Nothing of the sort! As a matter of fact, I was very careful. But," he proceeded, with a sudden wave of memory, "I don't think my heart will ever beat normally again. It seemed as though it would tear its way out of my side when I leaned towards you, and you knew, and you lay still."

She laughed.

"You surely didn't expect I was going to get up? It was quite encouragement enough to remain passive. As a matter of fact," she went on, "I couldn't have moved. I couldn't have uttered a sound. I suppose I must have been like one of those poor birds you read about, when some devouring animal crouches for its last spring."

"Compliments already!" he remarked. "You won't forget that my name is Francis, will you? Try and practise it while I carve the chicken."

"You carve very badly, Francis," she told him demurely.

"My dear," he said, "thank heavens we shall be able to afford a butler! By-the-bye, I told your father this morning that I was going to marry you, and he didn't seem to think it possible because he had two million pounds."

"Braggart!" she murmured. "When did you see my father?"

"He came to my rooms in the Temple soon after I arrived this morning. He seemed to think I might know where you were. I dare say he won't like me for a son-in-law," Francis continued with a smile. "I can't help that. He shouldn't have let me go out with you in a punt."

There was a discreet knock at the door. Brooks made his apologetic and somewhat troubled entrance.

Sir Timothy Brast is here to see you, sir," he

announced. "I ventured to say that you were not at home -"

"But I happened to know otherwise," a still voice remarked from outside. "May I come in, Mr. Ledsam?"

Sir Timothy stepped past the servant, who at a sign from Francis disappeared, closing the door behind him.

E. Phillips Oppenheim

CHAPTER XXII

After his first glance at Sir Timothy, Francis' only thought was for Margaret. To his intense relief, she showed no signs whatever of terror, or of any relapse to her former state. She was entirely mistress of herself and the occasion. Sir Timothy's face was cold and terrible.

"I must apologise for this second intrusion, Mr. Ledsam," he said cuttingly. "I think you will admit that the circumstances warrant it. Am I to understand that you lied to me this morning?"

"You are to understand nothing of the sort," Francis answered. "I told you everything I knew at that time of your daughter's movements."

"Indeed!" Sir Timothy murmured. "This little banquet, then, was unpremeditated?"

"Entirely," Francis replied. "Here is the exact truth, so far as I am concerned. I met your daughter little more than an hour ago, coming out of a steamship office, where she had booked a passage to Buenos Ayres to get away from me. I was fortunate enough to induce her to change her mind. She has consented instead to remain in England as my wife. We were, as you see, celebrating the occasion."

Sir Timothy laid his hat upon the sideboard and slowly removed his gloves.

"I trust," he said, "that this pint bottle does not represent your cellar. I will drink a glass of wine with you, and with your permission make myself a pate sandwich. I was just sitting down to luncheon when I received the information which brought me here."

Francis produced another bottle of wine from the sideboard and filled his visitor's glass.

"You will drink, I hope, to our happiness," he said.

"I shall do nothing of the sort," Sir Timothy declared, helping himself with care to the pate. "I have no superstitions about breaking bread with an enemy, or I should not have asked you to visit me at The Sanctuary, Mr. Ledsam. I object to your marriage with my daughter, and I shall take what steps I can to prevent it."

"Why?"

Sir Timothy did not at once reply. He seemed to be enjoying his sandwich; he also appreciated the flavour of his wine.

"Your question," he said, "strikes me as being a little ingenuous. You are at the present moment suspecting me of crimes beyond number. You encourage Scotland Yard detectives to make asses of themselves in my stream. Your myrmidons scramble on to the top of my walls and try to bribe my servants to disclose the mysteries of my household. You have accepted to the fullest extent my volunteered statement that I am a patron of crime. You are, in short - forgive me if I help myself to a little more of this pate - engaged in a strenuous attempt to bring me to justice."

None of these things affects your daughter," Francis pointed out.

"Pardon me," Sir Timothy objected. "You are a great and shining light of the English law. People speak of you as a future Chancellor. How can you contemplate an alliance with the widow of one criminal and the daughter of another?"

"As to Margaret being Oliver Hilditch's widow," Francis replied, "you were responsible for that, and no one else. He was your protege; you gave your consent to the marriage. As to your being her father, that again is not Margaret's fault. I should marry her if Oliver Hilditch had been three times the villain he was, and if you were the Devil himself."

"I am getting quite to like you, Mr. Ledsam," Sir Timothy declared, helping himself to another piece of toast and commencing to butter it. "Margaret, what have you to say about all this?"

"I have nothing to say," she answered. "Francis is speaking for me. I never dreamed that after what I have gone through I should be able to care for any one again in this world. I do care, and I am very happy about it. All last night I lay awake, making up my mind to run away, and this morning I actually booked my passage to Buenos Ayres. Then we met - just outside the steamship office - and I knew at once that I was making a mistake. I shall marry Francis exactly when he wants me to."

Sir Timothy passed his glass towards his proposed son-in-law.

"Might one suggest," he began - "thank you very much. This is of course very upsetting to me. I seem to be set completely at defiance. It is a very excellent wine, this, and a wonderful vintage."

Francis bent over Margaret.

"Please finish your lunch, dear," he begged. "It is perhaps just as well that your father came. We shall know exactly where we are."

"Just so," Sir Timothy agreed.

There was a queer constrained silence for several moments. Then Sir Timothy leaned back in his chair and with a word of apology lit a cigarette.

"Let us," he said, "consider the situation. Margaret is my daughter. You wish to marry her. Margaret is of age and has been married before. She is at liberty, therefore, to make her own choice. You agree with me so far?"

"Entirely," Francis assented.

"It happens," Sir Timothy went on, "that I disapprove of her choice. She desires to marry a young man who belongs to a profession which I detest, and whose efforts in life are directed towards the extermination of a class of people for whom I have every sympathy. To me he represents the smug as against the human, the artificially moral as against the freethinker. He is also my personal enemy. I am therefore naturally desirous that my daughter should not marry this young man."

"We will let it go at that," Francis commented, "but I should like to point out to you that the antagonism between us is in no way personal. You have declared yourself for forces with which I am at enmity, like any other decent-living citizen. Your declaration might at any time be amended."

Sir Timothy bowed.

"The situation is stated," he said. "I will ask you this question as a matter of form. Do you recognise my right to forbid your marriage with my daughter, Mr. Ledsam?"

"I most certainly do not," was the forcible reply.

"Have I any rights at all?" Sir Timothy asked. "Margaret has lived under my roof whenever it has suited her to do so. Since she has taken up her residence at Curzon Street, she has been her own mistress, her banking account has known no limit whatsoever. I may be a person of evil disposition, but I have shown no unkindness to her."

"It is quite true," Margaret Admitted, turning a little pale. "Since I have been alone, you have been kindness itself."

"Then let me repeat my question," Sir Timothy went on, "have I the right to any consideration at all?"

"Yes," Francis replied. "Short of keeping us apart, you have the ordinary rights of a parent."

"Then I ask you to delay the announcement of your engagement, or taking any further steps concerning it, for fourteen days," Sir Timothy said. "I place no restrictions on your movements during that time. Such hospitality as you, Mr. Ledsam, care to accept at my hands, is at your disposal. I am Bohemian enough, indeed, to find nothing to complain of in such little celebrations as you are at present indulging in - most excellent pate, that. But I request that no announcement of your engagement be made, or any further arrangements made concerning it, for that fourteen days."

"I am quite willing, father," Margaret acquiesced.

"And I, sir," Francis echoed.

"In which case," Sir Timothy concluded, rising to his feet, lighting a cigarette and taking up his hat and gloves, "I shall go peaceably away. You will admit, I trust," he added, with that peculiar smile at the corner of his lips, "that I have not in any way tried to come the heavy father? I can even command a certain amount of respect, Margaret, for a young man who is able to inaugurate his engagement by an impromptu meal of such perfection. I wish you both good morning. Any invitation which Margaret extends, Ledsam, please consider as confirmed by me."

He closed the door softly. They heard his footsteps descending the stairs. Francis leaned once more over Margaret. She seemed still dazed, confused with new thoughts. She responded, however, readily to his touch, yielded to his caress with an almost pathetic eagerness.

"Francis," she murmured, as his arms closed around her, "I want to forget."

CHAPTER XXIII

There followed a brief period of time, the most wonderful of his life, the happiest of hers. They took advantage of Sir Timothy's absolute license, and spent long days at The Sanctuary, ideal lovers' days, with their punt moored at night amongst the lilies, where her kisses seemed to come to him with an aroma and wonder born of the spot. Then there came a morning when he found a cloud on her face. She was looking at the great wall, and away at the minaret beyond. They had heard from the butler that Sir Timothy had spent the night at the villa, and that preparations were on hand for another of his wonderful parties. Francis, who was swift to read her thoughts, led her away into the rose garden where once she had failed him.

"You have been looking over the wall, Margaret," he said reproachfully.

She looked at him with a little twitch at the corners of her lips.

"Francis dear," she confessed, "I am afraid you are right. I cannot even look towards The Walled House without wondering why it was built - or catch a glimpse of that dome without stupid guesses as to what may go on underneath."

"I think very likely," he said soothingly, "we have both exaggerated the seriousness of your father's hobbies. We know that he has a wonderful gymnasium there, but the only definite rumour I have ever heard about the place is that men fight there who have a grudge against one another, and that they are not too particular about the weight of the gloves. That doesn't appeal to us, you know, Margaret, but it isn't criminal."

"If that were all!" she murmured.

"I dare say it is," he declared. "London, as you know, is a hot-bed of gossip. Everything that goes on is ridiculously exaggerated, and I think that it rather appeals to your father's curious sense of humour to pose as the law-breaker."

She pressed his arm a little. The day was overcast, a slight rain was beginning to fall.

"Francis," she whispered, "we had a perfect day here yesterday. Now the sun has gone and I am shivery."

He understood in a moment.

"We'll lunch at Ranelagh," he suggested. "It is almost on the way up. Then we can see what the weather is like. If it is bad, we can dine in town tonight and do a theatre."

"You are a dear," she told him fervently. "I am going in to get ready."

Francis went round to the garage for his car, and brought it to the front. While he was sitting there, Sir Timothy came through the door in the wall. He was smoking a cigar and he was holding an umbrella to protect his white flannel suit. He was as usual wonderfully groomed and turned out, but he walked as though he were tired, and his smile, as he greeted Francis, lacked a little of its usual light-hearted mockery.

"Are you going up to town?" he enquired.

Francis pointed to the grey skies.

"Just for the day," he answered. "Lady Cynthia went by the early train. We missed you last night."

"I came down late," Sir Timothy explained, "and I found it more convenient to stay at The Walled House. I hope you find that Grover looks after you while I am away? He has carte blanche so far as regards my cellar."

"We have been wonderfully served," Francis assured him.

In the distance they could hear the sound of hammering on the other side of the wall. Francis moved his head in that direction.

"I hear that they are preparing for another of your wonderful entertainments over there," he remarked.

"On Thursday," Sir Timothy assented. "I shall have something to say to you about it later on."

"Am I to take it that I am likely to receive an invitation?" Francis asked.

"I should think it possible," was the calm reply.

"What about Margaret?"

"My entertainment would not appeal to her," Sir Timothy declared. "The women whom I have been in the habit of asking are not women of Margaret's type."

"And Lady Cynthia?"

Sir Timothy frowned slightly.

"I find myself in some difficulty as regards Lady Cynthia," he admitted. "I am the guardian of nobody's morals, nor am I the censor of their tastes, but my entertainments are for men. The women whom I have hitherto asked have been women in whom I have taken no personal interest. They are necessary to form a picturesque background for my rooms, in the same way that I look to the gardeners to supply the floral decorations. Lady Cynthia's instincts, however, are somewhat adventurous. She would scarcely be content to remain a decoration."

"The issuing of your invitations," Francis remarked, "is of course a matter which concerns nobody else except yourself. If you do decide to favour me with one, I shall be delighted to come, provided Margaret has no objection."

"Such a reservation promises well for the future," Sir Timothy observed, with gentle sarcasm. "Here comes Margaret, looking very well, I am glad to see."

Margaret came forward to greet her father before stepping into the car. They exchanged only a few

E. Phillips Oppenheim

sentences, but Francis, whose interest in their relations was almost abnormally keen, fancied that he could detect signs of some change in their demeanour towards one another. The cold propriety of deportment which had characterised her former attitude towards her father, seemed to have given place to something more uncertain, to something less formal, something which left room even for a measure of cordiality. She looked at him differently. It was as though some evil thought which lived in her heart concerning him had perished.

"You are busy over there, father?" she asked.

"In a way," he replied. "We are preparing for some festivities on Thursday."

Her face fell.

"Another party?"

"One more," he replied. "Perhaps the last - for the present, at any rate."

She waited as though expecting him to explain. He changed the subject, however.

"I think you are wise to run up to town this morning," he said, glancing up at the grey skies. "By-the-bye, if you dine at Curzon Street to-night, do ask Hedges to serve you some of the '99 Cliquot. A marvellous wine, as you doubtless know, Ledsam, but it should be drunk. Au revoir!"

Francis, after a pleasant lunch at Ranelagh, and having arranged with Margaret to dine with her in Curzon

Street, spent an hour or two that afternoon at his chambers. As he was leaving, just before five, he came face to face with Shopland descending from a taxi.

"Are you busy, Mr. Ledsam?" the latter enquired. "Can you spare me half-an-hour?"

"An hour, if you like," Francis assented.

Shopland gave the driver an address and the two men seated themselves in the taxicab.

"Any news?" Francis asked curiously.

"Not yet," was the cautious reply. "It will not be long, however."

"Before you discover Reggie Wilmore?"

The detective smiled in a superior way.

"I am no longer particularly interested in Mr. Reginald Wilmore," he declared. "I have come to the conclusion that his disappearance is not a serious affair."

It's serious enough for his relatives," Francis objected.

"Not if they understood the situation," the detective rejoined. "Assure them from me that nothing of consequence has happened to that young man. I have made enquiries at the gymnasium in Holborn, and in other directions. I am convinced that his absence from home is voluntary, and that there is no cause for alarm as to his welfare."

"Then the sooner you make your way down to

Kensington and tell his mother so, the better," Francis said, a little severely. "Don't forget that I put you on to this."

"Quite right, sir," the detective acquiesced, "and I am grateful to you. The fact of it is that in making my preliminary investigations with regard to the disappearance of Mr. Wilmore, I have stumbled upon a bigger thing. Before many weeks are past, I hope to be able to unearth one of the greatest scandals of modern times."

"The devil!" Francis muttered.

He looked thoughtfully, almost anxiously at his companion. Shopland's face reflected to the full his usual confidence. He had the air of a man buoyant with hope and with stifled self-satisfaction.

"I am engaged," he continued, "upon a study of the methods and habits of one whom I believe to be a great criminal. I think that when I place my prisoner in the bar, Wainwright and these other great artists in crime will fade from the memory."

"Is Sir Timothy Brast your man?" Francis asked quietly.

His companion frowned portentously.

"No names," he begged.

"Considering that it was I who first put you on to him," Francis expostulated, "I don't think you need be so sparing of your confidence."

"Mr. Ledsam," the detective assured him, "I shall tell

you everything that is possible. At the same time, I will be frank with you. You are right when you say that it was you who first directed my attention towards Sir Timothy Brast. Since that time, however, your own relations with him, to an onlooker, have become a little puzzling."

"I see," Francis murmured. "You've been spying on me?"

Shopland shook his head in deprecating fashion.

"A study of Sir Timothy during the last month," he said, "has brought you many a time into the focus."

"Where are we going to now?" Francis asked, a little abruptly.

"Just a side show, sir. It's one of those outside things I have come across which give light and shade to the whole affair. We get out here, if you please."

The two men stepped on to the pavement. They were in a street a little north of Wardour Street, where the shops for the most part were of a miscellaneous variety. Exactly in front of them, the space behind a large plate-glass window had been transformed into a sort of show-place for dogs. There were twenty or thirty of them there, of all breeds and varieties.

"What the mischief is this?" Francis demanded.

"Come in and make enquiries," Shopland replied. "I can promise that you will find it interesting. It's a sort of dog's home."

Francis followed his companion into the place. A pleasant-looking, middle-aged woman came forward and greeted the latter.

"Do you mind telling my friend what you told me the other day?" he asked.

"Certainly, sir," she replied. "We collect stray animals here, sir," she continued, turning to Francis. "Every one who has a dog or a cat he can't afford to keep, or which he wants to get rid of, may bring it to us. We have agents all the time in the streets, and if any official of the Society for the Prevention of Cruelty to Animals brings us news of a dog or a cat being ill-treated, we either purchase it or acquire it in some way or other and keep it here."

"But your dogs in the window," Francis observed, "all seem to be in wonderful condition."

The woman smiled.

"We have a large dog and cat hospital behind," she explained, "and a veterinary surgeon who is always in attendance. The animals are treated there as they are brought in, and fed up if they are out of condition. When they are ready to sell, we show them."

"But is this a commercial undertaking," Francis enquired carefully, "or is it a branch of the S.P.C.A.?"

"It's quite a private affair, sir," the woman told him. "We charge only five shillings for the dogs and half-a-crown for the cats, but every one who has one must sign our book, promising to give it a good home, and has to be either known to us or to produce references.

We do not attempt, of course, to snake a profit."

"Who on earth is responsible for the upkeep?"

"We are not allowed to mention any names here, sir, but as a matter of fact I think that your friend knows. He met the gentleman in here one day. Would you care to have a look at the hospital, sir?"

Francis spent a quarter of an hour wandering around. When they left the place, Shopland turned to him with a smile.

"Now, sir," he said, "shall I tell you at whose expense that place is run?"

"I think I can guess," Francis replied. "I should say that Sir Timothy Brast was responsible for it."

The detective nodded. He was a little disappointed.

"You know about his collection of broken-down horses in the park at The Walled House, too, then, I suppose? They come whinnying after him like a flock of sheep whenever he shows himself."

"I know about them, too," Francis admitted. "I was present once when he got out of his car, knocked a carter down who was ill-treating a horse, bought it on the spot and sent it home."

Shopland smiled, inscrutably yet with the air of one vastly pleased.

"These little side-shows," he said, "are what help to make this, which I believe will be the greatest case of my life, so supremely interesting. Any one of my fraternity," he continued, with an air of satisfaction, "can take hold of a thread and follow it step by step, and wind up with the handcuffs, as I did myself with the young man Fairfax. But a case like this, which includes a study of temperament, requires something more."

They were seated once more in the taxicab, on their way westward. Francis for the first time was conscious of an utterly new sensation with regard to his companion. He watched him through half-closed eyes - an insignificant-looking little man whose clothes, though neat, were ill-chosen, and whose tie was an offense. There was nothing in the face to denote unusual intelligence, but the eyes were small and cunning and the mouth dogged. Francis looked away out of the window. A sudden flash of realisation had come to him, a wave of unreasoning but positive dislike.

"When do you hope to bring your case to an end?" he asked.

The man smiled once more, and the very smile irritated his companion.

"Within the course of the next few days, sir," he replied.

"And the charge?"

The detective turned around.

"Mr. Ledsam," he said, "we have been old friends, if you will allow me to use the word, ever since I was promoted to my present position in the Force. You have trusted me with a good many cases, and I acknowledge myself your debtor, but in the matter of Sir Timothy Brast, you will forgive my saying with all respect, sir, that our ways seem to lie a little apart."

"Will you tell me why you have arrived at that conclusion?" Francis asked. "It was I who first incited you to set a watch upon Sir Timothy. It was to you I first mentioned certain suspicions I myself had with regard to him. I treated you with every confidence. Why do you now withhold yours from me?"

"It is quite true, Mr. Ledsam," Shopland admitted, "that it was you who first pointed out Sir Timothy as an interesting study for my profession, but that was a matter of months ago. If you will forgive my saying so, your relations with Sir Timothy have altered since then. You have been his guest at The Sanctuary, and there is a rumour, sir - you will pardon me if I seem to be taking a liberty - that you are engaged to be married to his daughter, Oliver Hilditch's widow."

"You seem to be tolerably well informed as to my affairs, Shopland," Francis remarked.

"Only so far as regards your associations with Sir Timothy," was the deprecating reply. "If you will excuse me, sir, this is where I should like to descend."

"You have no message for Mr. Wilmore, then?" Francis asked.

"Nothing definite, sir, but you can assure him of this. His brother is not likely to come to any particular harm. I have no absolute information to offer, but it is

E. Phillips Oppenheim

my impression that Mr. Reginald Wilmore will be home before a week is past. Good afternoon, sir."

Shopland stepped out of the taxicab and, raising his hat, walked quickly away. Francis directed the man to drive to Clarges Street. As they drove off, he was conscious of a folded piece of paper in the corner where his late companion had been seated. He picked it up, opened it, realised that it was a letter from a firm of lawyers, addressed to Shopland, and deliberately read it through. It was dated from a small town not far from Hatch End:

DEAR SIR:

Mr. John Phillips of this firm, who is coroner for the district, has desired me to answer the enquiry contained in your official letter of the 13th. The number of inquests held upon bodies recovered from the Thames in the neighbourhood to which you allude, during the present year has been seven. Four of these have been identified. Concerning the remaining three nothing has ever been heard. Such particulars as are on our file will be available to any accredited representative of the police at any time.

Faithfully yours,

PHILLIPS & SON.

The taxicab came to a sudden stop. Francis glanced up. Very breathless, Shopland put his head in at the window.

"I dropped a letter," he gasped.

Francis folded it up and handed it to him.

"What about these three unidentified people, Shopland?" he asked, looking at him intently.

The man frowned angrily. There was a note of defiance in his tone as he stowed the letter away in his pocketbook.

"There were two men and one woman," he replied, "all three of the upper classes. The bodies were recovered from Wilson's lock, some three hundred yards from The Walled House."

"Do they form part of your case?" Francis persisted.

Shopland stepped back.

"Mr. Ledsam," he said, "I told you, some little time ago, that so far as this particular case was concerned I had no confidences to share with you. I am sorry that you saw that letter. Since you did, however, I hope you will not take it as a liberty from one in my position if I advise you most strenuously to do nothing which might impede the course of the law. Good day, sir!"

E. Phillips Oppenheim

CHAPTER XXIV

Francis, in that pleasant half-hour before dinner which he spent in Margaret's sitting-room, told her of the dogs' home near Wardour Street. She listened sympathetically to his description of the place.

"I had never heard of it," she acknowledged, "but I am not in anyway surprised. My father spends at least an hour of every day, when he is down at Hatch End, amongst the horses, and every time a fresh crock is brought down, he is as interested as though it were a new toy."

"It is a remarkable. trait in a very remarkable character," Francis commented.

I could tell you many things that would surprise you," Margaret continued. "One night, for instance, when we were staying at The Sanctuary, he and I were going out to dine with some neighbours and he heard a cat mewing in the hedge somewhere. He stopped the car, got out himself, found that the cat had been caught in a trap, released it, and sent me on to the dinner alone whilst he took the animal back to the veterinary surgeon at The Walled House. He was simply white with fury whilst he was tying up the poor thing's leg. I couldn't help asking him what he would have done if he could have found the farmer who set the trap. He looked up at me and I was almost frightened. 'I should have killed him,' be said, - and I believe he meant it. And, Francis, the very next day we were motoring to London and saw a terrible accident. A motor bicyclist came down a side road at full speed and ran into a motor-lorry. My father got out of the car, helped them lift the body from under the wheels of the lorry, and came back absolutely unmoved. 'Serve the silly young fool right!' was his only remark. He was so horribly callous that I could scarcely bear to sit by his side. Do you understand that?"

"It isn't easy," he admitted.

There was a knock at the door. Margaret glanced at the clock.

"Surely dinner can't be served already!" she exclaimed. "Come in."

Very much to their surprise, it was Sir Timothy himself who entered. He was in evening dress and wearing several orders, one of which Francis noted with surprise.

"My apologies," he said. "Hedges told me that there were cocktails here, and as I am on my way to a rather weary dinner, I thought I might inflict myself upon you for a moment."

Margaret rose at once to her feet.

"I am a shocking hostess," she declared. "Hedges brought the things in twenty minutes ago."

She took up the silver receptacle, shook it vigorously

and filled three glasses. Sir Timothy accepted his and bowed to them both.

"My best wishes," he said. "Really, when one comes to think of it, however much it may be against my inclinations I scarcely see how I shall be able to withhold my consent. I believe that you both have at heart the flair for domesticity. This little picture, and the thought of your tete-a-tete dinner, almost touches me."

"Don't make fun of us, father," Margaret begged. "Tell us where you are going in all that splendour?"

Sir Timothy shrugged his shoulders.

"A month or so ago," he explained, "I was chosen to induct a scion of Royalty into the understanding of fighting as it is indulged in at the National Sporting Club. This, I suppose, is my reward - an invitation to something in the nature of a State dinner, which, to tell you the truth, I had forgotten until my secretary pointed it out to me this afternoon. I have grave fears of being bored or of misbehaving myself. I have, as Ledsam here knows, a distressing habit of truthfulness, especially to new acquaintances. However, we must hope for the best. By-the-bye, Ledsam, in case you should have forgotten, I have spoken to Hedges about the '99 Cliquot."

"Shall we see you here later?" Margaret asked, after Francis had murmured his thanks.

"I shall probably return direct to Hatch End," Sir Timothy replied. "There are various little matters down there which are interesting me just now preparations for my party. Au revoir! A delicious cocktail, but I am inclined to resent the Angostura."

He sauntered out, after a glance at the clock. They heard his footsteps as he descended the stairs.

"Tell me, what manner of a man is your father?" Francis asked impulsively.

"I am his daughter and I do not know," Margaret answered. "Before he came, I was going to speak to you of a strange misunderstanding which has existed between us and which has just been removed. Now I have a fancy to leave it until later. You will not mind?"

"When you choose," Francis assented. "Nothing will make any difference. We are past the days when fathers or even mothers count seriously in the things that exist between two people like you and me, who have felt life. Whatever your father may be, whatever he may turn out to be, you are the woman I love - you are the woman who is going to be my wife."

She leaned towards him for a moment.

"You have an amazing gift," she whispered, "of saying just the thing one loves to hear in the way that convinces."

Dinner was served to them in the smaller of the two dining-rooms, an exquisite meal, made more wonderful still by the wine, which Hedges himself dispensed with jealous care. The presence of servants, with its restraining influence upon conversation, was not altogether unwelcome to Francis. He and Margaret had had so little opportunity for general conversation that to discuss other than personal subjects in this pleasant, leisurely way had its charm. They spoke of music, of which she knew far more than he; of foreign travel, where they met on common ground, for each had only the tourist's knowledge of Europe, and each was anxious for a more individual acquaintance with it. She had tastes in books which delighted him, a knowledge of games which promised a common resource. It was only whilst they were talking that he realised with a shock how young she was, how few the years that lay between her serene school-days and the tempestuous years of her married life. Her school-days in Naples were most redolent of delightful memories. She broke off once or twice into the language, and he listened with delight to her soft accent. Finally the time came when dessert was set upon the table.

"I have ordered coffee up in the little sitting-room again," she said, a little shyly. "Do you mind, or would you rather have it here?"

"I much prefer it there," he assured her.

They sat before an open window, looking out upon some elm trees in the boughs of which town sparrows twittered, and with a background of roofs and chimneys. Margaret's coffee was untasted, even her cigarette lay unlit by her side. There was a touch of the old horror upon her face. The fingers which he drew into his were as cold as ice.

"You must have wondered sometimes," she began, "why I ever married Oliver Hilditch."

"You were very young," he reminded her, with a little shiver, "and very inexperienced. I suppose he appealed to you in some way or another."

"It wasn't that," she replied. "He came to visit, me at Eastbourne, and he certainly knew all the tricks of making himself attractive and agreeable. But he never won my heart - he never even seriously took my fancy. I married him because I believed that by doing so I was obeying my father's wishes."

"Where was your father at the time, then?" Francis asked.

"In South America. Oliver Hilditch was nothing more than a discharged employe of his, discharged for dishonesty. He had to leave South America; within a week to escape prosecution, and on the way to Europe he concocted the plot which very nearly ruined my life. He forged a letter from my father, begging me, if I found it in any way possible, to listen to Oliver Hilditch's proposals, and hinting. guardedly at a very serious financial crisis which it was in his power to avert. It never occurred to me or to my chaperon to question his bona fides. He had lived under the same roof as my father, and knew all the intimate details of his life. He was very clever and I suppose I was a fool. I remember thinking I was doing quite a heroic action when I went to the registrar with him. What it led to you know."

There was a moment's throbbing silence. Francis, notwithstanding his deep pity, was conscious of an overwhelming sensation of relief. She had never cared for Oliver Hilditch! She had never pretended to! He put the thought into words.

"You never cared for him, then?"

"I tried to," she replied simply, "but I found it impossible. Within a week of our marriage I hated him."

Francis leaned back, his eyes half closed. In his ears was the sonorous roar of Piccadilly, the hooting of motor-cars, close at hand the rustling of a faint wind in the elm trees. It was a wonderful moment. The nightmare with which he had grappled so fiercely, which he had overthrown, but whose ghost still sometimes walked by his side, had lost its chief and most poignant terror. She had been tricked into the marriage. She had never cared or pretended to care. The primal horror of that tragedy which he had figured so often to himself, seemed to have departed with the thought. Its shadow must always remain, but in time his conscience would acquiesce in the pronouncement of his reason. It was the hand of justice, not any human hand, which had slain Oliver Hilditch.

"What did your father say when he discovered the truth?" he asked.

"He did not know it until he came to England - on the day that Oliver Hilditch was acquitted. My husband always pretended that he had a special mail bag going out to South America, so he took away all the letters I wrote to my father, and he took care that I received none except one or two which I know now were forgeries. He had friends in South America himself who helped him - one a typist in my father's office, of whom I discovered afterwards - but that really doesn't matter. He was a wonderful master of deceit."

Francis suddenly took her hands. He had an overwhelming desire to escape from the miasma of those ugly days, with their train of attendant thoughts and speculations.

"Let us talk about ourselves," he whispered.

After that, the evening glided away incoherently, with no sustained conversation, but with an increasing sense of well-being, of soothed nerves and happiness, flaming seconds of passion, sign-posts of the wonderful world which lay before them. They sat in the cool silence until the lights of the returning taxicabs and motor-cars became more frequent, until the stars crept into the sky and the yellow arc of the moon stole up over the tops of the houses. Presently they saw Sir Timothy's Rolls-Royce glide up to the front door below and Sir Timothy himself enter the house, followed by another man whose appearance was somehow familiar.

"Your father has changed his mind," Francis observed.

"Perhaps he has called for something," she suggested, "or he may want to change his clothes before he goes down to the country."

Presently, however, there was a knock at the door. Hedges made his diffident appearance.

"I beg your pardon, sir," he began, addressing Francis. "Sir Timothy has been asking if you are still here. He would be very glad if you could spare him a moment in the library."

Francis rose at once to his feet.

"I was just leaving," he said. "I will look in at the library and see Sir Timothy on my way out."

E. Phillips Oppenheim

CHAPTER XXV

Sir Timothy was standing upon the hearthrug of the very wonderful apartment which he called his library. By his side, on a black marble pedestal, stood a small statue by Rodin. Behind him, lit by a shielded electric light, was a Vandyck, "A Portrait of a Gentleman Unknown," and Francis, as he hesitated for a moment upon the threshold, was struck by a sudden quaint likeness between the face of the man in the picture, with his sunken cheeks, his supercilious smile, his narrowed but powerful eyes, to the face of Sir Timothy himself. There was something of the same spirit there - the lawless buccaneer, perhaps the criminal.

"You asked for me, Sir Timothy," Francis said.

Sir Timothy smiled.

"I was fortunate to find that you had not left," he answered. "I want you to be present at this forthcoming interview. You are to a certain extent in the game. I thought it might amuse you."

Francis for the first time was aware that his host was not alone. The room, with its odd splashes of light, was full of shadows, and he saw now that in an easy-chair a little distance away from Sir Timothy, a girl was seated. Behind her, still standing, with his hat in his hand, was a man. Francis recognised them both with surprise.

"Miss Hyslop!" he exclaimed.

She nodded a little defiantly. Sir Timothy smiled. "Ah!" he said. "You know the young lady, without a doubt. Mr. Shopland, your coadjutor in various works of philanthropy, you recognise, of course? I do not mind confessing to you, Ledsam, that I am very much afraid of Mr. Shopland. I am not at all sure that he has not a warrant for my arrest in his pocket."

The detective came a little further into the light. He was attired in an ill-fitting dinner suit, a soft-fronted shirt of unpleasing design, a collar of the wrong shape, and a badly arranged tie. He seemed, nevertheless, very pleased with himself.

"I came on here, Mr. Ledsam, at Sir Timothy's desire," he said. "I should like you to understand," he added, with a covert glance of warning, "that I have been devoting every effort, during the last few days, to the discovery of your friend's brother, Mr. Reginald Wilmore."

"I am very glad to hear it," Francis replied shortly. "The boy's brother is one of my greatest friends."

"I have come to the conclusion," the detective pronounced, "that the young man has been abducted, and is being detained at The Walled House against his will for some illegal purpose."

"In other respects," Sir Timothy said, stretching out his hand towards a cedar-wood box of cigarettes and selecting one, "this man seems quite sane. I have watched him very closely on the way here, but I could see no signs of mental aberration. I do not think, at any rate, that he is dangerous."

"Sir Timothy," Shopland explained, with some anger in his tone, "declines to take me seriously. I can of course apply for a search warrant, as I shall do, but it occurred to me to be one of those cases which could be better dealt with, up to a certain point, without recourse to the extremities of the law."

Sir Timothy, who had lit his cigarette, presented a wholly undisturbed front.

"What I cannot quite understand," he said, "is the exact meaning of that word 'abduction.' Why should I be suspected of forcibly removing a harmless and worthy young man from his regular avocation, and, as you term it, abducting him, which I presume means keeping him bound and gagged and imprisoned? I do not eat young men. I do not even care for the society of young men. I am not naturally a gregarious person, but I think I would go so far," he added, with a bow towards Miss Hyslop, "as to say that I prefer the society of young women. Satisfy my curiosity, therefore, I beg of you. For what reason do you suppose that I have been concerned in the disappearance of this Mr. Reginald Wilmore?"

Francis opened his lips, but Shopland, with a warning glance, intervened.

"I work sometimes as a private person, sir," he said, "but it is not to be forgotten that I am an officer of the law. It is not for us to state motives or even to afford explanations for our behaviour. I have watched your house at Hatch End, Sir Timothy, and I have come to the conclusion that unless you are willing to discuss this matter with me in a different spirit, I am justified in asking the magistrates for a search warrant."

Sir Timothy sighed.

"Mr. Ledsam," he said, "I think, after all, that yours is the most interesting end of this espionage business. It is you who search for motives, is it not, and pass them on to our more automatic friend, who does the rest. May I ask, have you supplied the motive in the present case?"

"I have failed to discover any motive at all for Reginald Wilmore's disappearance," Francis admitted, "nor have I at any time been able to connect you with it. Mr. Shopland's efforts, however, although he has not seen well to take me into his entire confidence, have my warmest approval and sympathy. Although I have accepted your very generous hospitality, Sir Timothy, I think there has been no misunderstanding between us on this matter."

"Most correct," Sir Timothy murmured. "The trouble seems to be, so far as I am concerned, that no one will tell me exactly of what I am suspected? I am to give Mr. Shopland the run of my house, or he will make his appearance in the magistrate's court and the evening papers will have placards with marvellous headlines at my expense. How will it run, Mr. Shopland -

"'MYSTERIOUS DISAPPEARANCE OF A YOUNG GENTLEMAN.
MILLIONAIRE'S HOUSE TO BE SEARCHED.'"

"We do not necessarily acquaint the press with our procedure," Shopland rejoined.

"Nevertheless," Sir Timothy continued, "I have known awkward consequences arise from a search warrant too rashly applied for or granted. However, we are scarcely being polite. So far, Miss Hyslop has had very little to say."

The young lady was not altogether at her ease.

"I have had very little to say," she repeated, "because I did not expect an audience."

Sir Timothy drew a letter from his pocket, opened it and adjusted his eyeglass.

"Here we are," he said. "After leaving my dinner-party tonight, I called at the club and found this note. Quite an inviting little affair, you see young lady's writing, faint but very delicate perfume, excellent stationery, Milan Court - the home of adventures!"

"DEAR SIR TIMOTHY BRAST:

"Although I am not known to you personally, there is a certain matter concerning which information has come into my possession, which I should like to discuss with you. Will you call and see me as soon as possible?"

Sincerely yours,

"DAISY HYSLOP."

"On receipt of this note," Sir Timothy continued, folding it up, "I telephoned to the young lady and as I was fortunate enough to find her at home I asked her to come here. I then took the liberty of introducing myself to Mr. Shopland, whose interest in my evening has been unvarying, and whose uninvited company I have been compelled to bear with, and suggested that, as I was on my way back to Curzon Street, he had better come in and have a drink and tell me what it was all about. I arranged that he should find Miss Hyslop here, and for a person of observation, which I flatter myself to be, it was easy to discover the interesting fact that Mr. Shopland and Miss Daisy Hyslop were not strangers. "Now tell me, young lady," Sir Timothy went on. "You see, I have placed myself entirely in your hands. Never mind the presence of these two gentlemen. Tell me exactly what you wanted to say to me?"

"The matter is of no great importance," Miss Hyslop declared, "in any case I should not discuss it before these two gentlemen."

"Don't go for a, moment, please," Sir Timothy begged, as she showed signs of departure. "Listen. I want to make a suggestion to you. There is an impression abroad that I was interested in the two young men, Victor Bidlake and Fairfax, and that I knew something of their quarrel. You were an intimate friend of young Bidlake's and presumably in his confidence. It occurs to me, therefore, that Mr. Shopland might very well have visited you in search of information, linking me up with that unfortunate affair. Hence your little note to me."

Miss Hyslop rose to her feet. She had the appearance of being very angry indeed.

"Do you mean to insinuate - " she began.

"Madam, I insinuate nothing," Sir Timothy interrupted sternly. "I only desire to suggest this. You are a young lady whose manner of living, I gather, is to a certain extent precarious. It must have seemed to you a likelier source of profit to withhold any information you might have to give at the solicitation of a rich man, than to give it free gratis and for nothing to a detective. Now am I right?"

Miss Hyslop turned towards the door. She had the air of a person who had been entirely misunderstood.

"I wrote you out of kindness, Sir Timothy," she said in an aggrieved manner. "I shall have nothing more to say on the matter - to you, at any rate."

Sir Timothy sighed.

"You see," he said, turning to the others, "I have lost my chance of conciliating a witness. My cheque-book remains locked up and she has gone over to your side."

She turned around suddenly.

"You know that you made Bobby Fairfax kill Victor!" she almost shouted.

Sir Timothy smiled in triumph.

"My dear young lady," he begged, "let us now be friends again. I desired to know your trump card. For that reason I fear that I have been a little brutal. Now please don't hurry away. You have shot your bolt. Already Mr. Shopland is turning the thing over in his mind. Was I lurking outside that night, Mr. Shopland, to guide that young man's flabby arm? He scarcely seemed man enough for a murderer, did he, when he sat quaking on that stool in Soto's Bar while Mr. Ledsam tortured him? I beg you again not to hurry, Miss Hyslop. At any rate wait while my servants fetch you a taxi. It was clouding over when I came in. We may even have a thunderstorm."

"I want to, get out of this house," Daisy Hyslop declared. "I think you are all horrible. Mr. Ledsam did behave like a gentleman when he came to see me, and Mr. Shopland asked questions civilly. But you -" she added, turning round to Sir Timothy.

"Hush, my dear," he interrupted, holding out his hand. "Don't abuse me. I am not angry with you - not in the least - and I am going to prove it. I shall oppose any search warrant which you might apply for, Mr. Shopland, and I think I can oppose it with success. But I invite you two, Miss Hyslop and Mr. Ledsam, to my party on Thursday night. Once under my roof you shall have carte blanche. You can wander where you please, knock the walls for secret hiding-places, stamp upon the floor for oubliettes. Upstairs or down, the cellars and the lofts, the grounds and the park, the whole of my domain is for you from midnight on Thursday until four o'clock. What do you say, Mr. Shopland? Does my offer satisfy you?"

The detective hesitated.

"I should prefer an invitation for myself," he declared bluntly.

Sir Timothy shook his head.

E. Phillips Oppenheim

"Alas, my dear Mr. Shopland," he regretted, "that is impossible! If I had only myself to consider I would not hesitate. Personally I like you. You amuse me more than any one I have met for a long time. But unfortunately I have my guests to consider! You must be satisfied with Mr. Ledsam's report."

Shopland stroked his stubbly moustache. It was obvious that he was not in the least disconcerted.

"There are three days between now and then," he reflected.

"During those three days, of course," Sir Timothy said drily, "I shall do my best to obliterate all traces of my various crimes. Still, you are a clever detective, and you can give Mr. Ledsam a few hints. Take my advice. You won't get that search warrant, and if you apply for it none of you will be at my party."

"I accept," Shopland decided.

Sir Timothy crossed the room, unlocked the drawer of a magnificent writing-table, and from a little packet drew out two cards of invitation. They were of small size but thick, and the colour was a brilliant scarlet. On one he wrote the name of Francis, the other he filled in for Miss Hyslop.

"Miss Daisy Hyslop," he said, "shall we drink a glass of wine together on Thursday evening, and will you decide that although, perhaps, I am not a very satisfactory correspondent, I can at least be an amiable host?"

The girl's eyes glistened. She knew very well that the

possession of that card meant that for the next few days she would be the envy of every one of her acquaintances.

"Thank you, Sir Timothy," she replied eagerly. "You have quite misunderstood me but I should like to come to your party."

Sir Timothy handed over the cards. He rang for a servant and bowed the others out. Francis he detained for a moment.

"Our little duel, my friend, marches," he said. "After Thursday night we will speak again of this matter concerning Margaret. You will know then what you have to face."

Margaret herself opened the door and looked in.

"What have those people been doing here?" she asked. "What is happening?"

Her father unlocked his drawer once more and drew out another of the red cards.

"Margaret," he said, "Ledsam here has accepted my invitation for Thursday night. You have never, up till now, honoured me, nor have I ever asked you. I suggest that for the first part of the entertainment, you give me the pleasure of your company."

"For the first part?"

"For the first part only," he repeated, as he wrote her name upon the card.

"What about Francis?" she asked. "Is he to, stay all the time?"

Sir Timothy smiled. He locked up his drawer and. slipped the key into his pocket.

"Ledsam and I," he said, "have promised one another a more complete mutual understanding on Thursday night. I may not be able to part with him quite so soon."

CHAPTER XXVI

Bored and listless, like a tired and drooping lily in the arms of her somewhat athletic partner, Lady Cynthia brought her dance to a somewhat abrupt conclusion.

"There is some one in the lounge there to whom I wish to speak," she said. "Perhaps you won't mind if we finish later. The floor seems sticky tonight, or my feet are heavy."

Her partner made the best of it, as Lady Cynthia's partners, nowadays, generally had to. She even dispensed with his escort, and walked across the lounge of Claridge's alone. Sir Timothy rose to his feet. He had been sitting in a corner, half sheltered by a pillar, and had fancied himself unseen.

"What a relief!" she exclaimed. "Another turn and I should have fainted through sheer boredom."

"Yet you are quite wonderful dancing," he said. "I have been watching you for some time."

"It is one of my expiring efforts," she declared, sinking into the chair by his side. "You know whose party it is, of course? Old Lady Torrington's. Quite a boy and girl affair. Twenty-four of us had dinner in the worst corner of the room. I can hear the old lady ordering the dinner now. Charles with a long menu. She shakes her head and taps him on the wrist with her fan. 'Monsieur Charles, I am a poor woman. Give me what there is - a small, plain dinner - and charge me at your minimum.' The dinner was very small and very plain, the champagne was horribly sweet. My partner talked of a new drill, his last innings for the Household Brigade, and a wonderful round of golf he played last Sunday week. I was turned on to dance with a man who asked me to marry him, a year ago, and I could feel him vibrating with gratitude, as he looked at me, that I had refused. I suppose I am very haggard."

"Does that matter, nowadays?" Sir Timothy asked.

She shrugged her shoulders.

"I am afraid it does. The bone and the hank of hair stuff is played out. The dairy-maid style is coming in. Plump little Fanny Torrington had a great success to-night, in one of those simple white dresses, you know, which look like a sack with a hole cut in the top. What are you doing here by yourself?"

"I have an engagement in a few minutes," he explained. "My car is waiting now. I looked in at the club to dine, found my favourite table taken and nearly every man I ever disliked sidling up to tell me that he hears I am giving a wonderful party on Thursday. I decided not to dine there, after all, and Charles found me a corner here. I am going in five minutes."

"Where to?" she asked. "Can't I come with you ?"

"I fear not," he answered. "I am going down in the East End."

"Adventuring?"

"More or less," he admitted.

Lady Cynthia became beautiful. She was always beautiful when she was not tired.

"Take me with you, please," she begged.

He shook his head.

"Not to be done!"

"Don't shake your head like that," she enjoined, with a little grimace. "People will think I am trying to borrow money from you and that you are refusing me! Just take me with you some of the way. I shall scream if I go back into that dancing-room again."

Sir Timothy glanced at the clock.

"If there is any amusement to you in a rather dull drive eastwards -"

She was on her feet with the soft, graceful speed which had made her so much admired before her present listlessness had set in.

"I'll get my cloak," she said.

They drove along the Embankment, citywards. The heat of the city seemed to rise from the pavements. The wall of the Embankment was lined with people, leaning over to catch the languid breeze that crept up with the tide. They crossed the river and threaded their way through a nightmare of squalid streets, where half-dressed men and women hung from the top windows and were even to be seen upon the roof, struggling for air. The car at last pulled up at the corner of a long street.

"I am going down here," Sir Timothy announced. "I shall be gone perhaps an hour. The neighbourhood is not a fit one for you to be left alone in. I shall have time to send you home. The car will be back here for me by the time I require it."

"Where are you going?" she asked curiously. "Why can't I come with you?"

"I am going where I cannot take you," was the firm reply. "I told you that before I started."

"I shall sit here and wait for you," she decided. "I rather like the neighbourhood. There is a gentleman in shirt-sleeves, leaning over the rail of the roof there, who has his eye on me. I believe I shall be a success here - which is more than I can say of a little further westwards."

Sir Timothy smiled slightly. He had exchanged his hat for a tweed cap, and had put on a long dustcoat.

"There is no gauge by which you may know the measure of your success," he said. "If there were -"

"If there were?" she asked, leaning a little forward and looking at him with a touch of the old brilliancy in her eyes.

"If there were," he said, with a little show of mock gallantry, "a very jealously-guarded secret might escape me. I think you will be quite all right here," he continued. "It is an open thoroughfare, and I see two policemen at the corner. Hassell, my chauffeur, too, is a reliable fellow. We will be back within the hour."

"We?" she repeated.

He indicated a man who had silently made his appearance during the conversation and was standing waiting on the sidewalk.

"Just a companion. I do not advise you to wait. If you insist - au revoir!"

Lady Cynthia leaned back in a corner of the car.

Through half-closed eyes she watched the two men on their way down the crowded thoroughfare - Sir Timothy tall, thin as a lath, yet with a certain elegance of bearing; the man at his side shorter, his hands thrust into the pockets of his coat, his manner one of subservience. She wondered languidly as to their errand in this unsavoury neighbourhood. Then she closed her eyes altogether and wondered about many things.

Sir Timothy and his companion walked along the crowded, squalid street without speech. Presently they turned to the right and stopped in front of a public-house of some pretensions.

"This is the place?" Sir Timothy asked.

"Yes, sir!"

Both men entered. Sir Timothy made his way to the

counter, his companion to a table near, where he took a seat and ordered a drink. Sir Timothy did the same. He was wedged in between a heterogeneous crowd of shabby, depressed but apparently not ill-natured men and women. A man in a flannel shirt and pair of shabby plaid trousers, which owed their precarious position to a pair of worn-out braces, turned a beery eye upon the newcomer.

"I'll 'ave one with you, guvnor," he said.

"You shall indeed," Sir Timothy assented.

"Strike me lucky but I've touched first time!" the man exclaimed. "I'll 'ave a double tot of whisky," he added, addressing the barman. "Will it run to it, guvnor?"

"Certainly," was the cordial reply, "and the same to your friends, if you will answer a question."

"Troop up, lads," the man shouted. "We've a toff 'ere. He ain't a 'tec - I know the cut of them. Out with the question."

"Serve every one who desires it with drinks," Sir Timothy directed the barman. "My question is easily answered. Is this the place which a man whom I understand they call Billy the Tanner frequents?"

The question appeared to produce an almost uncomfortable sensation. The enthusiasm for the free drinks, however, was only slightly damped, and a small forest of grimy hands was extended across the counter.

"Don't you ask no questions about 'im, guvnor," Sir

Timothy's immediate companion advised earnestly. "He'd kill you as soon as look at you. When Billy the Tanner's in a quarrelsome mood, I've see 'im empty this place and the whole street, quicker than if a mad dog was loose. 'E's a fair and 'oly terror, 'e is. 'E about killed 'is wife, three nights ago, but there ain't a living soul as 'd dare to stand in the witness-box about it."

"Why don't the police take a hand in the matter if the man is such a nuisance?" Sir Timothy asked.

His new acquaintance, gripping a thick tumbler of spirits and water with a hand deeply encrusted with the stains of his trade, scoffed.

"Police! Why, 'e'd take on any three of the police round these parts!" he declared. "Police! You tell one on 'em that Billy the Tanner's on the rampage, and you'll see 'em 'op it. Cheero, guvnor and don't you get curious about Billy. It ain't 'ealthy."

The swing-door was suddenly opened. A touslehaired urchin shoved his face in.

"Billy the Tanner's coming!" he shouted. "Cave, all! He's been 'avin' a rare to-do in Smith's Court."

Then a curious thing happened. The little crowd at the bar seemed somehow to melt away. Half-a-dozen left precipitately by the door. Half-a-dozen more slunk through an inner entrance into some room beyond. Sir Timothy's neighbour set down his tumbler empty. He was the last to leave.

"If you're going to stop 'ere, guvnor," he begged fervently, "you keep a still tongue in your 'ead. Billy ain't particular who it is. 'E'd kill 'is own mother, if 'e felt like it. 'E'll swing some day, sure as I stand 'ere, but 'e'll do a bit more mischief first. 'Op it with me, guvnor, or get inside there."

"Jim's right," the man behind the bar agreed. "He's a very nasty customer, Bill the Tanner, sir. If he's coming down, I'd clear out for a moment. You can go in the guvnor's sitting-room, if you like."

Sir Timothy shook his head.

"Billy the Tanner will not hurt me," he said. "As a matter of fact, I came down to see him."

His new friend hesitated no longer but made for the door through which most of his companions had already disappeared. The barman leaned across the counter.

"Guvnor," he whispered hoarsely, "I don't know what the game is, but I've given you the office. Billy won't stand no truck from any one. He's a holy terror."

Sir Timothy nodded.

"I quite understand," he said.

There was a moment's ominous silence. The barman withdrew to the further end of his domain and busied himself cleaning some glasses. Suddenly the door was swung open. A man entered whose appearance alone was calculated to inspire a certain amount of fear. He was tall, but his height escaped notice by reason of the extraordinary breadth of his shoulders. He had a coarse and vicious face, a crop of red hair, and an unshaven growth of the same upon his face. He wore what appeared to be the popular dress in the neighbourhood - a pair of trousers suspended by a belt, and a dirty flannel shirt. His hands and even his chest, where the shirt fell away, were discoloured by yellow stains. He looked around the room at first with an air of disappointment. Then he caught sight of Sir Timothy standing at the counter, and he brightened up.

"Where's all the crowd, Tom?" he asked the barman.

"Scared of you, I reckon," was the brief reply. "There was plenty here a few minutes ago."

"Scared of me, eh?" the other repeated, staring hard at Sir Timothy. "Did you 'ear that, guvnor?"

"I heard it," Sir Timothy acquiesced.

Billy the Tanner began to cheer up. He walked all round this stranger.

"A toff! A big toff! I'll 'ave a drink with you, guvnor," he declared, with a note of incipient truculence in his tone.

The barman had already reached up for two glasses but Sir Timothy shook his head.

"I think not," he said.

There was a moment's silence. The barman made despairing signs at Sir Timothy. Billy the Tanner was moistening his lips with his tongue.

"Why not?" he demanded.

"Because I don't know you and I don't like you," was the bland reply.

Billy the Tanner wasted small time upon preliminaries. He spat upon his hands.

"I dunno you and I don't like you," he retorted. "D'yer know wot I'm going to do?"

"I have no idea," Sir Timothy confessed.

"I'm going to make you look so that your own mother wouldn't know you - then I'm going to pitch you into the street," he added, with an evil grin. "That's wot we does with big toffs who come 'anging around 'ere."

"Do you?" Sir Timothy said calmly. "Perhaps my friend may have something to say about that."

The man of war was beginning to be worked up.

"Where's your big friend?" he shouted. "Come on! I'll take on the two of you."

The man who had met Sir Timothy in the street had risen to his feet. He strolled up to the two. Billy the Tanner eyed him hungrily.

"The two of you, d'yer 'ear?" he shouted. "And 'ere's just a flick for the toff to be going on with!"

He delivered a sudden blow at Sir Timothy - a full, vicious, jabbing blow which had laid many a man of the neighbourhood in the gutter. To his amazement, the chin at which he had aimed seemed to have mysteriously disappeared. Sir Timothy himself was standing about half-a-yard further away. Billy the Tanner was too used to the game to be off his balance, but he received at that moment the surprise of his life. With the flat of his hand full open, Sir Timothy struck him across the cheek such a blow that it resounded through the place, a blow that brought both the inner doors ajar, that brought peering eyes from every direction. There was a moment's silence. The man's fists were clenched now, there was murder in his face. Sir Timothy stepped on one side.

"I am not a fighter," he said coolly, leaning back against the marble table. "My friend will deal with you."

Billy the Tanner glared at the newcomer, who had glided in between him and Sir Timothy.

"You can come and join in, too," he shouted to Sir Timothy. "I'll knock your big head into pulp when I've done with this little job!"

The bully knew in precisely thirty seconds what had happened to him. So did the crowds who pressed back into the place through the inner door: So did the barman. So did the landlord, who had made a cautious appearance through a trapdoor. Billy the Tanner, for the first time in his life, was fighting a better man. For two years he had been the terror of the neighbourhood, and he showed now that at least he had courage. His smattering of science, however, appeared only ridiculous. Once, through sheer strength and blundering force, he broke down his opponent's guard and struck him in the place that had dispatched many a man before - just over the heart. His present opponent scarcely winced, and Billy the Tanner paid the penalty then for his years of bullying. His antagonist paused for a single second, as though unnerved by the blow. Red fire seemed to stream from his eyes. Then it was all over. With a sickening crash, Billy the Tanner went down upon the sanded floor. It was no matter of a count for him. He lay there like a dead man, and from the two doors the hidden spectators streamed into the room. Sir Timothy laid some money upon the table.

"This fellow insulted me and my friend," he said. "You see, he has paid the penalty. If he misbehaves again, the same thing will happen to him. I am leaving some money here with your barman. I shall be glad for every one to drink with me. Presently, perhaps, you had better send for an ambulance or a doctor."

A little storm of enthusiastic excitement, evidenced for the most part in expletives of a lurid note, covered the retreat of Sir Timothy and his companion. Out in the street a small crowd was rushing towards the place. A couple of policemen seemed to be trying to make up their minds whether it was a fine night. An inspector hurried up to them.

"What's doing in 'The Rising Sun'?" he demanded sharply.

"Some one's giving Billy the Tanner a hiding," one of the policemen replied.

"Honest?"

"A fair, ripe, knock-out hiding," was the emphatic confirmation. "I looked in at the window."

The inspector grinned.

"I'm glad you had the sense not to interfere," he remarked.

Sir Timothy and his companion reached the car. The latter took a seat by the chauffeur. Sir Timothy stepped in. It struck him that Lady Cynthia was a little breathless. Her eyes, too, were marvellously bright. Wrapped around her knees was the chauffeur's coat.

"Wonderful!" she declared. "I haven't had such a wonderful five minutes since I can remember! You are a dear to have brought me, Sir Timothy."

"What do you mean?" he demanded.

"Mean?" she laughed, as the car swung around and they glided away. "You didn't suppose I was going to sit here and watch you depart upon a mysterious errand? I borrowed your chauffeur's coat and his cap, and slunk down after you. I can assure you I looked the most wonderful female apache you ever saw! And I saw the fight. It was better than any of the prize fights I have ever been to. The real thing is better than the sham, isn't it?"

Sir Timothy leaned back in his place and remained silent. Soon they passed out of the land of tired people, of stalls decked out with unsavoury provender, of foetid smells and unwholesome-looking houses. They passed through a street of silent warehouses on to the Embankment. A stronger breeze came down between the curving arc of lights.

"You are not sorry that you brought me?" Lady Cynthia asked, suddenly holding out her hand.

Sir Timothy took it in his. For some reason or other, he made no answer at all.

CHAPTER XXVII

The car stopped in front of the great house in Grosvenor Square. Lady Cynthia turned to her companion.

"You must come in, please," she said. "I insist, if it is only for five minutes."

Sir Timothy followed her across the hall to a curved recess, where the footman who had admitted them touched a bell, and a small automatic lift came down.

"I am taking you to my own quarters," she explained. "They are rather cut off but I like them - especially on hot nights."

They glided up to the extreme top of the house. She opened the gates and led the way into what was practically an attic sitting-room, decorated in black and white. Wide-flung doors opened onto the leads, where comfortable chairs, a small table and an electric standard were arranged. They were far above the tops of the other houses, and looked into the green of the Park.

"This is where I bring very few people," she said. "This is where, even after my twenty-eight years of fraudulent life, I am sometimes myself. Wait."

E. Phillips Oppenheim

There were feminine drinks and sandwiches arranged on the table. She opened the cupboard of a small sideboard just inside the sitting-room, however, and produced whisky and a syphon of soda. There was a pail of ice in a cool corner. From somewhere in the distance came the music of violins floating through the window of a house where a dance was in progress. They could catch a glimpse of the striped awning and the long line of waiting vehicles with their twin eyes of fire. She curled herself up on a settee, flung a cushion at Sir Timothy, who was already ensconced in a luxurious easy-chair, and with a tumbler of iced sherbet in one hand, and a cigarette in the other, looked across at him.

"I am not sure," she said, "that you have not to-night dispelled an illusion."

"What manner of one?" he asked.

"Above all things," she went on, "I have always looked upon you as wicked. Most people do. I think that is one reason why so many of the women find you attractive. I suppose it is why I have found you attractive."

The smile was back upon his lips. He bowed a little, and, leaning forward, dropped a chunk of ice into his whisky and soda.

"Dear Lady Cynthia," he murmured, "don't tell me that I am going to slip back in your estimation into some normal place."

"I am not quite sure," she said deliberately. "I have always looked upon you as a kind of amateur criminal, a man who loved black things and dark ways. You know how weary one gets of the ordinary code of morals in these days. You were such a delightful antidote. And now, I am not sure that you have not shaken my faith in you."

"In what way?"

"You really seem to have been engaged to-night in a very sporting and philanthropic enterprise. I imagined you visiting some den of vice and mixing as an equal with these terrible people who never seem to cross the bridges. I was perfectly thrilled when I put on your chauffeur's coat and hat and followed you."

"The story of my little adventure is a simple one," Sir Timothy said. "I do not think it greatly affects my character. I believe, as a matter of fact, that I am just as wicked as you would have me be, but I have friends in every walk of life, and, as you know, I like to peer into the unexpected places. I had heard of this man Billy the Tanner. He beats women, and has established a perfect reign of terror in the court and neighbourhood where he lives. I fear I must agree with you that there were some elements of morality - of conforming, at any rate, to the recognised standards of justice - in what I did. You know, of course, that I am a great patron of every form of boxing, fencing, and the various arts of self-defence and attack. I just took along one of the men from my gymnasium who I knew was equal to the job, to give this fellow a lesson."

"He did it all right," Lady Cynthia murmured.

"But this is where I think I re-establish myself," Sir Timothy continued, the peculiar nature of his smile reasserting itself. "I did not do this for the sake of the neighbourhood. I did not do it from any sense of justice at all. I did it to provide for myself an enjoyable and delectable spectacle."

She smiled lazily.

"That does rather let you out," she admitted. "However, on the whole I am disappointed. I am afraid that you are not so bad as people think."

"People?" he repeated. "Francis Ledsam, for instance - my son-in-law in posse?"

"Francis Ledsam is one of those few rather brilliant persons who have contrived to keep sane without becoming a prig," she remarked.

"You know why?" he reminded her. "Francis Ledsam has been a tremendous worker. It is work which keeps a man sane. Brilliancy without the capacity for work drives people to the madhouse."

"Where we are all going, I suppose," she sighed.

"Not you," he answered. "You have just enough - I don't know what we moderns call it - soul, shall I say? - to keep you from the muddy ways."

She rose to her feet and leaned over the rails. Sir Timothy watched her thoughtfully. Her figure, notwithstanding its suggestions of delicate maturity, was still as slim as a young girl's. She was looking across the tree-tops towards an angry bank of clouds - long, pencil-like streaks of black on a purple background. Below, in the street, a taxi passed with grinding of brakes and noisy horn. The rail against which she leaned looked very flimsy. Sir Timothy stretched out his hand and held her arm.

"My nerves are going with my old age," he apologised. "That support seems too fragile."

She did not move. The touch of his fingers grew firmer.

"We have entered upon an allegory," she murmured. "You are preserving me from the depths."

He laughed harshly.

"I!" he exclaimed, with a sudden touch of real and fierce bitterness which brought the light dancing into her eyes and a spot of colour to her cheeks. "I preserve you! Why, you can never hear my name without thinking of sin, of crime of some sort! Do you seriously expect me to ever preserve any one from anything?"

"You haven't made any very violent attempts to corrupt me," she reminded him.

"Women don't enter much into my scheme of life," he declared. "They played a great part once. It was a woman, I think, who first headed me off from the pastures of virtue."

"I know," she said softly. "It was Margaret's mother."

His voice rang out like a pistol-shot.

"How did you know that?"

E. Phillips Oppenheim

She turned away from the rail and threw herself back in her chair. His hand, however, she still kept in hers.

"Uncle Joe was Minister at Rio, you know, the year it all happened," she explained. "He told us the story years ago - how you came back from Europe and found things were not just as they should be between Margaret's mother and your partner, and how you killed your partner."

His nostrils quivered a little. One felt that the fire of suffering had touched him again for a moment.

"Yes, I killed him," he admitted. "That is part of my creed. The men who defend their honour in the Law Courts are men I know nothing of. This man would have wronged me and robbed me of my honour. I bade him defend himself in any way he thought well. It was his life or mine. He was a poor fighter and I killed him."

"And Margaret's mother died from the shock."

"She died soon afterwards."

The stars grew paler. The passing vehicles, with their brilliant lights, grew fewer and fewer. The breeze which had been so welcome at first, turned into a cold night wind. She led the way back into the room.

"I must go," he announced.

"You must go," she echoed, looking up at him. "Goodbye!"

She was so close to him that his embrace, sudden and

passionate though it was, came about almost naturally. She lay in his arms with perfect content and raised her lips to his.

He broke away. He was himself again, self-furious.

"Lady Cynthia," he said, "I owe you my most humble apologies. The evil that is in me does not as a rule break out in this direction."

"You dear, foolish person," she laughed, "that was good, not evil. You like me, don't you? But I know you do. There is one crime you have always forgotten to develop - you haven't the simplest idea in the world how to lie."

"Yes, I like you," he admitted. "I have the most absurd feeling for you that any man ever found it impossible to put into words. We have indeed strayed outside the world of natural things," he added.

"Why?" she murmured. "I never felt more natural or normal in my life. I can assure you that I am loving it. I feel like muslin gowns and primroses and the scent of those first March violets underneath a warm hedge where the sun comes sometimes. I feel very natural indeed, Sir Timothy."

"What about me?" he asked harshly. "In three weeks' time I shall be fifty years old."

She laughed softly.

"And in no time at all I shall be thirty - and entering upon a terrible period of spinsterhood!"

"Spinsterhood!" he scoffed. "Why, whenever the Society papers are at a loss for a paragraph, they report a few more offers of marriage to the ever-beautiful Lady Cynthia."

"Don't be sarcastic," she begged. "I haven't yet had the offer of marriage I want, anyhow."

"You'll get one you don't want in a moment," he warned her.

She made a little grimace.

"Don't!" she laughed nervously. "How am I to preserve my romantic notions of you as the emperor of the criminal world, if you kiss me as you did just now - you kissed me rather well - and then ask me to marry you? It isn't your role. You must light a cigarette now, pat the back of my hand, and swagger off to another of your haunts of vice."

"In other words, I am not to propose?" Sir Timothy said slowly.

"You see how decadent I am," she sighed. "I want to toy with my pleasures. Besides, there's that scamp of a brother of mine coming up to have a drink - I saw him get out of a taxi - and you couldn't get it through in time, not with dignity."

The rattle of the lift as it stopped was plainly audible. He stooped and kissed her fingers.

"I fear some day," he murmured, "I shall be a great disappointment to you."

CHAPTER-XXVIII

There was a great deal of discussion, the following morning at the Sheridan Club, during the gossipy half-hour which preceded luncheon, concerning Sir Timothy Brast's forthcoming entertainment. One of the men, Philip Baker, who had been for many years the editor of a famous sporting weekly, had a ticket of invitation which he displayed to an envious little crowd.

"You fellows who get invitations to these parties," a famous actor declared, "are the most elusive chaps on earth. Half London is dying to know what really goes on there, and yet, if by any chance one comes across a prospective or retrospective guest, he is as dumb about it as though it were some Masonic function. We've got you this time, Baler, though. We'll put you under the inquisition on Friday morning."

"There a won't be any need," the other replied. "One hears a great deal of rot talked about these affairs, but so far as I know, nothing very much out of the way goes on. There are always one or two pretty stiff fights in the gymnasium, and you get the best variety show and supper in the world."

"Why is there this aroma of mystery hanging about the affair, then?" some one asked.

"Well, for one or two reasons," Baker answered. "One, no doubt, is because Sir Timothy has a great idea of arranging the fights himself, and the opponents actually don't know until the fight begins whom they are meeting, and sometimes not even then. There has been some gossiping, too, about the rules, and the weight of the gloves, but that I know, nothing about."

"And the rest of the show?" a younger member enquired. "Is it simply dancing and music and that sort of thing?"

"Just a variety entertainment," the proud possessor of the scarlet-hued ticket declared. "Sir Timothy always has something up his sleeve. Last year, for instance, he had those six African girls over from Paris in that queer dance which they wouldn't allow in London at all. This time no one knows what is going to happen. The house, as you know, is absolutely surrounded by that hideous stone wall, and from what I have heard, reporters who try to get in aren't treated too kindly. Here's Ledsam. Very likely he knows more about it."

"Ledsam," some one demanded, as Francis joined the group, "are you going to Sir Timothy Brast's show to-morrow night?"

"I hope so," Francis replied, producing his strip of pasteboard.

"Ever been before?"

"Never."

"Do you know what sort of a show it's going to be?" the actor enquired.

"Not the slightest idea. I don't think any one does. That's rather a feature of the affair, isn't it?"

"It is the envious outsider who has never received an invitation, like myself," some one remarked, "who probably spreads these rumours, for one always hears it hinted that some disgraceful and illegal exhibition is on tap there - a new sort of drugging party, or some novel form of debauchery."

"I don't think," Francis said quietly, "that Sir Timothy is quite that sort of man."

"Dash it all, what sort of man is he?" the actor demanded. "They tell me that financially he is utterly unscrupulous, although he is rolling in money. He has the most Mephistophelian expression of any man I ever met - looks as though he'd set his heel on any one's neck for the sport of it - and yet they say he has given at least fifty thousand pounds to the Society for the Prevention of Cruelty to Animals, and that the whole of the park round that estate of his down the river is full of lamed and decrepit beasts which he has bought himself off the streets."

"The man must have an interesting personality," a novelist who had joined the party observed. "Of course, you know that he was in prison for six months?"

"What for?" some one asked.

"Murder, only they brought it in manslaughter," was the terse reply. "He killed his partner. It was many years ago, and no one knows all the facts of the story."

"I am not holding a brief for Sir Timothy," Francis remarked, as he sipped his cocktail. "As a matter of fact, he and I are very much at cross-purposes. But as regards that particular instance, I am not sure that he was very much to be blamed, any more than you can blame any injured person who takes the law into his own hands."

"He isn't a man I should care to have for an enemy," Baker declared.

"Well, we'll shake the truth out of you fellows, somehow or other," one of the group threatened. "On Friday morning we are going to have the whole truth - none of this Masonic secrecy which Baker indulged in last year."

The men drifted in to luncheon and Francis, leaving them, took a taxi on to the Ritz. Looking about in the vestibule for Margaret, he came face to face with Lady Cynthia. She was dressed with her usual distinction in a gown of yellow muslin and a beflowered hat, and was the cynosure of a good many eyes.

"One would almost imagine, Lady Cynthia," he said, as they exchanged greetings, "that you had found that elixir we were talking about."

"Perhaps I have," she answered, smiling. "Are you looking for Margaret? She is somewhere about. We were just having a chat when I was literally carried off by that terrible Lanchester woman. Let's find her."

They strolled up into the lounge. Margaret came to meet them. Her smile, as she gave Francis her left hand, transformed and softened her whole appearance.

"You don't mind my having asked Cynthia to lunch with us?" she said. "I really couldn't get rid of the girl. She came in to see me this morning the most aggressively cheerful person I ever knew. I believe that she had an adventure last night. All that she will tell me is that she dined and danced at Claridge's with a party of the dullest people in town."

A tall, familiar figure passed down the vestibule. Lady Cynthia gave a little start, and Francis, who happened to be watching her, was amazed at her expression.

"Your father, Margaret!" she pointed out. "I wonder if he is lunching here."

"He told me that he was lunching somewhere with a South American friend - one of his partners, I believe," Margaret replied. "I expect he is looking for him."

Sir Timothy caught sight of them, hesitated for a moment and came slowly in their direction.

"Have you found your friend?" Margaret asked.

"The poor fellow is ill in bed," her father answered. "I was just regretting that I had sent the car away, or I should have gone back to Hatch End."

"Stay and lunch with us," Lady Cynthia begged, a little impetuously.

"I shall be very pleased if you will," Francis put in. "I'll go and tell the waiter to enlarge my table."

He hurried off. On his way back, a page-boy touched him on the arm.

"If you please, sir," he announced, "you are wanted on the telephone."

"I?" Francis exclaimed. "Some mistake, I should think. Nobody knows that I am here."

"Mr. Ledsam," the boy said. "This way, sir."

Francis walked down the vestibule to the row of telephone boxes at the further end. The attendant who was standing outside, indicated one of them and motioned the boy to go away. Francis stepped inside. The man followed, closing the door behind him.

"I am asking your pardon, sir, for taking a great liberty," he confessed. "No one wants you on the telephone. I wished to speak to you."

Francis looked at him in surprise. The man was evidently agitated. Somehow or other, his face was vaguely familiar.

"Who are you, and what do you want with me?" Francis asked.

"I was butler to Mr. Hilditch, sir," the man replied. "I waited upon you the night you dined there, sir - the night of Mr. Hilditch's death."

"Well?"

"I have a revelation to make with regard to that night, sir," the man went on, "which I should like to place in your hands. It is a very serious matter, and there are reasons why something must be done about it at once. Can I come and see you at your rooms, sir?"

Francis studied the man for a moment intently. He was evidently agitated - evidently, too, in very bad health. His furtive manner was against him. On the other hand, that might have arisen from nervousness.

"I shall be in at half-past three, number 13 b, Clarges Street," Francis told him.

"I can get off for half-an-hour then, sir," the man replied. "I shall be very glad to come. I must apologise for having troubled you, sir."

Francis went slowly back to his trio of guests. All the way down the carpeted vestibule he was haunted by the grim shadow of a spectral fear. The frozen horror of that ghastly evening was before him like a hateful tableau. Hilditch's mocking words rang in his cars: "My death is the one thing in the world which would make my wife happy." The Court scene, with all its gloomy tragedy, rose before his eyes - only in the dock, instead of Hilditch, he saw another!

E. Phillips Oppenheim

CHAPTER XXIX

There were incidents connected with that luncheon which Francis always remembered. In the first place, Sir Timothy was a great deal more silent than usual. A certain vein of half-cynical, half-amusing comment upon things and people of the moment, which seemed, whenever he cared to exert himself, to flow from his lips without effort, had deserted him. He sat where the rather brilliant light from the high windows fell upon his face, and Francis wondered more than once whether there were not some change there, perhaps some prescience of trouble to come, which had subdued him and made him unusually thoughtful. Another slighter but more amusing feature of the luncheon was the number of people who stopped to shake hands with Sir Timothy and made more or less clumsy efforts to obtain an invitation to his coming entertainment. Sir Timothy's reply to these various hints was barely cordial. The most he ever promised was that he would consult with his secretary and see if their numbers were already full. Lady Cynthia, as a somewhat blatant but discomfited Peer of the Realm took his awkward leave of them, laughed softly.

"Of course, I think they all deserve what they get," she declared. "I never heard such brazen impudence in my life - from people who ought to know better, too."

Lord Meadowson, a sporting peer, who was one of Sir Timothy's few intimates, came over to the table. He paid his respects to the two ladies and Francis, and turned a little eagerly to Sir Timothy.

"Well?" he asked.

Sir Timothy nodded.

"We shall be quite prepared for you," he said. "Better bring your cheque-book."

"Capital!" the other exclaimed. "As I hadn't heard anything, I was beginning to wonder whether you would be ready with your end of the show."

"There will be no hitch so far as we are concerned," Sir Timothy assured him.

"More mysteries?" Margaret enquired, as Meadowson departed with a smile of satisfaction.

Her father shrugged his shoulders.

"Scarcely that," he replied. "It is a little wager between Lord Meadowson and myself which is to be settled to-morrow."

Lady Torrington, a fussy little woman, her hostess of the night before, on her way down the room stopped and shook hands with Lady Cynthia.

"Why, my dear," she exclaimed, "wherever did you vanish to last night? Claude told us all that, in the middle of a dance with him, you excused yourself for a moment and he never saw you again. I quite expected to read in the papers this morning that you had eloped."

"Precisely what I did," Lady Cynthia declared. "The only trouble was that my partner had had enough of me before the evening was over, and deposited me once more in Grosvenor Square. It is really very humiliating," she went on meditatively, "how every one always returns me."

"You talk such nonsense, Cynthia!" Lady Torrington exclaimed, a little pettishly. "However, you found your way home all right?"

"Quite safely, thank you. I was going to write you a note this afternoon. I went away on an impulse. All I can say is that I am sorry. Do forgive me."

"Certainly!" was the somewhat chilly reply. "Somehow or other, you seem to have earned the right to do exactly as you choose. Some of my young men whom you had promised to dance with, were disappointed, but after all, I suppose that doesn't matter."

"Not much," Lady Cynthia assented sweetly. "I think a few disappointments are good for most of the young men of to-day."

"What did you do last night, Cynthia?" Margaret asked her presently, when Lady Torrington had passed on.

"I eloped with your father," Lady Cynthia confessed, smiling across at Sir Timothy. "We went for a little drive together and I had a most amusing time. The only trouble was, as I have been complaining to that tiresome woman, he brought me home again."

"But where did you go to?" Margaret persisted.

"It was an errand of charity," Sir Timothy declared.

"It sounds very mysterious," Francis observed. "Is that all we are to be told?"

"I am afraid," Sir Timothy complained, "that very few people sympathise with my hobbies or my prosecution of them. That is why such little incidents as last night's generally remain undisclosed. If you really wish to know what happened," he went on, after a moment's pause, "I will tell you. As you know, I have a great many friends amongst the boxing fraternity, and I happened to hear of a man down in the East End who has made himself a terror to the whole community in which he lives. I took Peter Fields, my gymnasium instructor, down to the East End last night, and Peter Fields - dealt with him."

"There was a fight?" Margaret exclaimed, with a little shudder.

"There was a fight," Sir Timothy repeated, "if you can call it such. Fields gave him some part of the punishment he deserved."

"And you were there, Cynthia?"

"I left Lady Cynthia in the car," Sir Timothy explained. "She most improperly bribed my chauffeur to lend her his coat and hat, and followed me."

"You actually saw the fight, then?" Francis asked.

"I did," Lady Cynthia admitted. " I saw it from the

beginning to the end."

Margaret looked across the table curiously. It seemed to her that her friend had turned a little paler.

"Did you like it?" she asked simply.

Lady Cynthia was silent for a moment. She glanced at Sir Timothy. He, too, was waiting for her answer with evident interest.

"I was thrilled," she acknowledged. "That was the pleasurable part of it I have been so, used to looking on at shows that bored me, listening to conversations that wearied me, attempting sensations which were repellent, that I just welcomed feeling, when it came - feeling of any sort. I was excited. I forgot everything else. I was so fascinated that I could not look away. But if you ask me whether I liked it, and I have to answer truthfully, I hated it! I felt nothing of the sort at the time, but when I tried to sleep I found myself shivering. It was justice, I know, but it was ugly."

She watched Sir Timothy, as she made her confession, a little wistfully. He said nothing, but there was a very curious change in his expression. He smiled at her in an altogether unfamiliar way,

"I suppose," she said, appealing to him, "that you are very disappointed in me?"

"On the contrary," he answered, "I am delighted."

"You mean that?" she asked incredulously.

"I do," he declared. "Companionship between our

sexes is very delightful so far as it goes, but the fundamental differences between a man's outlook and tastes and a woman's should never be bridged over. I myself do not wish to learn to knit. I do not care for the womenkind in whom I am interested to appreciate and understand fighting."

Margaret looked across the table in amazement.

"You are most surprising this morning, father," she declared.

"I am perhaps misunderstood," he sighed, "perhaps have acquired a reputation for greater callousness than I possess. Personally, I love fighting. I was born a fighter, and I should find no happier way of ending my life than fighting, but, to put it bluntly, fighting is a man's job."

"What about women going to see fights at the National Sporting Club?" Lady Cynthia asked curiously.

"It is their own affair, but if you ask my opinion I do not approve of it," Sir Timothy replied. "I am indifferent upon the subject, because I am indifferent upon the subject of the generality of your sex," he added, with a little smile, "but I simply hold that it is not a taste which should be developed in women, and if they do develop it, it is at the expense of those very qualities which make them most attractive."

Lady Cynthia took a cigarette from her case and leaned over to Francis for a light.

"The world is changing," she declared. "I cannot bear many more shocks. I fancied that I had written myself for ever out of Sir Timothy's good books because of my confession just now."

He smiled across at her. His words were words of courteous badinage, but Lady Cynthia was conscious of a strange little sense of pleasure.

"On the contrary," he assured her, "you found your way just a little further into my heart."

"It seems to me, in a general sort of way," Margaret observed, leaning back in her chair, "that you and my father are becoming extraordinarily friendly, Cynthia."

"I am hopefully in love with your father," Lady Cynthia confessed. "It has been coming on for a long time. I suspected it the first time I ever met him. Now I am absolutely certain."

"It's quite a new idea," Margaret remarked. "Shall we like her in the family, Francis?"

"No airs!" Lady Cynthia warned her. "You two are not properly engaged yet. It may devolve upon me to give my consent."

"In that case," Francis replied, "I hope that we may at least count upon your influence with Sir Timothy?"

"If you'll return the compliment and urge my suit with him," Lady Cynthia laughed. "I am afraid he can't quite make up his mind about me, and I am so nice. I haven't flirted nearly so much as people think, and my instincts are really quite domestic."

"My position," Sir Timothy remarked, as he made an unsuccessful attempt to possess himself of the bill which Francis had called for, "is becoming a little difficult."

"Not really difficult," Lady Cynthia objected, "because the real decision rests in your hands."

"Just listen to the woman!" Margaret exclaimed. "Do you realise, father, that Cynthia is making the most brazen advances to you? And I was going to ask her if she'd like to come back to The Sanctuary with us this evening!"

Lady Cynthia was suddenly eager. Margaret glanced across at her father. Sir Timothy seemed almost imperceptibly to stiffen a little.

"Margaret has carte blanche at The Sanctuary as regards her visitors," he said. "I am afraid that I shall be busy over at The Walled House."

"But you'd come and dine with us?"

Sir Timothy hesitated. An issue which had been looming in his mind for many hours seemed to be suddenly joined.

"Please!" Lady Cynthia begged.

Sir Timothy followed the example of the others and rose to his feet. He avoided Lady Cynthia's eyes. He seemed suddenly a little tired.

"I will come and dine," he assented quietly. "I am afraid that I cannot promise more than that. Lady

Cynthia, as she knows, is always welcome at The Sanctuary."

CHAPTER XXX

Punctual to his appointment that afternoon, the man who had sought an interview with Francis was shown into the latter's study in Clarges Street.

He wore an overcoat over his livery, and directly he entered the room Francis was struck by his intense pallor. He had been trying feverishly to assure himself that all that the man required was the usual sort of help, or assistance into a hospital. Yet there was something furtive in his visitor's manner, something which suggested the bearer of a guilty secret.

"Please tell me what you want as quickly as you can," Francis begged. "I am due to start down into the country in a few minutes."

"I won't keep you long, sir," the man replied. "The matter is rather a serious one."

"Are you ill?"

"Yes, sir!"

"You had better sit down."

The man relapsed gratefully into a chair.

"I'll leave out everything that doesn't count, sir," he said. "I'll be as brief as I can. I want you to go back to the night I waited upon you at dinner the night Mr. Oliver Hilditch was found dead. You gave evidence. The jury brought it in 'suicide.' It wasn't suicide at all, sir. Mr. Hilditch was murdered."

The sense of horror against which he had been struggling during the last few hours, crept once more through the whole being of the man who listened. He was face to face once more with that terrible issue. Had he perjured himself in vain? Was the whole structure of his dreams about to collapse, to fall about his ears?

"By whom?" he faltered.

"By Sir Timothy Brast, sir."

Francis, who had been standing with his hand upon the table, felt suddenly inclined to laugh. Facile though his brain was, the change of issues was too tremendous for him to readily assimilate it. He picked up a cigarette from an open box, with shaking fingers, lit it, and threw himself into an easy-chair. He was all the time quite unconscious of what he was doing.

"Sir Timothy Brast?" he repeated.

"Yes, sir," the man reiterated. "I wish to tell you the whole story."

"I am listening," Francis assured him.

"That evening before dinner, Sir Timothy Brast called to see Mr. Hilditch, and a very stormy interview took place. I do not know the rights of that, sir. I only know that there was a fierce quarrel. Mrs. Hilditch came in and Sir Timothy left the house. His last words to Mr. Hilditch were, 'You will hear from me again.' As you know, sir - I mean as you remember, if you followed the evidence - all the servants slept at the back of the house. I slept in the butler's room downstairs, next to the plate pantry. I was awake when you left, sitting in my easy-chair, reading. Ten minutes after you had left, there was a sound at the front door as though some one had knocked with their knuckles. I got up, to open it but Mr. Hilditch was before me. He admitted Sir Timothy. They went back into the library together. It struck me that Mr. Hilditch had had a great deal to drink, and there was a queer look on Sir Timothy's face that I didn't understand. I stepped into the little room which communicates with the library by folding doors. There was a chink already between the two. I got a knife from the pantry and widened it until I could see through. I heard very little of the conversation but there was no quarrel. Mr. Hilditch took up the weapon which you know about, sat in a chair and held it to his heart. I heard him say something like this. 'This ought to appeal to you, Sir Timothy. You're a specialist in this sort of thing. One little touch, and there you are.' Mrs. Hilditch said something about putting it away. My master turned to Sir Timothy and said something in a low tone. Suddenly Sir Timothy leaned over. He caught hold of Mr. Hilditch's hand which held the hilt of the dagger, and and - well, he just drove it in, sir. Then he stood away. Mrs. Hilditch sprang up and would have screamed, but Sir Timothy placed his hand over her mouth. In a moment I heard her say, 'What have you done?' Sir Timothy looked at Mr. Hilditch quite calmly. 'I have ridded the world of a verminous creature,' he said. My knees began to shake. My nerves were always bad. I crept back into my room, took off my clothes and got into bed. I had just put the light out when they called for me."

Francis was himself again. There was an immense relief, a joy in his heart. He had never for a single moment blamed Margaret, but he had never for a single moment forgotten. It was a closed chapter but the stain was on its pages. It was wonderful to tear it out and scatter the fragments.

"I remember you at the inquest," he said. "Your name is John Walter."

"Yes, sir."

"Your evidence was very different."

"Yes, sir."

"You kept all this to yourself."

"I did, sir. I thought it best."

"Tell me what has happened since?"

The man looked down at the table.

"I have always been a poor man, sir," he said. "I have had bad luck whenever I've made a try to start at anything. I thought there seemed a chance for me here. I went to Sir Timothy and I told him everything."

"Well?"

"Sir Timothy never turned a hair, sir. When I had finished he was very short with me, almost curt. 'You have behaved like a man of sense, Walter,' he said. 'How much?' I hesitated for some time. Then I could see he was getting impatient. I doubled what I had thought of first. 'A thousand pounds, sir,' I said. Sir Timothy he went to a safe in the wall and he counted out a thousand pounds in notes, there and then. He brought them over to me. 'Walter,' he said, 'there is your thousand pounds. For that sum I understand you promise to keep what you saw to yourself?' 'Yes, sir,' I agreed. 'Take it, then,' he said, 'but I want you to understand this. There have been many attempts but no one yet has ever succeeded in blackmailing me. No one ever will. I give you this thousand pounds willingly. It is what you have asked for. Never let me see your face again. If you come to me starving, it will be useless. I shall not part with another penny.'"

The man's simple way of telling his story, his speech, slow and uneven on account of his faltering breath, seemed all to add to the dramatic nature of his disclosure. Francis found himself sitting like a child who listens to a fairy story.

"And then?" he asked simply.

"I went off with the money," Walter continued, "and I had cruel bad luck. I put it into a pub. I was robbed a little, I drank a little, my wife wasn't any good. I lost it all, sir. I found myself destitute. I went back to Sir Timothy."

"Well?"

The man shifted his feet nervously. He seemed to have come to the difficult part of his story.

"Sir Timothy was as hard as nails," he said slowly. "He saw me. The moment I had finished, he rang the bell. 'Hedges,' he said to the manservant who came in, 'this man has come here to try and blackmail me. Throw him out. If he gives any trouble, send for the police. If he shows himself here again, send for the police.'"

"What happened then?"

"Well, I nearly blurted out the whole story," the man confessed, "and then I remembered that wouldn't do me any good, so I went away. I got a job at the Ritz, but I was took ill a few days afterwards. I went to see a doctor. From him I got my death-warrant, sir."

"Is it heart?"

"It's heart, sir," the man acknowledged. "The doctor told me I might snuff out at any moment. I can't live, anyway, for more than a year. I've got a little girl."

"Now just why have you come to see me?" Francis asked.

"For just this, sir," the man replied. "Here's my account of what happened," he went on, drawing some sheets of foolscap from his pocket. "It's written in my own hand and there are two witnesses to my signature - one a clergyman, sir, and the other a doctor, they thinking it was a will or something. I had it in my mind to send that to Scotland Yard, and then I remembered that I hadn't a penny to leave my little girl. I began to wonder - think as meanly of me as you like, sir - how I could still make some money out of this. I happened to know that you were none too friendly disposed towards Sir Timothy. This confession of mine, if it wouldn't mean hanging, would mean imprisonment for the rest of his life. You could make a better bargain with him than me, sir. Do you want to hold him in your power? If so, you can have this confession, all signed and everything, for two hundred pounds, and as I live, sir, that two hundred pounds is to pay for my funeral, and the balance for my little girl."

Francis took the papers and glanced them through.

"Supposing I buy this document from you," he said, "what is its actual value? You could write out another confession, get that signed, and sell it to another of Sir Timothy's enemies, or you could still go to Scotland Yard yourself."

"I shouldn't do that, sir, I assure you," the man declared nervously, "not on my solemn oath. I want simply to be quit of the whole matter and have a little money for the child."

Francis considered for a moment.

"There is only one way I can see," he said, "to make this document worth the money to me. If you will sign a confession that any statement you have made as to the death of Mr. Hilditch is entirely imaginary, that you did not see Sir Timothy in the house that night, that you went to bed at your usual time and slept until you were awakened, and that you only made this charge for the purpose of extorting money - if you will sign a confession to that effect and give it me with these papers, I will pay you the two hundred pounds and I will never use the confession unless you repeat the charge."

"I'll do it, sir," the man assented.

Francis drew up a document, which his visitor read through and signed. Then he wrote out an open cheque.

"My servant shall take you to the bank in a taxi," he said. "They would scarcely pay you this unless you were identified. We understand one another?"

"Perfectly, sir!"

Francis rang the bell, gave his servant the necessary orders, and dismissed the two men. Half-an-hour later, already changed into flannels, he was on his way into the country.

CHAPTER XXXI

Sir Timothy walked that evening amongst the shadows. Two hours ago, the last of the workmen from the great furnishing and catering establishments who undertook the management of his famous entertainments, had ceased work for the day and driven off in the motor-brakes hired to take them to the nearest town. The long, low wing whose use no one was able absolutely to divine, was still full of animation, but the great reception-rooms and stately hall were silent and empty. In the gymnasium, an enormous apartment as large as an ordinary concert hall, two or three electricians were still at work, directed by the man who had accompanied Sir Timothy to the East End on the night before. The former crossed the room, his footsteps awaking strange echoes.

"There will be seating for fifty, sir, and standing room for fifty," he announced. "I have had the ring slightly enlarged, as you suggested, and the lighting is being altered so that the start is exactly north and south."

Sir Timothy nodded thoughtfully. The beautiful oak floor of the place was littered with sawdust and shavings of wood. Several tiers of seats had been arranged on the space usually occupied by swings, punching-balls and other artifices. On a slightly raised dais at the further end was an exact replica of a ring,

E. Phillips Oppenheim

corded around and with sawdust upon the floor. Upon the walls hung a marvellous collection of weapons of every description, from the modern rifle to the curved and terrible knife used by the most savage of known tribes.

"How are things in the quarters?" Sir Timothy asked.

"Every one is well, sir. Doctor Ballantyne arrived this afternoon. His report is excellent."

Sir Timothy nodded and turned away. He looked into the great gallery, its waxen floors shining with polish, ready for the feet of the dancers on the morrow; looked into a beautiful concert-room, with an organ that reached to the roof; glanced into the banquetting hall, which extended far into the winter-garden; made his way up the broad stairs, turned down a little corridor, unlocked a door and passed into his own suite. There was a small dining-room, a library, a bedroom, and a bathroom fitted with every sort of device. A man-servant who had heard him enter, hurried from his own apartment across the way.

"You are not dining here, sir? "he enquired.

Sir Timothy shook his head.

"No, I am dining late at The Sanctuary," he replied. "I just strolled over to see how the preparations were going on. I shall be sleeping over there, too. Any prowlers?"

"Photographer brought some steps and photographed the horses in the park from the top of the wall this afternoon, sir," the man announced. "Jenkins let him go. Two or three pressmen sent in their cards to you, but they were not allowed to pass the lodge."

Sir Timothy nodded. Soon he left the house and crossed the park towards The Sanctuary. He was followed all the way by horses, of which there were more than thirty in the great enclosure. One mare greeted him with a neigh of welcome and plodded slowly after him. Another pressed her nose against his shoulder and walked by his side, with his hand upon her neck. Sir Timothy looked a little nervously around, but the park itself lay almost like a deep green pool, unobserved, and invisible from anywhere except the house itself. He spoke a few words to each of the horses, and, producing his key, passed through the door in the wall into The Sanctuary garden, closing it quickly as he recognised Francis standing under the cedar-tree.

"Has Lady Cynthia arrived yet?" he enquired.

"Not yet," Francis replied. "Margaret will be here in a minute. She told me to say that cocktails are here and that she has ordered dinner served on the terrace."

"Excellent!" Sir Timothy murmured. "Let me try one of your cigarettes."

"Everything ready for the great show to-morrow night?" Francis asked, as he served the cocktails.

"Everything is in order. I wonder, really," Sir Timothy went on, looking at Francis curiously, "what you expect to see?"

"I don't think we any of us have any definite idea,"

Francis replied. "We have all, of course, made our guesses."

"You will probably be disappointed," Sir Timothy warned him. "For some reason or other - perhaps I have encouraged the idea - people look upon my parties as mysterious orgies where things take place which may not be spoken of. They are right to some extent. I break the law, without a doubt, but I break it, I am afraid, in rather a disappointing fashion."

A limousine covered in dust raced in at the open gates and came to a standstill with a grinding of brakes. Lady Cynthia stepped lightly out and came across the lawn to them.

"I am hot and dusty and I was disagreeable," she confided, "but the peace of this wonderful place, and the sight of that beautiful silver thing have cheered me. May I have a cocktail before I go up to change? I am a little late, I know," she went. on, "but that wretched garden-party! I thought my turn would never come to receive my few words. Mother would have been broken-hearted if I had left without them. What slaves we are to royalty! Now shall I hurry and change? You men have the air of wanting your dinner, and I am rather that way myself. You look tired, dear host," she added, a little hesitatingly.

"The heat," he answered.

"Why you ever leave this spot I can't imagine," she declared, as she turned away, with a lingering glance around. "It seems like Paradise to come here and breathe this air. London is like a furnace."

The two men were alone again. In Francis' pocket were the two documents, which he had not yet made up his mind how to use. Margaret came out to them presently, and he strolled away with her towards the rose garden.

"Margaret," he said, "is it my fancy or has there been a change in your father during the last few days?"

"There is a change of some sort," she admitted. "I cannot describe it. I only know it is there. He seems much more thoughtful and less hard. The change would be an improvement," she went on, "except that somehow or other it makes me feel uneasy. It is as though he were grappling with some crisis."

They came to a standstill at the end of the pergola, where the masses of drooping roses made the air almost faint with their perfume. Margaret stretched out her hand, plucked a handful of the creamy petals and held them against her cheek. A thrush was singing noisily. A few yards away they heard the soft swish of the river.

"Tell me," she asked curiously, "my father still speaks of you as being in some respects an enemy. What does he mean?"

"I will tell you exactly," he answered. "The first time I ever spoke to your father I was dining at Soto's. I was talking to Andrew Wilmore. It was only a short time after you had told me the story of Oliver Hilditch, a story which made me realise the horror of spending one's life keeping men like that out of the clutch of the law."

"Go on, please," she begged.

"Well, I was talking to Andrew. I told him that in future I should accept no case unless I not only believed in but was convinced of the innocence of my client. I added that I was at war with crime. I think, perhaps, I was so deeply in earnest that I may have sounded a little flamboyant. At any rate, your father, who had overheard me, moved up to our table. I think he deduced from what I was saying that I was going to turn into a sort of amateur crime-investigator, a person who I gathered later was particularly obnoxious to him. At any rate, he held out a challenge. 'If you are a man who hates crime,' he said, or something like it, 'I am one who loves it.' He then went on to prophesy that a crime would be committed close to where we were, within an hour or so, and he challenged me to discover the assassin. That night Victor Bidlake was murdered just outside Soto's."

"I remember! Do you mean to tell me, then," Margaret went on, with a little shiver, "that father told you this was going to happen?"

"He certainly did," Francis replied. "How his knowledge came I am not sure - yet. But he certainly knew."

"Have you anything else against him?" she asked.

"There was the disappearance of Andrew Wilmore's younger brother, Reginald Wilmore. I have no right to connect your father with that, but Shopland, the Scotland Yard detective, who has charge of the case, seems to believe that the young man was brought into this neighbourhood, and some other indirect evidence which came into my hands does seem to point towards your father being concerned in the matter. I appealed to him at once but he only laughed at me. That matter, too, remains a mystery."

Margaret was thoughtful for a moment. Then she turned towards the house. They heard the soft ringing of the gong.

"Will you believe me when I tell you this?" she begged, as they passed arm in arm down the pergola. "I am terrified of my father, though in many ways he is almost princely in his generosity and in the broad view he takes of things. Then his kindness to all dumb animals, and the way they love him, is the most amazing thing I ever knew. If we were alone here to-night, every animal in the house would be around his chair. He has even the cats locked up if we have visitors, so that no one shall see it. But I am quite honest when I tell you this - I do not believe that my father has the ordinary outlook upon crime. I believe that there is a good deal more of the Old Testament about him than the New."

"And this change which we were speaking about?" he asked, lowering his voice as they reached the lawn.

"I believe that somehow or other the end is coming," she said. "Francis, forgive me if I tell you this - or rather let me be forgiven - but I know of one crime my father has committed, and it makes me fear that there may be others. And I have the feeling, somehow, that the end is close at hand and that he feels it, just as we might feel a thunder-storm in the air."

"I am going to prove the immemorial selfishness of my sex," he whispered, as they drew near the little table. "Promise me one thing and I don't care if your father is Beelzebub himself. Promise me that, whatever happens, it shall not make any difference to us?"

She smiled at him very wonderfully, a smile which had to take the place of words, for there were servants now within hearing, and Sir Timothy himself was standing in the doorway.

CHAPTER XXXII

Lady Cynthia and Sir Timothy strolled after dinner to the bottom of the lawn and watched the punt which Francis was propelling turn from the stream into the river.

"Perfectly idyllic," Lady Cynthia sighed.

"We have another punt," her companion suggested.

She shook her head.

"I am one of those unselfish people," she declared, "whose idea of repose is not only to rest oneself but to see others rest. I think these two chairs, plenty of cigarettes, and you in your most gracious and discoursive mood, will fill my soul with content."

"Your decision relieves my mind," her companion declared, as he arranged the cushions behind her back. "I rather fancy myself with a pair of sculls, but a punt-pole never appealed to me. We will sit here and enjoy the peace. To-morrow night you will find it all disturbed - music and raucous voices and the stampede of my poor, frightened horses in the park. This is really a very gracious silence."

"Are those two really going to marry?" Lady Cynthia

asked, moving her head lazily in the direction of the disappearing punt.

"I imagine so."

"And you? What are you going to do then?"

"I am planning a long cruise. I telegraphed to Southampton to-day. I am having my yacht provisioned and prepared. I think I shall go over to South America."

She was silent for a moment.

"Alone?" she asked presently.

"I am always alone," he answered.

"That is rather a matter of your own choice, is it not?"

"Perhaps so. I have always found it hard to make friends. Enemies seem to be more in my line."

"I have not found it difficult to become your friend," she reminded him.

"You are one of my few successes," he replied.

She leaned back with half-closed eyes. There was nothing new about their environment - the clusters of roses, the perfume of the lilies in the rock garden, the even sweeter fragrance of the trim border of mignonette. Away in the distance, the night was made momentarily ugly by the sound of a gramophone on a passing launch, yet this discordant note seemed only to bring the perfection of present things closer. Back across the velvety lawn, through the feathery strips of foliage, the lights of The Sanctuary, shaded and subdued, were dimly visible. The dining-table under the cedar-tree had already been cleared. Hedges, newly arrived from town to play the major domo, was putting the finishing touches to a little array of cool drinks. And beyond, dimly seen but always there, the wall. She turned to him suddenly.

"You build a wall around your life," she said, "like the wall which encircles your mystery house. Last night I thought that I could see a little way over the top. To-night you are different."

"If I am different," he answered quietly, "it is because, for the first time for many years, I have found myself wondering whether the life I had planned for myself, the things which I had planned should make life for me, are the best. I have had doubts - perhaps I might say regrets."

"I should like to go to South America," Lady Cynthia declared softly.

He finished the cigarette which he was smoking and deliberately threw away the stump. Then he turned and looked at her. His face seemed harder than ever, clean-cut, the face of a man able to defy Fate, but she saw something in his eyes which she had never seen before.

"Dear child," he said, "if I could roll back the years, if from all my deeds of sin, as the world knows sin, I could cancel one, there is nothing in the world would make me happier than to ask you to come with me as my cherished companion to just whatever part of the world you cared for. But I have been playing pitch and toss with fortune all my life, since the great trouble came which changed me so much. Even at this moment, the coin is in the air which may decide my fate."

"You mean?" she ventured.

"I mean," he continued, "that after the event of which we spoke last night, nothing in life has been more than an incident, and I have striven to find distraction by means which none of you - not even you, Lady Cynthia, with all your breadth of outlook and all your craving after new things - would justify."

"Nothing that you may have done troubles me in the least," she assured him. "I do wish that you could put it all out of your mind and let me help you to make a fresh start."

"I may put the thing itself out of my mind," he answered sadly, "but the consequences remain."

"There is a consequence which threatens?" she asked.

He was silent for a moment. When he spoke again, he had recovered all his courage.

"There is the coin in the air of which I spoke," he replied. "Let us forget it for a moment. Of the minor things I will make you my judge. Ledsam and Margaret are coming to my party to-morrow night. You, too, shall be my guest. Such secrets as lie on the other side of that wall shall be yours. After that, if I survive your judgment of them, and if the coin which I have thrown into the air comes, down to the tune I call - after that - I will remind you of something which happened last night - of something which, if I live for many years, I shall never forget."

She leaned towards him. Her eyes were heavy with longing. Her arms, sweet and white in the dusky twilight, stole hesitatingly out.

"Last night was so long ago. Won't you take a later memory?"

Once again she lay in his arms, still and content.

As they crossed the lawn, an hour or so later, they were confronted by Hedges - who hastened, in fact, to meet them.

"You are being asked for on the telephone, sir," he announced. "It is a trunk call. I have switched it through to the study."

"Any name?" Sir Timothy asked indifferently.

The man hesitated. His eyes sought his master's respectfully but charged with meaning.

"The person refuses to give his name, sir, but I fancied that I recognised his voice. I think it would be as well for you to speak, sir."

Lady Cynthia sank into a chair.

"You shall go and answer your telephone call," she said, "and leave Hedges to serve me with one of these strange drinks. I believe I see some of my favourite orangeade."

Sir Timothy made his way into the house and into the low, oak-beamed study with its dark furniture and latticed windows. The telephone bell began to ring again as he entered. He took up the receiver.

"Sir Timothy?" a rather hoarse, strained voice asked.

"I am speaking," Sir Timothy replied. "Who is it?"

The man at the other end spoke as though he were out of breath. Nevertheless, what he said was distinct enough.

"I am John Walter."

"Well?"

"I am just ringing you up," the voice went on, "to give you what's called a sporting chance. There's a boat from Southampton midday tomorrow. If you're wise, you'll catch it. Or better still, get off on your own yacht. They carry a wireless now, these big steamers. Don't give a criminal much of a chance, does it?"

"I am to understand, then," Sir Timothy said calmly, "that you have laid your information?"

"I've parted with it and serve you right," was the bitter reply. "I'm not saying that you're not a brave man, Sir Timothy, but there's such a thing as being foolhardy, and that's what you are. I wasn't asking you for half your fortune, nor even a dab of it, but if your life wasn't worth a few hundred pounds - you, with all that money - well, it wasn't worth saving. So now you know. I've spent ninepence to give you a chance to hop it, because I met a gent who has been good to me. I've had a good dinner and I feel merciful. So there you are."

"Do I gather," Sir Timothy asked, in a perfectly level tone, "that the deed is already done?"

"It's already done and done thoroughly," was the uncompromising answer. "I'm not ringing up to ask you to change your mind. If you were to offer me five thousand now, or ten, I couldn't stop the bally thing. You've a sporting chance of getting away if you start at once. That's all there is to it."

"You have nothing more to say?"

"Nothing! Only I wish to God I'd never stepped into that Mayfair agency. I wish I'd never gone to Mrs. Hilditch's as a temporary butler. I wish I'd never seen any one of you! That's all. You can go to Hell which way you like, only, if you take my advice, you'll go by the way of South America. The scaffold isn't every man's fancy."

There was a burr of the instrument and then silence. Sir Timothy carefully replaced the receiver, paused on his way out of the room to smell a great bowl of lavender, and passed back into the garden.

"More applicants for invitations?" Lady Cynthia enquired lazily.

Her host smiled.

"Not exactly! Although," he added, "as a matter of fact my party would have been perhaps a little more complete with the presence of the person to whom I have been speaking."

Lady Cynthia pointed to the stream, down which the punt was slowly drifting. The moon had gone behind a cloud, and Francis' figure, as he stood there, was undefined and ghostly. A thought seemed to flash into her mind. She leaned forward.

"Once," she said, "he told me that he was your enemy."

"The term is a little melodramatic," Sir Timothy protested. "We look at certain things from opposite points of view. You see, my prospective son-in-law, if ever he becomes that, represents the law - the Law with a capital 'L' - which recognises no human errors or weaknesses, and judges crime out of the musty books of the law-givers of old. He makes of the law a mechanical thing which can neither bend nor give, and he judges humanity from the same standpoint. Yet at heart he is a good fellow and I like him."

"And you?"

"My weakness lies the other way," he confessed, "and my sympathy is with those who do not fear to make their own laws."

She held out her hand, white and spectral in the momentary gloom. At the other end of the lawn, Francis and Margaret were disembarking from the punt.

"Does it sound too shockingly obvious," she murmured, "if I say that I want to make you my law?"

CHAPTER XXXIII

It would have puzzled anybody, except, perhaps, Lady Cynthia herself, to have detected the slightest alteration in Sir Timothy's demeanour during the following day, when he made fitful appearances at The Sanctuary, or at the dinner which was served a little earlier than usual, before his final departure for the scene of the festivities. Once he paused in the act of helping himself to some dish and listened for a moment to the sound of voices in the hall, and when a taxicab drove up he set down his glass and again betrayed some interest.

"The maid with my frock, thank heavens!" Lady Cynthia announced, glancing out of the window. "My last anxiety is removed. I am looking forward now to a wonderful night."

"You may very easily be disappointed," her host warned her. "My entertainments appeal more, as a rule, to men."

"Why don't you be thoroughly original and issue no invitations to women at all?" Margaret enquired.

"For the same reason that you adorn your rooms and the dinner-table with flowers," he answered. "One needs them - as a relief. Apart from that, I am really

E. Phillips Oppenheim

proud of my dancing-room, and there again, you see, your sex is necessary."

"We are flattered," Margaret declared, with a little bow. "It does seem queer to think that you should own what Cynthia's cousin, Davy Hinton, once told me was the best floor in London, and that I have never danced on it."

"Nor I," Lady Cynthia put in. "There might have been some excuse for not asking you, Margaret, but why an ultra-Bohemian like myself has had to beg and plead for an invitation, I really cannot imagine."

"You might find," Sir Timothy said, "you may even now - that some of my men guests are not altogether to your liking."

"Quite content to take my risk," Lady Cynthia declared cheerfully. "The man with the best manners I ever met - it was at one of Maggie's studio dances, too - was a bookmaker. And a retired prize-fighter brought me home once from an Albert Hall dance."

"How did he behave?" Francis asked.

"He was wistful but restrained," Lady Cynthia replied, "quite the gentleman, in fact."

"You encourage me to hope for the best," Sir Timothy said, rising to his feet. "You will excuse me now? I have a few final preparations to make."

"Are we to be allowed," Margaret enquired, "to come across the park?"

"You would not find it convenient," her father assured her. "You had better order a car, say for ten o'clock. Don't forget to bring your cards of invitation, and find me immediately you arrive. I wish to direct your proceedings to some extent."

Lady Cynthia strolled across with him to the postern-gate and stood by his side after he had opened it. Several of the animals, grazing in different parts of the park, pricked up their ears at the sound. An old mare came hobbling towards him; a flea-bitten grey came trotting down the field, his head in the air, neighing loudly.

"You waste a great deal of tenderness upon your animal friends, dear host," she murmured.

He deliberately looked away from her.

"The reciprocation, at any rate, has its disadvantages," he remarked, glancing a little disconsolately at the brown hairs upon his coat-sleeve. "I shall have to find another coat before I can receive my guests - which is a further reason," he added, "why I must hurry."

At the entrance to the great gates of The Walled House, two men in livery were standing. One of them examined with care the red cards of invitation, and as soon as he was satisfied the gates were opened by some unseen agency. The moment the car had passed through, they were closed again.

"Father seems thoroughly mediaeval over this business," Margaret remarked, looking about her with interest. "What a quaint courtyard, too! It really is quite Italian."

"It seems almost incredible that you have never been here!" Lady Cynthia exclaimed. "Curiosity would have brought me if I had had to climb over the wall!"

"It does seem absurd in one way," Margaret agreed, "but, as a matter of fact, my father's attitude about the place has always rather set me against it. I didn't feel that there was any pleasure to be gained by coming here. I won't tell you really what I did think. We must keep to our bargain. We are not to anticipate."

At the front entrance, under the covered portico, the white tickets which they had received in exchange for their tickets of invitation, were carefully collected by another man, who stopped the car a few yards from the broad, curving steps. After that, there was no more suggestion of inhospitality. The front doors, which were of enormous size and height, seemed to have been removed, and in the great domed hall beyond Sir Timothy was already receiving his guests. Being without wraps, the little party made an immediate entrance. Sir Timothy, who was talking to one of the best-known of the foreign ambassadors, took a step forward to meet them.

"Welcome," he said, "you, the most unique party, at least, amongst my guests. Prince, may I present you to my daughter, Mrs. Hilditch? Lady Cynthia Milton and Mr. Ledsam you know, I believe."

"Your father has just been preparing me for this pleasure," the Prince remarked, with a smile. "I am delighted that his views as regards these wonderful parties are becoming a little more - would it be correct to say latitudinarian? He has certainly been very strict up to now."

"It is the first time I have been vouchsafed an invitation," Margaret confessed.

"You will find much to interest you," the Prince observed. "For myself, I love the sport of which your father is so noble a patron. That, without doubt, though, is a side of his entertainment of which you will know nothing."

Sir Timothy, choosing a moment's respite from the inflowing stream of guests, came once more across to them.

"I am going to leave you, my honoured guests from The Sanctuary," he said, with a faint smile, "to yourselves for a short time. In the room to your left, supper is being served. In front is the dancing-gallery. To the right, as you see, is the lounge leading into the winter-garden. The gymnasium is closed until midnight. Any other part of the place please explore at your leisure, but I am going to ask you one thing. I want you to meet me in a room which I will show you, at a quarter to twelve."

He led them down one of the corridors which opened from the hall. Before the first door on the right a man-servant was standing as though on sentry duty. Sir Timothy tapped the panel of the door with his forefinger.

"This is my sanctum," he announced. "I allow no one in here without special permission. I find it useful to have a place to which one can come and rest quite quietly sometimes. Williams here has no other duty except to guard the entrance. Williams, you will allow this gentleman and these two ladies to pass in at a quarter to twelve."

The man looked at them searchingly.

"Certainly, sir," he said. "No one else?"

"No one, under any pretext."

Sir Timothy hurried back to the hall, and the others followed him in more leisurely fashion. They were all three full of curiosity.

"I never dreamed," Margaret declared, as she looked around her, "that I should ever find myself inside this house. It has always seemed to me like one great bluebeard's chamber. If ever my father spoke of it at all, it was as of a place which he intended to convert into a sort of miniature Hell."

Sir Timothy leaned back to speak to them as they passed.

"You will find a friend over there, Ledsam," he said.

Wilmore turned around and faced them. The two men exchanged somewhat surprised greetings.

"No idea that I was coming until this afternoon," Wilmore explained. "I got my card at five o'clock, with a note from Sir Timothy's secretary. I am racking my brains to imagine what it can mean."

"We're all a little addled," Francis confessed. "Come and join our tour of exploration. You know Lady Cynthia. Let me present you to Mrs. Hilditch."

The introduction was effected and they all, strolled on together. Margaret and Lady Cynthia led the way into the winter-garden, a palace of glass, tall palms, banks of exotics, flowering shrubs of every description, and a fountain, with wonderfully carved water nymphs, brought with its basin from Italy. Hidden in the foliage, a small orchestra was playing very softly. The atmosphere of the place was languorous and delicious.

"Leave us here," Margaret insisted, with a little exclamation of content. "Neither Cynthia nor I want to go any further. Come back and fetch us in time for our appointment."

The two men wandered off. The place was indeed a marvel of architecture, a country house, of which only the shell remained, modernised and made wonderful by the genius of a great architect. The first room which they entered when they left the winter-garden, was as large as a small restaurant, panelled in cream colour, with a marvellous ceiling. There were tables of various sizes laid for supper, rows of champagne bottles in ice buckets, and servants eagerly waiting for orders. Already a sprinkling of the guests had found their way here. The two men crossed the floor to the cocktail bar in the far corner, behind which a familiar face grinned at them. It was Jimmy, the bartender from Soto's, who stood there with a wonderful array of bottles on a walnut table.

"If it were not a perfectly fatuous question, I should ask what you were doing here, Jimmy?" Francis remarked.

"I always come for Sir Timothy's big parties, sir," Jimmy explained. "Your first visit, isn't it, sir?"

"My first," Francis assented.

"And mine," his companion echoed.

"What can I have the pleasure of making for you, sir?" the man enquired.

"A difficult question," Francis admitted. "It is barely an hour and a half since we finished diner. On the other hand, we are certainly going to have some supper some time or other."

Jimmy nodded understandingly.

"Leave it to me, sir," he begged.

He served them with a foaming white concoction in tall glasses. A genuine lime bobbed up and down in the liquid.

"Sir Timothy has the limes sent over from his own estate in South America," Jimmy announced. "You will find some things in that drink you don't often taste."

The two men sipped their beverage and pronounced it delightful. Jimmy leaned a little across the table.

"A big thing on to-night, isn't there, sir?" he asked cautiously.

"Is there?" Francis replied. "You mean -?"

Jimmy motioned towards the open window, close to which the river was flowing by.

"You going down, sir?"

Francis shook his head dubiously.

"Where to?"

The bartender looked with narrowed eyes from one to the other of the two men. Then he suddenly froze up. Wilmore leaned a little further over the impromptu counter.

"Jimmy," he asked, "what goes on here besides dancing and boxing and gambling?"

"I never heard of any gambling," Jimmy answered, shaking his head. "Sir Timothy doesn't care about cards being played here at all."

"What is the principal entertainment, then?" Francis demanded. "The boxing?"

The bartender shook his head.

"No one understands very much about this house, sir," he said, "except that it offers the most wonderful entertainment in Europe. That is for the guests to find out, though. We servants have to attend to our duties. Will you let me mix you another drink, sir?"

"No, thanks," Francis answered. "The last was too good to spoil. But you haven't answered my question, Jimmy. What did you mean when you asked if we were going down?"

Jimmy's face had become wooden.

"I meant nothing, sir," he said. "Sorry I spoke."

The two men turned away. They recognised many acquaintances in the supper-room, and in the long gallery beyond, where many couples were dancing now to the music of a wonderful orchestra. By slow stages they made their way back to the winter-garden, where Lady Cynthia and Margaret were still lost in admiration of their surroundings. They all walked the whole length of the place. Beyond, down a flight of stone steps, was a short, paved way to the river. A large electric launch was moored at the quay. The grounds outside were dimly illuminated with cunningly-hidden electric lights shining through purple-coloured globes into the cloudy darkness. In the background, enveloping the whole of the house and reaching to the river on either side, the great wall loomed up, unlit, menacing almost in its suggestions. A couple of loiterers stood within a few yards of them, looking at the launch.

"There she is, ready for her errand, whatever it may be," one said to the other curiously. "We couldn't play the stowaway, I suppose, could we?"

"Dicky Bell did that once," the other answered. "Sir Timothy has only one way with intruders. He was thrown into the river and jolly nearly drowned."

The two men passed out of hearing.

"I wonder what part the launch plays in the night's entertainment," Wilmore observed.

Francis shrugged his shoulders.

"I have given up wondering," he said. "Margaret, do you hear that music?"

She laughed.

"Are we really to dance?" she murmured. "Do you want to make a girl of me again?"

"Well, I shouldn't be a magician, should I?" he answered.

They passed into the ballroom and danced for some time. The music was seductive and perfect, without any of the blatant notes of too many of the popular orchestras. The floor seemed to sway under their feet.

"This is a new joy come back into life!" Margaret exclaimed, as they rested for a moment.

"The first of many," he assured her.

They stood in the archway between the winter-garden and the dancing-gallery, from which they could command a view of the passing crowds. Francis scanned the faces of the men and women with intense interest. Many of them were known to him by sight, others were strangers. There was a judge, a Cabinet Minister, various members of the aristocracy, a sprinkling from the foreign legations, and although the stage was not largely represented, there were one or two well-known actors. The guests seemed to belong to no universal social order, but to Francis, watching them almost eagerly, they all seemed to have something of the same expression, the same slight air of weariness, of restless and unsatisfied desires.

"I can't believe that the place is real, or that these people we see are not supers," Margaret whispered.

"I feel every moment that a clock will strike and that it will all fade away."

"I'm afraid I'm too material for such imaginings," Francis replied, "but there is a quaintly artificial air about it all. We must go and look for Wilmore and Lady Cynthia."

They turned back into the enervating atmosphere of the winter-garden, and came suddenly face to face with Sir Timothy, who had escorted a little party of his guests to see the fountain, and was now returning alone.

"You have been dancing, I am glad to see," the latter observed. "I trust that you are amusing yourselves?"

"Excellently, thank you," Francis replied.

"And so far," Sir Timothy went on, with a faint smile, "you find my entertainment normal? You have no question yet which you would like to ask?"

"Only one - what do you do with your launch up the river on moonless nights, Sir Timothy?"

Sir Timothy's momentary silence was full of ominous significance.

"Mr. Ledsam," he said, after a brief pause, "I have given you almost carte blanche to explore my domains here. Concerning the launch, however, I think that you had better ask no questions at present."

"You are using it to-night?" Francis persisted.

"Will you come and see, my venturesome guest?"

"With great pleasure," was the prompt reply.

Sir Timothy glanced at his watch.

"That," he said, "is one of the matters of which we will speak at a quarter to twelve. Meanwhile, let me show you something. It may amuse you as it has done me."

The three moved back towards one of the arched openings which led into the ballroom.

"Observe, if you please," their host continued, "the third couple who pass us. The girl is wearing green - the very little that she does wear. Watch the man, and see if he reminds you of any one."

Francis did as he was bidden. The girl was a well-known member of the chorus of one of the principal musical comedies, and she seemed to be thoroughly enjoying both the dance and her partner. The latter appeared to be of a somewhat ordinary type, sallow, with rather puffy cheeks, and eyes almost unnaturally dark. He danced vigorously and he talked all the time. Something about him was vaguely familiar to Francis, but he failed to place him.

"Notwithstanding all my precautions," Sir Timothy continued, "there, fondly believing himself to be unnoticed, is an emissary of Scotland Yard. Really, of all the obvious, the dry-as-dust, hunt-your-criminal-by-rule-of-three kind of people I ever met, the class of detective to which this man belongs can produce the most blatant examples."

"What are you going to do about him?" Francis asked.

Sir Timothy shrugged his shoulders.

"I have not yet made up my mind," he said. "I happen to know that he has been laying his plans for weeks to get here, frequenting Soto's and other restaurants, and scraping acquaintances with some of my friends. The Duke of Tadchester brought him - won a few hundreds from him at baccarat, I suppose. His grace will never again find these doors open to him."

Francis' attention had wandered. He was gazing fixedly at the man whom Sir Timothy had pointed out.

"You still do not fully recognise our friend," the latter observed carelessly. "He calls himself Manuel Loito, and he professes to be a Cuban. His real name I understood, when you introduced us, to be Shopland."

"Great heavens, so it is!" Francis exclaimed.

"Let us leave him to his precarious pleasures," Sir Timothy suggested. "I am free for a few moments. We will wander round together."

They found Lady Cynthia and Wilmore, and looked in at the supper-room, where people were waiting now for tables, a babel of sound and gaiety. The grounds and winter-gardens were crowded. Their guide led the way to a large apartment on the, other side of the hall, from which the sound of music was proceeding.

"My theatre," he said. "I wonder what is going on."

They passed inside. There was a small stage with steps leading down to the floor, easy-chairs and round tables everywhere, and waiters serving refreshments. A girl was dancing. Sir Timothy watched her approvingly.

"Nadia Ellistoff," he told them. "She was in the last Russian ballet, and she is waiting now for the rest of the company to start again at Covent Garden. You see, it is Metzger who plays there. They improvise. Rather a wonderful performance, I think."

They watched her breathlessly, a spirit in grey tulle, with great black eyes now and then half closed.

"It is 'Wind before Dawn,'" Lady Cynthia whispered. "I heard him play it two days after he composed it, only there are variations now. She is the soul of the south wind."

The curtain went down amidst rapturous applause. The dancer had left the stage, floating away into some sort of wonderfully-contrived nebulous background. Within a few moments, the principal comedian of the day was telling stories. Sir Timothy led them away.

"But how on earth do you get all these people?" Lady Cynthia asked.

"It is arranged for me," Sir Timothy replied. "I have an agent who sees to it all. Every man or woman who is asked to perform, has a credit at Cartier's for a hundred guineas. I pay no fees. They select some little keepsake."

Margaret laughed softly.

"No wonder they call this place a sort of Arabian Nights!" she declared.

"Well, there isn't much else for you to see," Sir Timothy said thoughtfully. "My gymnasium, which is one of the principal features here, is closed just now for a special performance, of which I will speak in a moment. The concert hall I see they are using for an overflow dance-room. What you have seen, with the grounds and the winter-garden, comprises almost everything."

They moved back through the hall with difficulty. People were now crowding in. Lady Cynthia laughed softly.

"Why, it is like a gala night at the Opera, Sir Timothy!" she exclaimed. "How dare you pretend that this is Bohemia!"

"It has never been I who have described my entertainments," he reminded her. "They have been called everything - orgies, debauches - everything you can think of. I have never ventured myself to describe them."

Their passage was difficult. Every now and then Sir Timothy was compelled to shake hands with some of his newly-arriving guests. At last, however, they reached the little sitting-room. Sir Timothy turned back to Wilmore, who hesitated.

"You had better come in, too, Mr. Wilmore, if you will," he invited. "You were with Ledsam, the first day we met, and something which I have to say now may interest you."

"If I am not intruding," Wilmore murmured.

They entered the room, still jealously guarded. Sir Timothy closed the door behind them.

CHAPTER XXXIV

The apartment was one belonging to the older portion of the house, and had been, in fact, an annex to the great library. The walls were oak-panelled, and hung with a collection of old prints. There were some easy-chairs, a writing-table, and some well-laden bookcases. There were one or two bronze statues of gladiators, a wonderful study of two wrestlers, no minor ornaments. Sir Timothy plunged at once into what he had to say.

"I promised you, Lady Cynthia, and you, Ledsam," he said, "to divulge exactly the truth as regards these much-talked-of entertainments here. You, Margaret, under present circumstances, are equally interested. You, Wilmore, are Ledsam's friend, and you happen to have an interest in this particular party. Therefore, I am glad to have you all here together. The superficial part of my entertainment you have seen. The part which renders it necessary for me to keep closed doors, I shall now explain. I give prizes here of considerable value for boxing contests which are conducted under rules of our own. One is due to take place in a very few minutes. The contests vary in character, but I may say that the chief officials of the National Sporting Club are usually to be found here, only, of course, in an unofficial capacity. The difference between the contests arranged by me, and others, is that my men are here to fight. They use sometimes an illegal weight of glove and they sometimes hurt one another. If any two of the boxing fraternity have a grudge against one another, and that often happens, they are permitted here to fight it out, under the strictest control as regards fairness, but practically without gloves at all. You heard of the accident, for instance, to Norris? That happened in my gymnasium. He was knocked out by Burgin. It was a wonderful fight.

"However, I pass on. There is another class of contest which frequently takes place here. Two boxers place themselves unreservedly in my hands. The details of the match are arranged without their knowledge. They come into the ring without knowing whom they are going to fight. Sometimes they never know, for my men wear masks. Then we have private matches. There is one to-night. Lord Meadowson and I have a wager of a thousand guineas. He has brought to-night from the East End a boxer who, according to the terms of our bet, has never before engaged in a professional contest. I have brought an amateur under the same conditions. The weight is within a few pounds the same, neither has ever seen the other, only in this case the fight is with regulation gloves and under Queensberry rules."

"Who is your amateur, Sir Timothy?" Wilmore asked harshly.

"Your brother, Mr. Wilmore," was the prompt reply. "You shall see the fight if I have your promise not to attempt in any way to interfere."

Wilmore rose to his feet.

"Do you mean to tell me," he demanded, "that my

E. Phillips Oppenheim

brother has been decoyed here, kept here against his will, to provide amusement for your guests?"

"Mr. Wilmore, I beg that you will be reasonable," Sir Timothy expostulated. "I saw your brother box at his gymnasium in Holborn. My agent made him the offer of this fight. One of my conditions had to be that he came here to train and that whilst he was here he held no communication whatever with the outside world. My trainer has ideas of his own and this he insists upon. Your brother in the end acquiesced. He was at first difficult to deal with as regards this condition, and he did, in fact, I believe, Mr. Ledsam, pay a visit to your office, with the object of asking you to become an intermediary between him and his relatives."

"He began a letter to me," Francis interposed, "and then mysteriously disappeared."

"The mystery is easily explained," Sir Timothy continued. "My trainer, Roger Hagon, a Varsity blue, and the best heavyweight of his year, occupies the chambers above yours. He saw from the window the arrival of Reginald Wilmore - which was according to instructions, as they were to come down to Hatch End together - went down the stairs to meet him, and, to cut a long story short, fetched him out of your office, Ledsam, without allowing him to finish his letter. This absolute isolation seems a curious condition, perhaps, but Hagon insists upon it, and I can assure you that he knows his business. The mystery, as you have termed it, of his disappearance that morning, is that he went upstairs with Hagon for several hours to undergo a medical examination, instead of leaving the building forthwith."

"Queer thing I never thought of Hagon," Francis remarked. "As a matter of fact, I never see him in the Temple, and I thought that he had left."

"May I ask," Wilmore intervened, "when my brother will be free to return to his home?"

"To-night, directly the fight is over," Sir Timothy replied. "Should he be successful, he will take with him a sum of money sufficient to start him in any business he chooses to enter."

Wilmore frowned slightly.

"But surely," he protested, "that would make him a professional pugilist?"

"Not at all," Sir Timothy replied. "For one thing, the match is a private one in a private house, and for another the money is a gift. There is no purse. If your brother loses, he gets nothing. Will you see the fight, Mr. Wilmore?"

"Yes, I will see it," was the somewhat reluctant assent.

"You will give me your word not to interfere in any way?"

"I shall not interfere," Wilmore promised. "If they are wearing regulation gloves, and the weights are about equal, and the conditions are what you say, it is the last thing I should wish to do."

"Capital!" Sir Timothy exclaimed. "Now to pass on. There is one other feature of my entertainments concerning which I have something to say - a series of performances which takes place on my launch at odd times. There is one fixed for tonight. I can say little about it except that it is unusual. I am going to ask you, Lady Cynthia, and you, Ledsam, to witness it. When you have seen that, you know everything. Then you and I, Ledsam, can call one another's hands. I shall have something else to say to you, but that is outside the doings here."

"Are we to see the fight in the gymnasium?" Lady Cynthia enquired.

Sir Timothy shook his head.

"I do not allow women there under any conditions," he said. "You and Margaret had better stay here whilst that takes place. It will probably be over in twenty minutes. It will be time then for us to find our way to the launch. After that, if you have any appetite, supper. I will order some caviare sandwiches for you," Sir Timothy went on, ringing the bell, "and some wine."

Lady Cynthia smiled.

"It is really a very wonderful party," she murmured.

Their host ushered the two men across the hall, now comparatively deserted, for every one had settled down to his or her chosen amusement - down a long passage, through a private door which he unlocked with a Yale key, and into the gymnasium. There were less than fifty spectators seated around the ring, and Francis, glancing at them hastily, fancied that he recognised nearly every one of them. There was Baker, a judge, a couple of actors, Lord Meadowson, the most renowned of sporting peers, and a dozen who followed in his footsteps; a little man who had once been amateur champion in the bantam class, and who was now considered the finest judge of boxing in the world; a theatrical manager, the present amateur boxing champion, and a sprinkling of others. Sir Timothy and his companions took their chairs amidst a buzz of welcome. Almost immediately, the man who was in charge of the proceedings, and whose name was Harrison, rose from his place.

"Gentlemen," he said, "this is a sporting contest, but one under usual rules and usual conditions. An amateur, who tips the scales at twelve stone seven, who has never engaged in a boxing contest in his life, is matched against a young man from a different sphere of life, who intends to adopt the ring as his profession, but who has never as yet fought in public. Names, gentlemen, as you know, are seldom mentioned here. I will only say that the first in the ring is the nominee of our friend and host, Sir Timothy Brast; second comes the nominee of Lord Meadowson."

Wilmore, notwithstanding his pre-knowledge, gave a little gasp. The young man who stood now within a few yards of him, carelessly swinging his gloves in his hand, was without a doubt his missing brother. He looked well and in the pink of condition; not only well but entirely confident and at his ease. His opponent, on the other hand, a sturdier man, a few inches shorter, was nervous and awkward, though none the less determined-looking. Sir Timothy rose and whispered in Harrison's ear. The latter nodded. In a very few moments the preliminaries were concluded, the fight begun.

CHAPTER XXXV

Francis, glad of a moment or two's solitude in which to rearrange his somewhat distorted sensations, found an empty space in the stern of the launch and stood leaning over the rail. His pulses were still tingling with the indubitable excitement of the last half-hour. It was all there, even now, before his eyes like a cinematograph picture - the duel between those two men, a duel of knowledge, of strength, of science, of courage. From beginning to end, there had been no moment when Francis had felt that he was looking on at what was in any way a degrading or immoral spectacle. Each man had fought in his way to win. Young Wilmore, graceful as a panther, with a keen, joyous desire of youth for supremacy written in his face and in the dogged lines of his mouth; the budding champion from the East End less graceful, perhaps, but with even more strength and at least as much determination, had certainly done his best to justify his selection. There were no points to be scored. There had been no undue feinting, no holding, few of the tricks of the professional ring. It was a fight to a finish, or until Harrison gave the word. And the better man had won. But even that knock-out blow which Reggie Wilmore had delivered after a wonderful feint, had had little that was cruel in it. There was something beautiful almost in the strength and grace with which it had been delivered - the breathless eagerness, the waiting, the end.

Francis felt a touch upon his arm and looked around. A tall, sad-faced looking woman, whom he had noticed with a vague sense of familiarity in the dancing-room, was standing by his side.

"You have forgotten me, Mr. Ledsam," she said.

"For the moment," he admitted.

I am Isabel Culbridge," she told him, watching his face.

"Lady Isabel?" Francis repeated incredulously. "But surely -"

"Better not contradict me," she interrupted. "Look again."

Francis looked again.

"I am very sorry," he said. "It is some time, is it not, since we met?"

She stood by his side, and for a few moments neither of them spoke. The little orchestra in the bows had commenced to play softly, but there was none of the merriment amongst the handful of men and women generally associated with a midnight river picnic. The moon was temporarily obscured, and it seemed as though some artist's hand had so dealt with the few electric lights that the men, with their pale faces and white shirt-fronts, and the three or four women, most of them, as it happened, wearing black, were like some ghostly figures in some sombre procession. Only the music kept up the pretence that this was in any way an ordinary-excursion. Amongst the human element there

E. Phillips Oppenheim

was an air of tenseness which seemed rather to increase as they passed into the shadowy reaches of the river.

"You have been ill, I am afraid?" Francis said tentatively.

"If you will," she answered, "but my illness is of the soul. I have become one of a type," she went on, "of which you will find many examples here. We started life thinking that it was clever to despise the conventional and the known and to seek always for the daring and the unknown. New experiences were what we craved for. I married a wonderful husband. I broke his heart and still looked for new things. I had a daughter of whom I was fond - she ran away with my chauffeur and left me; a son whom I adored, and he was killed in the war; a lover who told me that he worshipped me, who spent every penny I had and made me the laughing-stock of town. I am still looking for new things."

"Sir Timothy's parties are generally supposed to provide them," Francis observed.

The woman shrugged her shoulders.

"So far they seem very much like anybody's else," she said. "The fight might have been amusing, but no women were allowed. The rest was very wonderful in its way, but that is all. I am still hoping for what we are to see downstairs."

They heard Sir Timothy's voice a few yards away, and turned to look at him. He had just come from below, and had paused opposite a man who had been standing a little apart from the others, one of the few who was wearing an overcoat, as though he felt the cold. In the background were the two servants who had guarded the gangway.

"Mr. Manuel Loito," Sir Timothy said - "or shall I say Mr. Shopland? - my invited guests are welcome. I have only one method of dealing with uninvited ones."

The two men suddenly stepped forward. Shopland made no protest, attempted no struggle. They lifted him off his feet as though he were a baby, and a moment later there was a splash in the water. They threw a life-belt after him.

"Always humane, you see," Sir Timothy remarked, as he leaned over the side. "Ah! I see that even in his overcoat our friend is swimmer enough to reach the bank. You find our methods harsh, Ledsam?" he asked, turning a challenging gaze towards the latter.

Francis, who had been watching Shopland come to the surface, shrugged his shoulders. He delayed answering for a moment while he watched the detective, disdaining the life-belt, swim to the opposite shore.

"I suppose that under the circumstances," Francis said, "he was prepared to take his risk."

"You should know best about that," Sir Timothy rejoined. "I wonder whether you would mind looking after Lady Cynthia? I shall be busy for a few moments."

Francis stepped across the deck towards where Lady Cynthia had been sitting by her host's side. They had passed into the mouth of a tree-hung strip of the river. The engine was suddenly shut off. A gong was sounded. There was a murmur, almost a sob of relief, as the little sprinkling of men and women rose hastily to their feet and made their way towards the companion-way. Downstairs, in the saloon, with its white satinwood panels and rows of swing chairs, heavy curtains were drawn across the portholes, all outside light was shut out from the place. At the further end, raised slightly from the floor, was a sanded circle. Sir Timothy made his way to one of the pillars by its side and turned around to face the little company of his guests. His voice, though it seemed scarcely raised above a whisper, was extraordinarily clear and distinct. Even Francis, who, with Lady Cynthia, had found seats only just inside the door, could hear every word he said.

"My friends," he began, "you have often before been my guests at such small fights as we have been able to arrange in as unorthodox a manner as possible between professional boxers. There has been some novelty about them, but on the last occasion I think it was generally observed that they had become a little too professional, a little ultra-scientific. There was some-thing which they lacked. With that something I am hoping to provide you to-night. Thank you, Sir Edgar," he murmured, leaning down towards his neighbour.

He held his cigarette in the flame of a match which the other had kindled. Francis, who was watching intently, was puzzled at the expression with which for a moment, as he straightened himself, Sir Timothy glanced down the room, seeking for Lady Cynthia's eyes. In a sense it was as though he were seeking for something he needed - approbation, sympathy, understanding.

"Our hobby, as you know, has been reality," he continued. "That is what we have not always been able to achieve. Tonight I offer you reality. There are two men here, one an East End coster, the other an Italian until lately associated with an itinerant vehicle of musical production. These two men have not outlived sensation as I fancy so many of us have. They hate one another to the death. I forget their surnames, but Guiseppe has stolen Jim's girl, is living with her at the present moment, and proposes to keep her. Jim has sworn to have the lives of both of them. Jim's career, in its way, is interesting to us. He has spent already six years in prison for manslaughter, and a year for a brutal assault upon a constable. Guiseppe was tried in his native country for a particularly fiendish murder, and escaped, owing, I believe, to some legal technicality. That, however, has nothing to do with the matter. These men have sworn to fight to the death, and the girl, I understand, is willing to return to Jim if he should be successful, or to remain with Guiseppe if he should show himself able to retain her. The fight between these men, my friends, has been transferred from Seven Dials for your entertainment. It will take place before you here and now."

There was a little shiver amongst the audience. Francis, almost to his horror, was unable to resist the feeling of queer excitement which stole through his veins. A few yards away, Lady Isabel seemed to have become transformed. She was leaning forward in her chair, her eyes glowing, her lips parted, rejuvenated, dehumanised. Francis' immediate companion, however, rather surprised him. Her eyes were fixed intently upon Sir Timothy's. She seemed to have been weighing every word he had spoken. There was none of that hungry pleasure in her face which shone from the other woman's and was reflected in the faces of many of the others. She seemed to be bracing herself for a shock. Sir Timothy looked over his shoulder towards the door which opened upon the sanded space.

"You can bring your men along," he directed.

One of the attendants promptly made his appearance. He was holding tightly by the arm a man of apparently thirty years of age, shabbily dressed, barefooted, without collar or necktie, with a mass of black hair which looked as though it had escaped the care of any barber for many weeks. His complexion was sallow; he had high cheekbones and a receding chin, which gave him rather the appearance of a fox. He shrank a little from the lights as though they hurt his eyes, and all the time he looked furtively back to the door, through which in a moment or two his rival was presently escorted. The latter was a young man of stockier build, ill-conditioned, and with the brutal face of the lowest of his class. Two of his front teeth were missing, and there was a livid mark on the side of his cheek. He looked neither to the right nor to the left. His eyes were fixed upon the other man, and they looked death.

"The gentleman who first appeared," Sir Timothy observed, stepping up into the sanded space but still half facing the audience, "is Guiseppe, the Lothario of this little act. The other is Jim, the wronged husband. You know their story. Now, Jim," he added, turning towards the Englishman, "I put in your trousers pocket these notes, two hundred pounds, you will perceive. I place in the trousers pocket of Guiseppe here notes to the same amount. I understand you have a little quarrel to fight out. The one who wins will naturally help himself to the other's money, together with that other little reward which I imagine was the first cause of your quarrel. Now ... let them go."

Sir Timothy resumed his seat and leaned back in leisurely fashion. The two attendants solemnly released their captives. There was a moment's intense silence. The two men seemed fencing for position. There was something stealthy and horrible about their movements as they crept around one another. Francis realised what it was almost as the little sobbing breath from those of the audience who still retained any emotion, showed him that they, too, foresaw what was going to happen. Both men had drawn knives from their belts. It was murder which had been let loose.

Francis found himself almost immediately upon his feet. His whole being seemed crying out for inter-ference. Lady Cynthia's death-white face and pleading eyes seemed like the echo of his own passionate aversion to what was taking place. Then he met Sir Timothy's gaze across the room and he remembered his promise. Under no conditions was he to protest or interfere. He set his teeth and resumed his seat. The fight went on. There were little sobs and tremors of excitement, strange banks of silence. Both men seemed out of condition. The sound of their hoarse breathing was easily heard against the curtain of spellbound silence. For a time their knives stabbed the empty air, but from the first the end seemed certain. The Englishman attacked wildly. His adversary waited his time, content with avoiding the murderous blows struck at him, striving all the time to steal underneath the other's guard. And then, almost without warning, it was all over. Jim was on his back in a crumpled heap. There was a horrid stain upon his coat. The other man was kneeling by his side, hate, glaring out of his eyes, guiding all the time the rising and falling of his knife. There was one more shriek - then silence only the sound of the victor's breathing as he rose slowly from his ghastly task. Sir Timothy rose to his feet and waved his hand. The curtain went down.

"On deck, if you please, ladies and gentlemen," he said calmly.

No one stirred. A woman began to sob. A fat, unhealthy-looking man in front of Francis reeled over in a dead faint. Two other of the guests near had risen from their seats and were shouting aimlessly like lunatics. Even Francis was conscious of that temporary imprisonment of the body due to his lacerated nerves. Only the clinging of Lady Cynthia to his arm kept him from rushing from the spot.

"You are faint?" he whispered hoarsely.

"Upstairs - air," she faltered.

They rose to their feet. The sound of Sir Timothy's voice reached them as they ascended the stairs.

"On deck, every one, if you please," he insisted. "Refreshments are being served there. There are inquisitive people who watch my launch, and it is inadvisable to remain here long."

People hurried out then as though their one desire was to escape from the scene of the tragedy. Lady Cynthia, still clinging to Francis' arm, led him to the furthermost corner of the launch. There were real tears in her eyes, her breath was coming in little sobs.

"Oh, it was horrible!" she cried. "Horrible! Mr. Ledsam - I can't help it - I never want to speak to Sir Timothy again!"

One final horror arrested for a moment the sound of voices. There was a dull splash in the river. Something had been thrown overboard. The orchestra began to play dance music. Conversation suddenly burst out. Every one was hysterical. A Peer of the Realm, red-eyed and shaking like an aspen leaf, was drinking champagne out of the bottle. Every one seemed to be trying to outvie the other in loud conversation, in outrageous mirth. Lady Isabel, with a glass of champagne in her hand, leaned back towards Francis.

"Well," she asked, "how are you feeling, Mr. Ledsam?"

"As though I had spent half-an-hour in Hell," he answered.

She screamed with laughter.

"Hear this man," she called out, "who will send any poor ragamuffin to the gallows if his fee is large enough! Of course," she added, turning back to him, "I ought to remember you are a normal person and to-night's entertainment was not for normal persons. For myself I am grateful to Sir Timothy. For a few moments of this aching aftermath of life, I forgot."

Suddenly all the lights around the launch flamed out, the music stopped. Sir Timothy came up on deck. On either side of him was a man in ordinary dinner clothes. The babel of voices ceased. Everyone was oppressed by some vague likeness. A breathless silence ensued.

"Ladies and gentlemen," Sir Timothy said, and once more the smile upon his lips assumed its most mocking curve, "let me introduce you to the two artists who have given us to-night such a realistic performance, Signor Guiseppe Elito and Signor Carlos Marlini. I had the good fortune," he went on, "to witness this very marvellous performance in a small music-hall at Palermo, and I was able to induce the two actors to pay us a visit over here. Steward, these gentlemen will take a glass of champagne."

The two Sicilians raised their glasses and bowed expectantly to the little company. They received, however, a much greater tribute to their performance than the applause which they had been expecting. There reigned everywhere a deadly, stupefied silence. Only a half-stifled sob broke from Lady Cynthia's lips as she leaned over the rail, her face buried in her hands, her whole frame shaking.

CHAPTER XXXVI

Francis and Margaret sat in the rose garden on the following morning. Their conversation was a little disjointed, as the conversation of lovers in a secluded and beautiful spot should be, but they came back often to the subject of Sir Timothy.

"If I have misunderstood your father," Francis, declared, "and I admit that I have, it has been to some extent his own fault. To me he was always the deliberate scoffer against any code of morals, a rebel against the law even if not a criminal in actual deeds. I honestly believed that The Walled House was the scene of disreputable orgies, that your father was behind Fairfax in that cold-blooded murder, and that he was responsible in some sinister way for the disappearance of Reggie Wilmore. Most of these things seem to have been shams, like the fight last night."

She moved uneasily in her place.

"I am glad I did not see that," she said, with a shiver.

"I think," he went on, "that the reason why your father insisted upon Lady Cynthia's and my presence there was that he meant it as a sort of allegory. Half the vices in life he claims are unreal."

E. Phillips Oppenheim

Margaret passed her arm through his and leaned a little towards him.

"If you knew just one thing I have never told you," she confided, "I think that you would feel sorry for him. I do, more and more every day, because in a way that one thing is my fault."

Notwithstanding the warm sunshine, she suddenly shivered. Francis took her hands in his. They were cold and lifeless.

"I know that one thing, dear," he told her quietly.

She looked at him stonily. There was a questioning fear in her eyes.

"You know -"

"I know that your fattier killed Oliver Hilditch."

She suddenly broke out into a stream of words. There was passion in her tone and in her eyes. She was almost the accuser.

"My father was right, then!" she exclaimed. "He told me this morning that he believed that it was to you or to your friend at Scotland Yard that Walter had told his story. But you don't know you don't know how terrible the temptation was how - you see I say it quite coolly - how Oliver Hilditch deserved to die. He was trusted by my father in South America and he deceived him, he forged the letters which induced me to marry him. It was part of his scheme of revenge. This was the first time we had any of us met since. I told my father the truth that afternoon. He knew for the first time how my marriage came about. My husband had prayed me to keep silent. I refused. Then he became like a devil. We were there, we three, that night after you left, and Francis, as I live, if my father had not killed him, I should have!"

"There was a time when I believed that you had," he reminded her. "I didn't behave like a pedagogic upholder of the letter of the law then, did I?"

She drew closer to him.

"You were wonderful," she whispered.

"Dearest, your father has nothing to fear from me," he assured her tenderly. "On the contrary, I think that I can show him the way to safety."

She rose impulsively to her feet.

"He will be here directly," she said. "He promised to come across at half-past twelve. Let us go and meet him. But, Francis -"

For a single moment she crept into his arms. Their lips met, her eyes shone into his. He held her away from him a moment later. The change was amazing. She was no longer a tired woman. She had become a girl again. Her eyes were soft with happiness, the little lines had gone from about her mouth, she walked with all the spring of youth and happiness.

"It is marvellous," she whispered. "I never dreamed that I should ever be happy again."

They crossed the rustic bridge which led on to the

lawn. Lady Cynthia came out of the house to meet them. She showed no signs of fatigue, but her eyes and her tone were full of anxiety.

"Margaret," she cried, "do you know that the hall is filled with your father's luggage, and that the car is ordered to take him to Southampton directly after lunch?"

Margaret and Francis exchanged glances.

"Sir Timothy may change his mind," the latter observed. "I have news for him directly he arrives."

On the other side of the wall they heard the whinnying of the old mare, the sound of galloping feet from all directions.

"Here he comes!" Lady Cynthia exclaimed. "I shall go and meet him."

Francis laid his hand upon her arm.

"Let me have a word with him first," he begged.

She hesitated.

"You are not going to say anything - that will make him want to go away?"

"I am going to tell him something which I think will keep him at home."

Sir Timothy came through the postern-gate, a moment or two later. He waved his hat and crossed the lawn in their direction. Francis went alone to meet him and, as he drew near, was conscious of a little shock. His host, although he held himself bravely, seemed to have aged in the night.

"I want one word with you, sir, in your study, please," Francis said.

Sir Timothy shrugged his shoulders and led the way. He turned to wave his hand once more to Margaret and Lady Cynthia, however, and he looked with approval at the luncheon-table which a couple of servants were laying under the cedar tree.

"Wonderful thing, these alfresco meals," he declared. "I hope Hedges won't forget the maraschino with the melons. Come into my den, Ledsam."

He led the way in courtly fashion. He was the ideal host leading a valued guest to his sanctum for a few moments' pleasant conversation. But when they arrived in the little beamed room and the door was closed, his manner changed. He looked searchingly, almost challengingly at Francis.

"You have news for me?" he asked.

"Yes!" Francis answered.

Sir Timothy shrugged his shoulders. He threw himself a little wearily into an easy-chair. His hands strayed out towards a cigarette box. He selected one and lit it.

"I expected your friend, Mr. Shopland," he murmured. "I hope he is none the worse for his ducking."

"Shopland is a fool," Francis replied. "He has nothing

to do with this affair, anyway. I have something to give you, Sir Timothy."

He took the two papers from his pocket and handed them over.

"I bought these from John Walter the day before yesterday," he continued. "I gave him two hundred pounds for them. The money was just in time. He caught a steamer for Australia late in the afternoon. I had this wireless from him this morning."

Sir Timothy studied the two documents, read the wireless. There was little change in his face. Only for a single moment his lips quivered.

"What does this mean?" he asked, rising to his feet with the documents in his hand.

"It means that those papers are yours to do what you like with. I drafted the second one so that you should be absolutely secure against any further attempt at blackmail. As a matter of fact, though, Walter is on his last legs. I doubt whether he will live to land in Australia."

"You know that I killed Oliver Hilditch?" Sir Timothy said, his eyes fixed upon the other's.

"I know that you killed Oliver Hilditch," Francis repeated. "If I had been Margaret's father, I think that I should have done the same."

Sir Timothy seemed suddenly very much younger. The droop of his lips was no longer pathetic. There was a little humourous twitch there.

"You, the great upholder of the law?" he murmured.

"I have heard the story of Oliver Hilditch's life," Francis replied. "I was partially responsible for saving him from the gallows. I repeat what I have said. And if you will -"

He held out his hand. Sir Timothy hesitated for one moment. Instead of taking it, he laid his hand upon Francis' shoulder.

"Ledsam," he said, "we have thought wrong things of one another. I thought you a prig, moral to your finger-tips with the morality of the law and the small places. Perhaps I was tempted for that reason to give you a wrong impression of myself. But you must understand this. Though I have had my standard and lived up to it all my life, I am something of a black sheep. A man stole my wife. I did not trouble the Law Courts. I killed him."

"I have the blood of generations of lawyers in my veins," Francis declared, "but I have read many a divorce case in which I think it would have been better and finer if the two men had met as you and that man met."

"I was born with the love of fighting in my bones," Sir Timothy went on. "In my younger days, I fought in every small war in the southern hemisphere. I fought, as you know, in our own war. I have loved to see men fight honestly and fairly."

"It is a man's hobby," Francis pronounced.

"I encouraged you deliberately to think," Sir Timothy

E. Phillips Oppenheim

went on, "what half the world thinks that - my parties at The Walled House were mysterious orgies of vice. They have, as a matter of fact, never been anything of the sort. The tragedies which are supposed to have taken place on my launch have been just as much mock tragedies as last night's, only I have not previously chosen to take the audiences into my confidence. The greatest pugilists in the world have fought in my gymnasium, often, if you will, under illegal conditions, but there has never been a fight that was not fair."

"I believe that," Francis said.

"And there is another matter for which I take some blame," Sir Timothy went on, "the matter of Fairfax and Victor Bidlake. They were neither of them young men for whose loss the world is any the worse. Fairfax to some extent imposed upon me. He was brought to The Walled House by a friend who should have known better. He sought my confidence. The story he told was exactly that of the mock drama upon the launch. Bidlake had taken his wife. He had no wish to appeal to the Courts. He wished to fight, a point of view with which I entirely sympathised. I arranged a fight between the two. Bidlake funked it and never turned up. My advice to Fairfax was, whenever he met Bidlake, to give him the soundest thrashing he could. That night at Soto's I caught sight of Fairfax some time before dinner. He was talking to the woman who had been his wife, and he had evidently been drinking. He drew me on one side. 'To-night,' he told me, 'I am going to settle accounts with Bidlake.' 'Where?' I asked. 'Here,' he answered. He went out to the theatre, I upstairs to dine. That was the extent of the knowledge I possessed which enabled me to predict some unwonted happening that night. Fairfax was a bedrugged and bedrunken decadent who had not the courage afterwards to face what he had done. That is all."

The hand slipped from Francis' shoulder. Francis, with a smile, held out his own. They stood there for a moment with clasped hands - a queer, detached moment, as it seemed to Francis, in a life which during the last few months had been full of vivid sensations. From outside came the lazy sounds of the drowsy summer morning - the distant humming of a mowing machine, the drone of a reaper in the field beyond, the twittering of birds in the trees, even the soft lapping of the stream against the stone steps. The man whose hand he was holding seemed to Francis to have become somehow transformed. It was as though he had dropped a mask and were showing a more human, a more kindly self. Francis wondered no longer at the halting gallop of the horses in the field.

"You'll be good to Margaret?" Sir Timothy begged. "She's had a wretched time."

Francis smiled confidently.

"I'm going to make up for it, sir," he promised. "And this South American trip," he continued, as they turned towards the French windows, "you'll call that off?"

Sir Timothy hesitated.

"I am not quite sure."

When they reached the garden, Lady Cynthia was alone. She scarcely glanced at Francis. Her eyes were

E. Phillips Oppenheim

anxiously fixed upon his companion.

"Margaret has gone in to make the cocktails herself," she explained. "We have both sworn off absinthe for the rest of our lives, and we know Hedges can't be trusted to make one without."

"I'll go and help her," Francis declared.

Lady Cynthia passed her arm through Sir Timothy's.

"I want to know about South America," she begged. "The sight of those trunks worries me."

Sir Timothy's casual reply was obviously a subterfuge. They crossed the lawn and the rustic bridge, almost in silence, passing underneath the pergola of roses to the sheltered garden at the further end. Then Lady Cynthia paused.

"You are not going to South America," she pleaded, "alone?"

Sir Timothy took her hands.

"My dear," he said, "listen, please, to my confession. I am a fraud. I am not a purveyor of new sensations for a decadent troop of weary, fashionable people. I am a fraud sometimes even to myself. I have had good luck in material things. I have had bad luck in the precious, the sentimental side of life. It has made something of an artificial character of me, on the surface at any rate. I am really a simple, elderly man who loves fresh air, clean, honest things, games, and a healthy life. I have no ambitions except those connected with sport. I don't even want to climb to the topmost niches in the world of finance. I think you have looked at me through the wrong-coloured spectacles. You have had a whimsical fancy for a character which does not exist."

"What I have seen," Lady Cynthia answered, "I have seen through no spectacles at all - with my own eyes. But what I have seen, even, does not count. There is something else."

"I am within a few weeks of my fiftieth birthday," Sir Timothy reminded her, "and you, I believe, are twenty-nine."

"My dear man," Lady Cynthia assured him fervently, "you are the only person in the world who can keep me from feeling forty-nine."

"And your people -"

"Heavens! My people, for the first time in their lives, will count me a brilliant success," Lady Cynthia declared. "You'll probably have to lend dad money, and I shall be looked upon as the fairy child who has restored the family fortunes."

Sir Timothy leaned a little towards her.

"Last of all," he said, and this time his voice was not quite so steady, "are you really sure that you care for me, dear, because I have loved you so long, and I have wanted love so badly, and it is so hard to believe -"

It was the moment, it seemed to her, for which she had prayed. She was in his arms, tired no longer, with all the splendid fire of life in her love-lit eyes and throbbing pulses. Around them the bees were humming, and a soft summer breeze shook the roses and brought little wafts of perfume from the carnation bed.

"There is nothing in life," Lady Cynthia murmured brokenly, "so wonderful as this."

Francis and Margaret came out from the house, the former carrying a silver tray. They had spent a considerable time over their task, but Lady Cynthia and Sir Timothy were still absent. Hedges followed them, a little worried.

"Shall I ring the gong, madam?" he asked Margaret. "Cook has taken such pains with her omelette."

"I think you had better, Hedges," Margaret assented.

The gong rang out - and rang again. Presently Lady Cynthia and Sir Timothy appeared upon the bridge and crossed the lawn. They were walking a little apart. Lady Cynthia was looking down at some roses which she had gathered. Sir Timothy's unconcern seemed a trifle overdone. Margaret laughed very softly.

"A stepmother, Francis!" she whispered. "Just fancy Cynthia as a stepmother!"